After all this time, they were here, together again.

Matt rolled onto his back, laced his fingers behind his head and stared at the sky. "This farm is the only place in Cedar Grove I like to be. Even the sky seems bluer. Do you remember the time we tried to cross the creek on that log, and you fell in?"

It wasn't falling into the creek Allie remembered. It was the kiss that had followed after he'd fished her out.

Matt sat up, his knees dangerously close to hers.

The woodsy scent of his aftershave sent a shiver through her body, and she looked away from his warm gaze, aware that he was recalling the kiss, as well. When he leaned toward her, she wanted him to kiss her again. But he was marrying Jessica.

A current she couldn't ignore charged the air between them, pulling her toward Matt. He cupped her face in his hands and hesitantly kissed her, his lips tender. Seconds passed, and she began to speak.

He put his finger on her lips. "Shh."

This time there was no hesitation as he claimed her mouth. She slipped her arms around him and gave in to the moment, losing herself to the passion she'd locked away for so long.

He's going to marry someone else.

Allie stopped. She couldn't do this.

She couldn't let him break her heart again....

Dear Reader,

I am so excited you have chosen *Matthew's Choice*. Have you ever wanted something so much that you would do almost anything to get it? That describes Matthew Jefferies. Growing up on the wrong side of the small Mississippi town of Cedar Grove instilled a desire in Matthew to be rich and successful. But he believes he has to change who he is to attain that goal. After college, he cuts ties with his family and leaves his fiancée, Allie, behind to seek his fortune. Now, ten years later, he's well on his way. A high-paying job, an expensive car, a fancy apartment and an engagement to the woman of his dreams, who happens to be the boss's daughter—he's on top of the world.

When he returns to Cedar Grove to care for his sister's son after she becomes critically ill, Matthew is thrown together with his ex-fiancée, and a struggle for his heart ensues. Allie is his past and Jessica is his future, and both have a strong hold on him.

In this book I've tried to show Matthew's struggle as he learns what true success is. I hope you enjoy his journey and feel that he makes the right choice.

Patricia Bradley

HEARTWARMING

Matthew's Choice

—

Patricia Bradley

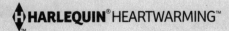

⬥HARLEQUIN®HEARTWARMING™

Recycling programs
for this product may
not exist in your area.

ISBN-13: 978-0-373-36694-1

Matthew's Choice

Copyright © 2014 by Patricia Bradley

Printed in U.S.A.

PATRICIA BRADLEY

lives in north Mississippi with her rescue cat, Suzy. She presents workshops on healthy relationships and writing. But her heart is tuned to writing stories of love and hope with happily-ever-after endings. When she's not writing or presenting workshops, she likes to throw mud on a wheel and see what happens. She loves to connect with readers on Facebook.

In memory of my mother, Frances Bradley

CHAPTER ONE

"NOAH, COME DANCE with me."

His mom's voice floated like a feather from the tiny living room to the equally tiny kitchen, where Noah searched the bare pantry for something to eat.

"Not now, Mom." Bleach from the big pan on the stove made his eyes water. He had to remember to take his socks and stuff out before he went to bed.

"Noah! Get in here this instant!"

His stomach twisted. He closed the pantry door and trudged into the living room, where his mom waltzed around the room to music playing on a CD player, her skinny arms crooked as if she were being held. She had that "look" he'd come to dread. She barely missed the small cedar tree with its paper ornaments and cardboard star on top. Dry needles lay scattered on the tile floor. He'd have to drag it to the street tomorrow. New Year's Day. His shoulders dropped. Then school would start back again next week.

His mom stopped when she spied him.

"There's my boy. C'mere. You'll be a teenager before I know it, and you need to know how to dance. Those girls are gonna be knockin' our door down."

"Aw, Mom, do I have to? I won't even be ten until next month."

"No-ah…"

He sighed and let her lead him around the room as she sang to the music.

"Did you know I could've been a famous singer?"

"Yeah, you told me." Over and over she'd told him that a big producer in Nashville had wanted to sign her, but she'd gotten sick. And he knew what kind of sick. She twirled and then guided him around the room again. At least they didn't have to worry about bumping into any furniture. Unless a worn-out couch and wooden crates counted.

"You're gonna be a lady-killer, you know." She chucked him under the chin.

Finally the waltz ended, and she released him.

"I'm gonna fix you some supper now," she said.

He frowned. "I don't think we have anything. Maybe I could go next door to Mrs. Adams. She said anytime we didn't have anything to eat she'd—"

His mother shook him. "Don't you dare go

beggin' for food. We don't ask anyone for anything. And you'd better not forget that."

Noah broke free and stumbled back.

She caught him and dropped to her knees. "Oh, Noah! I'm so sorry."

He wrapped his arms around her, her bony shoulders sharp against his hands. "It's okay, Mom. I think I saw a package of ramen noodles. I'll go fix 'em. Why don't you rest on the couch?" Her eyes searched his, and he nodded, willing her to do it. "Okay? I'll bring you a bowl."

She smiled, but it didn't reach her eyes. "You're a good boy. You deserve so much better than me."

"I love you, Mom."

"I don't know why."

He stood still as she steadied herself and stood, and then he helped her to the couch. "I'll be right back."

Her eyes drooped and she murmured something he couldn't understand. He waited a few minutes longer, until he was certain she was asleep. In the kitchen, he turned off the stove. When he returned he'd get his clothes out of the pan and hang them up to dry. Noah shrugged on his thin jacket and eased out the back door. He knew a place to get food without asking for it.

Noah slipped through the dark streets, shivering in the chilly air. At least it wasn't freezing. It'd been unusually warm for December in Mississippi. Everyone in Cedar Grove said so. It hadn't seemed like Christmas at all.

He passed the jewelry store where he and his mom had stood Christmas Day, picking out gifts they would give each other if they had the money. She'd picked out a watch for him—he didn't even know jewelry stores had watches for kids. He'd picked out a pearl necklace, and she'd almost cried. It'd made her sad to leave the ones her mom had given her at Joe's Pawn Shop last month. But the rent had to be paid, she'd said. He didn't want to think about this month.

Loud music boomed to the sound of an electric guitar at the bar on the corner, and he crossed to the other side, keeping in the shadows. Two blocks later, the First State Bank sign blinked the time and temperature. Mike's Café was across the street, dark and shuttered. He groaned. A Closed sign hung on the door.

It's New Year's Eve, dummy. The owner had probably left a long time ago, and any food he threw away would be gone already. Noah wasn't the only one who knew about the food the man threw away. Perfectly good food. He didn't understand why the guy didn't just use it the next day. He went behind the building just as the back door scraped open and a man exited with two black bags in his hands.

Noah's knees almost buckled with relief. He wasn't too late. The man tossed the bigger bag in the Dumpster then looked straight toward where Noah stood in the shadows. Noah tried to make himself smaller, and it must've worked. The man turned back to the bag and set it on a box before returning inside the building.

Noah waited for fifteen minutes, counting the time on the bank sign, shivering in the chilly air. Darting from the shadows, he ran to the box, grabbed the bag and took off. Two blocks later, he leaned against a brick building, panting for breath. As soon as he could breathe again, he untied the bag.

Wow! He'd expected bread or maybe cookies, but not a bag with sliced meat. He pulled out a slice. Just one, and he'd take the rest of it to his mom.

Ham. He loved ham and couldn't resist another slice. Noah broke off a chunk of bread and crammed it in his mouth, and then he closed the bag. Wait until Mom saw this.

When he reached his house, Noah entered by the back door and ran to the living room. "Mom! Look what I found."

She didn't respond, and Noah shook her. Why was she so pale? "Wake up, Mom."

A throat cleared behind him. "So this is where you live."

Noah whirled around, and his mouth dropped.

A guy in a cop's uniform stood in the doorway.

"My mom. You gotta help her."

MATTHEW JEFFERIES BUZZED away the five-o'clock shadow then splashed Dior aftershave on his face. Where was Clint with his tuxedo? Matt had exactly one hour to get dressed and pick up his soon-to-be fiancée, and his friend hadn't made it to Matt's apartment with his tux. If he were late, Jessica would be furious.

His feet tangled with the black towel he'd dropped on the floor, tossing him off balance until he snagged the sink rim and righted himself. Matt snatched the towel and slipped it back over the chrome bar. Jessica had picked the towel and the other black accessories for his bathroom to go with the black-and-white tile. She'd die if she discovered he'd actually used the towel. *They're only for looks, Matthew.* When it came to decorating, or hosting parties for that matter, Jessica had no equal. Not that she wouldn't be perfect without those talents. They'd make a great couple, and thirty was the perfect age to get married.

At his dresser, he rummaged through an ebony case for the platinum-and-black onyx cuff links she'd given him for Christmas. His gaze caught a small velvet ring box, and he flipped it open, revealing a two-carat diamond engagement ring. The seven square-cut diamonds along the shank were duplicated in the wedding band.

His mother's voice, weak from the cancer's toll on her body, echoed through the recesses of his mind. *These rings were your Grandmother Rae's, and they're all I have to leave you. Choose well. Find someone worthy to wear them.* Mom would have liked Jessica.

Tonight he would ask her father for Jessica's hand in marriage, and tomorrow morning, after he wowed her with his famous eggs Benedict, he'd ask her to marry him. Matt held the solitaire up to the light, and it shimmered like white fire. Jessica would be impressed.

Matt dialed Clint's number once again. "Come on, answer." Voice mail picked up, and he pressed End then tapped his fingers against his leg. When Clint got here, he was going to kill him. He never should've trusted his friend to get his tux here on time and wouldn't have if J. Phillip Bradford hadn't requested an audience an hour before the cleaners closed.

"Probably forgot to charge his phone," he muttered and took his dress shoes from the closet. Five minutes later, after he'd put the finishing touches to a shoeshine that a soldier would be proud of, his phone rang and he grabbed it. It better be Clint telling him he was parking.

He dropped his head, wanting to bang it on the wall. J. Phillip Bradford again. Matt shook off his frustration and answered. "Yes, sir, Mr. Bradford, what can I do for you?"

Bradford wasted no time on pleasantries. "I need you to drop by tomorrow at nine to go over page five of your proposal."

"Sir? Tomorrow's New Year's Day. I—"

"All the more reason to work—start the New Year off right. You do know Valentine's is only six weeks away, and while I like your proposal over the other five, if you expect to win the contract Wednesday, I need clarification on page five."

Matt smothered the sigh trying to get past his lips. It'd been bad enough that he'd had to drop everything today and rush over to Bradford's office, now he had to change his breakfast plans with Jessica tomorrow. But that was his lot as director of food and beverage for the Winthrop Corporation. The title was a catch-all for everything from securing business to overseeing the chef. Not to mention the budget. With a company that rivaled any of the big high-end chains, it was a significant job.

Matt wanted that contract for the corporation, even though working with J. Phillip would be a royal pain. The old man fired the original event planner after they'd butted heads over the ballroom, the menu and the decorations. If Phillip awarded Matt the contract, he had six weeks to pull the event together. He could do it—he could do anything that helped him climb the Winthrop corporate ladder.

"Yes, sir. I'll be there at nine sharp."

Bradford broke the connection without ceremony, leaving Matt holding a dead cell phone. He picked up his other shoe, attacking it with a vengeance. Getting the Valentine's Day contract was only the start. J. Phillip Bradford headed the Bradford Foundation, which was made up of three nonprofits, and each one hosted an extravagant fund-raiser every year. He would convince the old curmudgeon that the Winthrop Hotel was the perfect location for each, and at Matt's price.

The doorbell chimed, and he fumbled the shoe. That had to be Clint. Shrugging out of the shirt he'd worn to work this morning, he rushed to the door, jerking it open. "Do you know what time it is?"

His breath caught at the shock of seeing Allie Carson, a gray garment bag slung over her shoulder. She blinked and stepped back from the door. The bag did nothing to detract from the way the slinky black gown hugged her curves. Or the way her blond hair fell softly around her shoulders. "A-Allie? Where's Clint?"

She recovered, rolling her eyes. "Having his car towed from I-240. I told my brother six months ago he needed a new car. May I come in? Or do you want me to just hand you the tux and be on my way?"

"No, no, come in." He stepped back, catching the light scent of something sweet and exotic as she glided past him. Echoes of late-night dates and study sessions in college ricocheted across his mind. How long had it been since he'd seen her?

"Six years, eight months and twenty-one days," she said.

Almost seven years? He swallowed. "How did—"

Her lopsided grin teased him. "The question was written all over your face. What I want to know is why in the world you trusted Clint with your tux if you needed it tonight? My brother was late the day he was born."

Allie chuckled, her laugh throaty, husky, just the way he remembered it. Her blue eyes danced that same mischievous two-step they always had, then flitted from his face to his feet and back. Suddenly conscious of being shirtless, he grabbed the bag and held it in front of him.

"Trust me, he was a last resort." He didn't

want to tell her Clint was the only friend he had in Memphis, or that he was too busy to get together with him that often. "My fault anyway for waiting until today to pick it up." Matt shifted his weight. That black dress fit Allie like a glove. She'd lost at least twenty pounds since college. Yeah, she definitely looked good, but she reminded him of everything he'd left behind. "You would've thought in all that time we would've run in to each other."

Allie gave him that throaty laugh again. "Well, I rarely come to Memphis, and you never come to Cedar Grove."

She handed him a smaller bag he hadn't noticed. "Clint said something about me staying long enough to do your tie, or do you think you can manage it?"

She knew he couldn't. Clint knew he couldn't. As far back as when Matt had shared an apartment with Clint, his best friend always made sure Matt's bow tie was correctly knotted for the once a-year formal affairs he attended. He grabbed the smaller bag, as well.

"I think I can handle it," Matt mumbled and headed to his bedroom. "Be out in a minute."

"Clint told me not to leave until you were properly attired," she called after him.

After he'd changed into the pants and a pleated

tuxedo shirt, he stuck his head out the door. "Sodas are in the fridge."

"I'm good."

He left the door open and adjusted the cummerbund, making sure the pleats faced up. "What brings you to Memphis?"

"I came over for Christmas and Clint talked me into staying for this party he's going to." Her voice floated through the doorway. "I think they have a 'friend' they want to introduce."

So that's why she was all dolled up. He glanced down at the ring box, still open. Matt snapped the lid shut. Once he'd thought Allie would be the one wearing his grandmother's rings. Shrugging the thought off, he slid the tie around his neck, his fingers fumbling with the silk. After a few minutes, he gave up and grabbed his shoes. He'd give the tie one more shot after he donned his Oxfords.

Or maybe he'd search online for instructions first. Why hadn't he thought of that before? While his laptop booted up, he slipped on his shoes then typed his search words into Google. Oh, good…a video. Matt clicked on the link and leaned over the computer, studying the fat guy meticulously detailing how to knot a bow tie. He paused the video and draped the tie around his neck, making sure one side hung lower than the other.

What was it he said to do next? He clicked Play and stared hard at the computer screen. Do what? Matt backed the video up and played it again. No doubt about it, the guy was talking Greek. He yanked the tie off and headed for his living room.

"I give up! Would you please do this stupid—"

The room was empty. His heart sank. She had to still be here—somebody had to help him. Movement on the balcony caught his eye. He tapped on the sliding door, and when she turned, he dangled the tie. "Help?" he mouthed.

She slid the door open, shivering as she came back into the room. "Sorry, I just had to get some fresh air. It's chilly out there, but a beautiful night."

Then she took the tie without even an I-told-you-so glance and smoothed it out before handing it back to him. "Slip it around your neck."

He did as he was instructed. "Thanks for doing this."

"No prob…that's what friends are for. Now, be still."

He tried not to move, acutely aware of how close she stood to him. Maybe he should've tried harder to tie it. He cleared his throat. "You haven't said anything about the apartment. Do you like it?"

ALLIE HAD DREADED that question from the minute she'd stepped into the place. She supposed some people like the minimalist look—sparse white walls, chrome and glass tables and a thin, hard sofa that no doubt cost a mint. The room reminded her of a spread in an architectural magazine. And it fit Matthew to a T.

"It's…" *Cold* and *sterile* were the only words that came to mind. *Just tell him what he wants to hear.* Her gaze locked on the one dash of color, an abstract painting with a flowing crimson line in the center. "It's nice. I really like the painting. Did your girlfriend pick it out?" Allie nodded toward the silver frame that held a photo of Matt with his arms around a willowy redhead.

"It's actually her painting, and she put all of this together." His Adam's apple bobbed. "Her name is Jessica Winthrop, and she likes to paint, like you. We…we're kind of talking about getting married." He shook his head. "No, we're not just talking, we're making plans. She loves big-city living."

Implying Allie didn't. But it hadn't been the move to the big city she'd fought. She forced a thousand-watt smile to her lips. "I'm glad for you."

Liar, liar, pants on fire. She'd known one day he'd get married, and it wouldn't be to her, but did he have to be the one to tell her? If she hadn't come to Memphis over the holidays, hadn't agreed to deliver Matt's tux, she would've found out through the grapevine, which would've been bad enough.

And did he have to find someone who was an artist? She glanced at the painting again. Especially one so talented. She stifled a sigh. Focus on the task at hand. Get the tie on his neck and get out of here. Matt shifted his weight as she made a half knot and pulled it against his collar. "Be still so I can get this tied."

A pregnant pause filled the room as Allie forced her fingers through the mechanics of knotting the tie. Finally she had the black silk material transformed into a presentable bow, and his collar turned back down. The pause grew heavier. "I saw your sister just before the Christmas break," she said, more to fill the dead air than to pass information.

"What? Where?"

"At school. I double as the reading teacher and elementary school counselor. Her son has been having problems in the classroom."

"Son?" His brow wrinkled into a frown. "What are you talking about?"

"When is the last time you saw Mariah?"

"Ten years ago, when Mother died." He shrugged. "You were there—she was wasted."

She definitely remembered Matt's older sister

that day. Allie had held Mariah's head while she threw up in the commode. But now she understood his confusion—Mariah hadn't told Matt she was pregnant. The son born to her was in Allie's third-grade reading class and a frequent visitor to her counselor's room. "And you haven't talked to her since?"

"Sometimes. She calls every year or so, and for a while I have a number to reach her on, then it gets disconnected or she changes phones. But she never said anything about a kid." His cell phone dinged. Matt checked it and winced.

"Your girlfriend?"

He nodded. "Jessica has decided she wants to drive, and she'll be here in five minutes. Look, could I call you tomorrow to talk about my sister? Maybe we could get together for coffee."

No way. Ending the year with a visit to Matt Jefferies was one thing. Starting the New Year off having coffee with the only man she'd ever loved and couldn't have just was not happening. "I'm sorry. I have to go back to Cedar Grove tomorrow. Why don't you simply call Mariah?"

"Why? So she can lie to me again? Besides, the number I have has been disconnected. Where are my sister and the boy living?"

"His name is Noah." Allie dropped her gaze. "She works as a waitress at Loco Jim's."

Matt waited.

"And they live in a little house on Beaker Street."

His shoulders sagged. "That's next to the projects. Why didn't she tell me? She could've stayed in Mom's house. At least it would've been safer."

"Last time I passed by your mom's house, someone was living there."

"I would have helped her find something better than that end of Beaker Street."

Allie shook her head. "You don't have a clue, do you? She would never ask you for anything."

"What do you mean? Why not?"

"Really?" She grabbed her silk purse. "Look, I don't think you want me here when your girlfriend arrives, so I'd better go."

At the door, Allie turned around. "I know you're mad at Mariah for running off with that Connors kid, and maybe she doesn't live up to your expectations, but she and Noah need you. Call her tomorrow. Or even better, go back to Cedar Grove and see her, meet Noah."

From the set of his jaw, she knew that wasn't happening. "At least call her."

"Wait," he said. "Thanks for helping me."

THE ELEVATOR DOORS CLOSED, and Allie slumped against the stainless-steel wall as the elevator descended from the penthouse floor to the parking garage. What had possessed her to let Clint talk her into delivering the tux? Thoughts of wowing Matt with her new, slim body? Ha! He hadn't even noticed.

No doubt about it, Matt Jefferies had succeeded in putting his past behind him. Evidently he'd made his dreams come true. Money, great job, great apartment and definitely way out of her league.

And with that success, he needed a corporate wife. From the looks of that photo, he'd found one in Jessica. Who liked big-city living. Who would probably laugh at Allie's job in the school system in tiny Cedar Grove. Allie squared her shoulders as the elevator stopped on the ground floor. Why should she even care what this fiancée thought?

Matt was getting married. She'd make it a point to avoid him in the future. No need in getting her heartbeat up again. Besides, she had a party to get to, one where maybe *her* Prince Charming waited. Or not. With her luck, Clint had fixed her up with one of the old geezers living at the retirement home where his girlfriend worked. The doors opened and she stepped out, almost colliding with a model-thin woman in a flaming red gown that was definitely not off-the-rack.

Allie jerked up short. "Oh! I'm sorry."

The woman shook her head, her diamond teardrop earrings shimmering with the movement. "Oh, no, it was my fault entirely."

Whoever said women with red hair shouldn't wear red had never seen the girl in Matt's photo. She sighed as the elevator doors closed. Oh, yeah. Matt was definitely out of Allie's league.

As Allie walked to her car, her cell beeped, and she snagged the phone from the black satin clutch. Clint. Where are you?

Instead of texting, she speed-dialed her brother's number. "I'm on my way," she said when he answered.

"Well, we're waiting on you at the hotel, and your date is here."

Oh, joy. *I'm* not the one who sent me over here, mister. And how did you get there so quick? Last I saw of you, the tow truck was pulling your car off I-240."

"My date picked me up."

"Oh. Well, what about my date? Who is this mystery man, anyway?"

"It wouldn't be a mystery if I told you. Now, get a move on."

"I need an address."

"It's on Main Street at the Winthrop. Put the hotel in your GPS, and when you get here, ask at the desk for the Savannah Room and tell them Jessica Winthrop invited you."

Clint lost her at the Winthrop. Double joy.

Her brother never told Allie she was attending a party hosted by Matt's girlfriend. Now she'd see her ex-boyfriend twice on New Year's Eve. Could it get any better?

Twenty-five minutes later, she'd managed to get lost, not once, but twice. When she finally found the Savannah Room, she spied Clint pacing back and forth outside the door, all six feet of him.

He rubbed his jaw. "Where have you been? I was worried sick that you'd had an accident… or worse."

"I'm sorry, I got turned around." She glanced left, then right. "Where's your girlfriend?"

Clint winced. "She had to leave right after I talked with you. An emergency at the assisted living where she works. Said she might make it later. For a while, I thought you both were dumping me."

Allie linked her arm in his, patting it. "I'm here now, so let's go meet this guy you've managed to snooker."

"That's where you're wrong." Clint winked at her. "Your date twisted my arm to finagle an evening with you."

Allie tilted her head toward him. "What? Who is this person?"

"See for yourself. Voilà." He extended his hand, palm out.

She turned. "Peter?"

What was he doing here?

CHAPTER TWO

MATT SLIPPED INTO his jacket on the way to answer the doorbell again. He paused to look in the mirror and straighten his tie before sweeping the door open with a bow. "Good evening, madame."

Jessica breezed through the doorway, a sensual aroma swirling in her wake. With her coppery hair pinned up, the diamond earrings she wore dangled against her bare neck. His gaze traveled the length of the red dress that fit perfectly. He'd never seen this one before. "Wow! You look gorgeous. I'll have to fight the single men off tonight."

For half a second, he considered proposing right then and there. But no, he wanted to do it right and speak with her father first.

She slipped her left leg through the slit. "So you like it?"

"Hmmm," he said and pulled her to him.

Jessica pressed her lips against Matt's, making his toes curl inside his Oxfords. When they parted he trailed his finger along her jaw.

"So why didn't you let me pick you up like we planned?"

"I forgot to get my mail from the box, and when I ran down to get it, there was a young mother with her baby outside the door. Found out she was waiting for a cab to come by." The green flecks in her hazel eyes darkened. "It's New Year's Eve. She probably would have still been waiting if I hadn't offered to give her a ride. After I found her destination was near your apartment, I went to plan B. And here I am."

Knowing Jessica, it wouldn't have mattered if the young woman needed to go clear across town.

"Who was your blond visitor?"

He blanked for a second. "Visitor?"

"The elevator. While I was waiting for it, I noticed someone came down from this floor. Female, blond, black dress? Hello?"

"Oh, that was Clint's sister, delivering my tux."

She glanced toward the door. "*That* was Clint's sister? She looks nothing like the girl in your photo album."

"She, um, lost a little weight."

"That's putting it mildly. Do you suppose she'll be at the party with Clint?"

"Clint's coming to the party?" Oh, wait, Clint

had mentioned a party. Matt just didn't realize it was *this* party. His mind had been on Bradford.

"You never listen to me." Jessica punched him lightly on the shoulder. She glanced at the mirror and tucked a copper curl that had escaped the clasp back into place. "I told you last week I invited him, told him to bring guests if he wanted to. The more the merrier. Is my hair spray still here? This twig is driving me crazy."

"Top shelf in the bathroom." Thank goodness he'd rehung the towel.

"Oh, good." She held up her finger. "Won't take me but a sec."

Why hadn't Allie mentioned she'd be at the party? Why hadn't Clint, for that matter? Matt's stomach gulped at the thought of seeing Allie again. He'd seen the disapproval in her eyes when Mariah's name came up. And the kid… what was his name? *Noah.* Just what did Allie expect him to do? Take the two of them in? He pressed his lips together. Mariah had made her choices long ago, and he'd tried to help her then. He wasn't sure bailing her out now was the right answer. Matt checked his own hair in the mirror and frowned. Maybe a squirt of that hair spray would help his cowlick. He started into his bedroom and braked at the door as his heart crashed against his chest. He'd forgotten to put away his grandmother's rings, and Jessica had found them. She stood with her back to him, holding them up to the light, and once more he was tempted. No. He had it all planned for tomorrow. He stepped back into the living room and cleared his throat. "Are you finished? I need to get in there."

"Coming," Jessica answered.

"Oh, and by the way," Matt called, "Phillip Bradford wants to meet with me tomorrow morning at nine. Shouldn't take long. What do you say I pick you up at eleven?"

"You hadn't planned anything earlier, had you? I won't be up until ten at the earliest."

Check mark. That problem solved itself. A minute later she hurried back into the room. He examined her face, but it didn't give him a single clue as to how she felt about the rings.

"I forgot to tell you…Daddy wants us there early." She tapped her watch. "Like five minutes ago."

"And you're just now telling me?" He shook his head. "Let me put my cuff links in, and we'll go."

In the bedroom, he glanced at the ring box and smiled. Jessica wasn't giving anything away. The box was closed, and exactly where he'd left it. Now if he could just corner Mr. Winthrop before his nerves got the best of him.

What if Winthrop thought Matt was crazy,

asking for Jessica's hand? Or he thought it was too old-fashioned. Matt hadn't considered that. He fumbled with the cuff link as the stud hung in the material. Winthrop *seemed* to like him, but what if he'd misread her father? No, Winthrop liked him. Matt manhandled the stud through the buttonholes and straightened the cuffs.

Tonight he'd ask the father, tomorrow the daughter.

WHEN THEY ARRIVED, the party in the Savannah Room rocked the walls. Glittering gold letters proclaimed Happy New Year from the ceiling as music flowed from the string ensemble, providing the backdrop for dancing or mingling. Already the party was a success. Before Matt had even had time to mix with the crowd, Mr. Winthrop pulled him aside.

"Matthew. I'd like to speak privately with you. This way."

Matt followed the older man to a side room, feeling much like he did as a kid when his dad led him to the woodshed. Only expensive walnut paneling lined this woodshed, along with carpet deep enough to sink his feet into.

"Cigar?" Winthrop picked one then offered Matt the box

An Ashton Cabinet. He hesitated. What if Winthrop expected him to light up? The thought almost made him green. But offending the man would be worse, and he took one from the middle.

"The Ashton Cabinet is a mild but subtly complex cigar," Winthrop said as he clipped the end off and handed Matt the cutter. "I think you will enjoy it."

Matt swallowed and copied the older man's actions, then waited as Winthrop lit his cigar. Oh, cool. A lighter with a double flame.

Winthrop rotated the cigar under the fire. "The secret, Matt, is to toast the end, not burn it." He puffed on the fat roll of tobacco then blew on the end.

Once again, Matt copied Winthrop. On his third puff, queasiness rolled in his stomach, and he clamped his mouth shut. It was awfully hot in the room, and he adjusted his collar. What did Winthrop just say? "Sir? I didn't quite catch that."

Winthrop pointed to a pair of wingback chairs and a small table in the corner. "I asked if you'd like to sit."

Thank goodness. After they were seated, a heavy silence surrounded them. Winthrop puffed his cigar while Matt rolled his in his fingers. "I guess you can tell I'm not much of a cigar connoisseur."

"So I see."

Matt cleared his throat. "Actually, sir, I'd like to talk with you about your daughter."

Winthrop puffed his stogie once more. He blew the smoke toward the ceiling, and a series of small O's floated above his head. "That's why I brought you in here. How long have you been with the Winthrop Corporation, Matt?"

He blinked. "Seven years, sir. Right out of college."

"If I remember correctly, you started on the front desk, and now you're director of food and beverages. I understand you've gone after the J. Phillip Bradford account. You're ambitious. I like that." He fixed a hard stare on Matt. "I want that contract, even if we have to lose money on the Valentine's Day banquet."

Lose money? Matt adjusted his collar. "I don't understand."

"Do you know how many years I've tried to get Bradford's accounts? Did you know he doesn't always take the lowest bid? I know. I've had the lowest bid." Winthrop rubbed his jaw with his thumb. "No, he weighs the services offered against the cost. Whoever comes up with what he's looking for, wins. I've never been able to figure out exactly what he wants. I hope you're up to the challenge."

Great. Nothing like more pressure. "You can quit worrying, sir. I will get Bradford's business, starting with the Valentine's Day banquet." He spoke the words with more conviction than he felt.

Winthrop stared at the end of his cigar. After a long minute he shifted his gaze back to Matt and seemed to measure him. Matt sat a little straighter and waited.

"Matthew, how do you feel about family?"

"Sir?"

"I've never heard you discuss your family. And naturally, as I watch this growing relationship you have with my daughter, I want to know a little more about you beyond your business side. Family is very important, don't you agree?"

"Yes, sir. Unfortunately, the only family I have is my sister and her son." What would Winthrop say if he knew Matt had never met the boy? Maybe after he closed the deal with J. Phillip Bradford, he'd take a day off and drive to Cedar Grove and look them up. "We haven't been close in some time. She married and moved away."

"Perhaps you could bring them to dinner some night."

Matt's palms sweated. Mariah had been stoned at his mother's funeral, and he doubted she'd cleaned up her act. "Yes, sir."

"Good." Winthrop wafted *O*'s toward the ceiling again, then leveled his gaze at Matt. "Just so you know, my daughter is very precious to me.

She's my only child, and I'll admit, more than a little spoiled. I even have in mind buying the house next door for her and her future husband."

Matt swallowed. If Jessica agreed to marry him, he was not living next door to the Winthrops. Even if it *was* a mansion. But that discussion could wait until another night.

Her father stared at the white ash on the end of his cigar then stubbed the cigar in an ashtray. "Matthew, if you in any way hurt Jessica, I—"

"I can assure you, Mr. Winthrop, I will not hurt your daughter. With your blessing, and if she'll have me, I want to marry her."

ALLIE CAUGHT HER breath as Peter Elliott walked toward them, his light blue eyes fixed on her. He'd joked about them going out last week, but she hadn't a clue he was serious. With his blond good looks, the broad-shouldered director of social services in Cedar Grove could date any number of women.

"You could've told me," she muttered.

Clint laughed. "And have you say no?"

Not necessarily. But probably. Since the fiasco with Matt, she'd been reluctant to risk her heart again. Besides, she and Peter had been buddies since grade school, and she'd simply never thought of him in a romantic way. Maybe it was time to rethink their relationship.

Peter gave a slight bow when he reached them and took her hand. "I hope you don't mind that I invited myself to your New Year's Eve celebration."

"Mind?" She shook her head. "Just a little surprised."

Clint touched her arm. "I'm going to our table, over there in the corner."

She followed his gaze to an empty table just below a huge TV that played images of New Year's Eve celebrations from all over the world. Allie glanced around the room, counting ten TVs interspersed around the gold and silver streamers that hung from the ceiling.

"May I have this dance?" Peter said.

She hadn't even heard the music and glanced toward the front of the room, where a string ensemble played "Moonlight Serenade." Dancing seemed preferable to making small talk at the table. "As long as you don't step on my toes, I'll try not to step on yours."

"I'm sure you won't." Peter held his hand out.

Allie wrinkled her nose at him. "You haven't seen me dance."

She accepted his hand and followed him to the dance floor, where he took her lightly in his arms. It never entered her mind that he might actually trample her feet. No, it would be the other way around. Peter Elliott came from old money in Cedar Grove, and his social graces were impeccable, as were his clothes. The black tux had *high quality* written all over it, and she'd bet he even tied his own bow tie. The memory of Matt holding his out to her brought a quick smile to her lips.

"Did I say something funny?"

An *oops* shivered down her spine, and she looked up into his questioning blue eyes.

"No...it was something that happened earlier tonight."

Peter tightened his hold on her. "I'm sure Matthew Jefferies did any number of things that were amusing. I couldn't believe it when your brother told me he and Jessica Winthrop were an item." He leaned her back. "Weren't you sweet on him once?"

"Once." She almost stumbled, then concentrated on following Peter as he whirled her around. When the music ended, the ensemble slipped into a tango, and she shook her head at the invitation written on his face. "I think I'll sit this one out."

She allowed Peter to lead her through the crowd to their table, where Clint sat alone. Hopefully, with this many people at the party, she'd be able to avoid Matt and his girlfriend. Correction, make that his almost-fiancée. At the table, Peter offered to get her something to drink.

"Lime water," she said. After he left, she turned on her brother. "Just how did this date come about? And why didn't you tell me?"

"Last question first—I can count on one hand the number of men you've dated since you and Matt broke up. I figured you'd say no and so did Peter, so we decided not to tell you."

"Why were you even talking to him?"

"Last week a sixteen-year-old girl from Cedar Grove showed up at my Boys and Girls Club. One of my older girls had dragged her there after finding her living in her car. Since Peter is head of social services in Cedar Grove, I called him so he could notify the parents and ended up inviting him to the party—I knew Jessica wouldn't mind if I brought a few extra people."

Allie traced the fleur-de-lis pattern on the linen tablecloth. "How...do you like Jessica?"

"She's great. You'd like her if you met her. She volunteers at the club, teaching etiquette and art—the kids all love her."

Allie swallowed the lump that suddenly clogged her throat. She licked her lips. Good. Matt had someone worthy of him.

"Your drink, ma'am." Peter set down a crystal water glass with a wedge of lime adorning the rim.

At eleven on all the screens around the room, the ball dropped in New York City and confetti rained from an overhead vent as a rousing cheer went up. The evening was flying by. And without a glimpse of Matt.

"So, you forgive me for going behind your back to get a date with you?" Peter brushed confetti from her shoulder.

Allie tilted her head. "Why me?"

"You've got to be kidding."

"About—?"

"Allie, you're a beautiful woman. I'm surprised you're still single. When Clint called and mentioned the party, I jumped on it. At least I'd have one night to convince you to date me."

His confession stunned her into silence. Before she could recover, he touched his chest, frowning.

"It's my cell, it must be important given how late it is. Excuse me," he said and turned toward the wall as he fished his phone from inside his tux. "Elliott speaking."

He fell silent, listening to whomever was on the other end. Allie turned her gaze to the dance floor, not wanting to eavesdrop. Even so, she couldn't help overhearing his end of the conversation.

"I see." Silence followed again. "No, you did right by calling. Take the boy to the shelter, and I'll look into the matter in the morning."

He touched her arm. "I'm so sorry for the interruption."

"Don't worry about it. And I couldn't help overhearing. Trouble?"

"The usual. An overdose, with a nine-year-old child involved. Apparently there is no family for the child to stay with. Thank goodness for the shelter."

Chill bumps raced over her body. Nine-year-old. The age of her third-grade readers. "Is there anything I can do to help?"

"Dance with me again."

She cocked her head. The band had fired up the old Johnny Mathis song "Chances Are." She could do that.

On the dance floor, Peter held her lightly, both of them moving to the music. Once she scuffed against his shoe. "Sorry."

She focused on recapturing her rhythm as he leaned closer. "Have breakfast with me in the morning."

Allie almost stumbled. "I…need to get back to Cedar Grove. School starts Tuesday, and I have a lot to do."

"You would turn down the person who expedited your home study so you could become a foster parent?"

Peter had been responsible for her application being fast-tracked?

"That is blackmail," she said as the song ended, and they walked back to their table.

"Just joking. The paperwork should be completed next week."

They both turned as Clint called to them. "Look who I found!"

Matt and the girl in the photo trailed Clint.

"Matt..." Allie shifted her gaze to the girl who smiled at her. "And you must be Jessica."

Her smile faded. "Have we met?"

"Earlier tonight, at the elevator in Matt's building."

Recognition flashed in her hazel eyes. "Ohh..."

Clint spoke up. "Jessica, this is my sister, Allie Carson and her date, Peter Elliott." He punched Matt. "You remember Peter, don't you?"

"Oh, yeah. Peter would be hard to forget."

Whatever was wrong with Matt? He looked like he had indigestion.

"Clint mentioned you'd returned to Cedar Grove," Matt said. "Something about working for the state?"

Peter's lips pressed together. "I'm director of social services. Clint keeps me informed as well—he says you're doing quite well. In sales of some sort?"

"You could call it that. I put together this little soiree. In fact, there are a couple of details I need to attend to." He nodded then looped his arm through Jessica's. "Come with me?"

Jessica turned toward her and smiled. "Happy New Year, in case I don't see you all later."

"Yes…" Matt glanced around, and his eyes settled on Allie. "Happy New Year."

"You, too," Allie said.

As they walked away, Peter raised his eyebrows. "Another dance?"

She lifted her gaze, and her breath quickened at the warm twinkle in his blue eyes. "You are a glutton for punishment, but yes, that would be nice."

THE NIGHT SKY detonated in bursts of light and window-shaking explosions. In the backseat of a patrol car, Noah counted as church bells tolled in the New Year. The cop had stuck him there after Noah had tried to escape. He kicked the back of the driver's seat in a steady rhythm. "I want to go see my mom."

"Sorry, kid. My orders are to take you to the shelter."

Tears burned the backs of Noah's eyes. He didn't know what would happen there, but no way was he going there.

"But my mom, she'll need me when she wakes up." He tried to keep the whining out of his voice. Whining just made adults mad.

"Someone will come and get you, probably Monday, and take you to see her."

Monday? That was three days away. She might be dead by then. He was going tonight. A plan popped into his mind. "You promise?"

"Kid, if nobody comes, you call the station, and I'll come personally and take you. Just ask for Jason."

Yeah, he knew those kinds of promises. His mom made them all the time. Besides, if the cop could take him Monday, he could take him right now. "Thanks."

The cruiser turned into a dark drive and pulled up to an equally dark house. The cop spoke to him over his shoulder. "I'm going to open the door, and if you run again, I'll catch you, and I'll put handcuffs on you. Understand?"

Noah pressed his lips together to keep them from trembling. The cop's eyes were kind, but Noah knew he was serious about what he said. "Y-yes, sir." He'd just have to make sure the cop didn't catch him.

At the back of the house, a light glowed in the window, and the door opened before they reached it. A thick black woman met them at the steps in her bare feet and ushered them into the kitchen. The door clicked shut as butterflies fluttered in Noah's stomach. The door had some kind of box beside it that the black lady punched.

Had to be a lock. His breath hung in his chest. He was trapped.

"Jason," she said, nodding at the cop. Then she held out her hand. "I'm glad you made it, Noah."

She knew his name? He gazed up. And up. She must be ten feet tall. He swallowed, and she knelt in front of him, making them eye level.

"I'm sorry, son." She chuckled and the warm sound washed over him like a gentle rain. "Sometimes I forget that I can scare little people. My name is Miss Sarah."

He stood a little taller. "I wasn't scared."

She still had her hand extended, and he stuck his out. Immediately it was swallowed in her dark one.

"Are you hungry?" She widened her eyes like adults did sometimes when they talked to kids. "Could you eat some scrambled eggs and biscuits?"

His mouth watered, but he shook his head, remembering the last time he'd been put in a shelter in another state. That lady was all nice as long as somebody was around, too. Probably as soon as the cop left, this one would do the same thing—get mad 'cause she had to clean up his mess.

She ruffled his hair, and her knees popped as she stood. "Well, maybe you don't want anything, but I bet Jason here does. Right, Jason?"

"Some of your biscuits, Miss Sarah? Yes, *ma'am*." The cop took off his hat and laid it on the table. "Noah, you sit there in the middle, and I'll just take the end chair."

Noah did as he was told. The kitchen was warm, and his eyelids drooped. If he weren't so hungry…

Something smelled so good…he woke with a start. Jason and Miss Sarah were laughing, but not in a mean way.

"Didn't know whether to let you sleep or wake you up." Miss Sarah scooted him closer to the table, then slathered butter on a biscuit and put it on his plate beside a mound of scrambled eggs.

"I thought he was going to fall out of the seat," Jason said. He leaned back in his chair. "Thank you, Miss Sarah. That was really good."

The food tempted Noah. The last he'd eaten was the couple of slices of ham he'd found at the Dumpster, and before that, it'd been a bowl of ramen noodles. That'd been lunch, yesterday. *Don't be taking any handouts. We don't ask anybody for anything.* Butter oozed from the middle of the bread. Maybe just one bite…

The cop stood and picked up his cap.

"You gonna tell him about your phone call?" she asked.

"Oh, yeah." He smiled down at Noah. "I called

the hospital, and they told me your mom was doing better."

Noah swallowed the lump that threatened to choke him. "Is she awake?"

Jason hesitated. "Not yet."

"Then she's not all right. I gotta be there when she wakes up." His voice cracked, and he fought the tears that threatened to spill.

"What you need to do, son—" Miss Sarah cupped his face in her huge brown hands "—is to eat so you can keep your strength up. You won't be able to help your momma if you get sick. Okay?"

He stared into her chocolate-brown eyes.

"Trust me, Noah. I won't steer you wrong, and I won't ever lie to you."

Something inside him said she was telling the truth. At last, he nodded.

"Good. Now eat your food, and then we'll get you into bed."

He attacked the eggs, keeping his eye on Sarah and Jason as they walked to the back door. She punched in something on the box before Jason left, but he couldn't see exactly what she did. He'd have to watch if he wanted to get out of here. He figured there were bars on the windows like the last place. The door was probably the only way out.

CHAPTER THREE

"SO YOU'RE GUARANTEEING me you can pull this off for this price?" The silver-haired building magnate drew a line under the dollar figure Matt had quoted for the Valentine's Day banquet. "That's all-inclusive?"

"Yes, sir, Mr. Bradford," Matt said, "Except for the entertainment, and I can provide you with a list of bands and ensembles I've worked with in the past. I can even contact them for you, unless you want to bring in a comedian from Las Vegas. Then you're on your own."

J. Phillip Bradford rested his forearms on the table in the small conference room where Matt and the CEO were meeting. Bradford's silver eyebrows arched in perpetual skepticism. He didn't respond to Matt's attempt at humor.

Matt swallowed the impulse to add another sales pitch. He'd laid it all out and there was no reason to go over it again. The older man's steel-gray eyes bored into Matt's, and he forced himself not to move. Keeping his mouth shut was harder.

Finally, Bradford nodded. "Thank you for coming in. Of the five hotels who have submitted a proposal, you're the only representative who agreed to meet with me today."

Surely that counted for something. Matt pushed to his feet as the older man stood, his hand extended. Even at seventy, J. Phillip Bradford was as tall as Matt's six-one, his posture ramrod-straight, his grip firm as he still seemed to take Matt's measure.

"This gala is very important to me. At last year's affair, we raised enough money to fund an orphanage for a year. With the ambience you, or one of your competitors, provide, I expect to do even better this year. Thank you for coming by, Matthew."

Outside the conference room, Matt allowed his shoulders to relax as he mentally ticked the meeting off his to-do list for the day and hurried to the elevator. When he stepped off on the ground floor, he dialed Jessica. Today was the day. Pick her up in twenty minutes, take her to his apartment and make his *special* breakfast, then pop the question.

"Good morning, love." Sleepiness edged her soft voice.

She wasn't up, much less dressed. Disappointment stole a little of his excitement. "The meeting is over, and I'm on my way to pick you up."

"Now? What time is it?"

"Yes, now, and it's eleven-thirty. I have a special day planned."

"And I'm almost ready," she said with a low chuckle. "Fooled you, didn't I? But, since I'm not quite dressed yet, why don't I drive myself to your apartment?"

Punctuality wasn't Jessica's strong suit so he was a little surprised. "See me in the next thirty minutes?"

"Forty-five. I'll call you before I leave."

Back at his apartment, he set the dining room table then picked up a magazine he'd left flopped open on the bar. He looked around for a place to stash it.

Allie materialized in his mind, how she'd hesitated when he asked her thoughts about the apartment. She hadn't liked what she'd seen. It'd been written all over her face. Not that she would ever like anything about his new lifestyle.

Allie had looked good, and he wondered what made her lose all that weight? Not that she'd ever looked bad, or at least he hadn't thought so. She'd been the one bothered by her Rubenesque figure.

Was it because of Peter? Surely, not that smug egotist. What was it Peter said he did? Director of social services. Perfect. A bureaucratic job suited him to a T. He just couldn't see Allie and Peter together.

Matt glanced down at the magazine still in his hand. Maybe next week he and Jessica could pick out a new end table with a drawer. And maybe a couple of landscapes for the walls to go with the abstract painting. Scratch that thought. He'd mentioned that before. *No, no, Matthew, space and light will flow, creating the perfect decor for this room. Besides, this room is you.*

His cell vibrated in his pocket, and he fished it out. Jessica. "Yes?"

"Just so you'll know, I'm walking out the door. And did you remember to pick up the caramel coffee at Starbucks?"

His heart sank. Would Starbucks be open on New Year's Day? It had to be. If not, maybe there was a number on the door for emergencies. "It will be waiting for you."

"Good. See you soon."

Matt had fifteen minutes to drive to Starbucks and get back. He grabbed his car keys and hit the door. *Please let the coffee shop be open.* He repeated the mantra all the way to his BMW convertible, and then for the next two blocks. Cars in the parking lot. There *was* a God in heaven. As he got out of the car, a plaintive meow halted him, and he glanced around. Sounded like a kitten. Another meow. Matt ignored it. Inside the store he grabbed a bag of caramel coffee and hurried to the checkout.

Back at his car, the meows intensified. He didn't see a cat, but neither did he look too hard. Humming, he pulled from the parking space and turned onto the street, glancing one last time at the parking lot. A tiny kitten wobbled in the space he'd just left.

No! He didn't have time for any distractions, especially a kitten. Maybe the mother cat would come and take care of it. He drove on. But what if someone ran over it? Someone with small children. Groaning, he made a left onto the next street and circled back to the coffee shop. Maybe the mother cat had made an appearance.

No such luck. Matt parked and, using his finger and thumb, picked up the still mewling kitten. "Aw, kitty, you've got blood seeping from your nose."

The kitten stared at him through one opened eye. Just what he needed. An injured kitten and no vets open, but he couldn't just leave it like this in the cold parking lot. Matt looked around for something to put the kitten in and spied a cardboard box. He hurried to get it, trying not to think about how Jessica was allergic to cats. He would put it in his bedroom. She'd never have to know. "All right, kitty, just for today. Tomorrow you go to animal rescue."

NOAH BLINKED HIS eyes open and stretched his arms. The bed above him creaked, and seconds later a boy about his age popped his head over the side, his solemn brown eyes unwavering.

"You can't have the top bunk. It's ours."

Noah glared at him. "I don't want your old top bunk." He hoped he fell out of it.

Another blond head popped over the side, and Noah rubbed his eyes. Was he seeing double? No, there were two of them—they wore different pajama tops. The new boy had stars on his pajamas.

"Don't pay any attention to Lucas," star man said. "I'm Logan. We're twins. Why are you here? Our mom died and our dad got put in jail."

Lucas nodded. "Nobody wanted us so they brought us here. Didn't nobody want you, either?"

"I don't have anyone but my mom." Noah laced his fingers behind his head. "Doesn't matter—I'm not going to be here long."

"You'll be here longer than you think." Lucas swiped his nose with his white pajama sleeve. He poked his brother. "Come on. I smell breakfast."

Both heads disappeared, and when the twins descended the ladder at the foot of the bed, Noah got a good look at them. They were identical down to the freckles across their noses, except for their pajamas. Logan was an astronaut. Noah squinted. Was that a sad donkey on the pajamas Lucas had on? Boy, did somebody know him.

"You coming?" asked Logan.

"I'm not waiting," Lucas said and left, but Logan lingered.

"I'll be there in a minute." Noah had to figure a way to get out of here. A few minutes later, after Logan had exited and when no plan on how to get past the locked door came to him, he sniffed the air. Definitely wasn't bacon he smelled, more like sausage. Maybe there'd be some more of those biscuits like last night. *Last night.* His mom, so white, not saying anything. He threw back the blanket and scrambled out of bed. Miss Sarah might have heard something from the hospital.

Where were his shoes? He dropped to the floor and searched under the bed. They weren't there. He fought to get his breath. He couldn't leave if he didn't have his shoes. Maybe they were with his clothes. He looked in the chair, where he'd neatly folded his shirt and jeans the night before. They were gone. The room spun. He fisted his hands. "No!"

"Noah, honey, what's wrong?" Miss Sarah's arms wrapped around him, and the spinning stopped.

"You took my shoes. And my clothes. Give them back. They're mine."

"Oh, sugar, I just put your clothes in the wash,

and your shoes needed cleaning. You can have them back as soon as they're dry."

He gulped and searched her face. Her brown eyes smiled back at him. "You promise?" he whispered.

"No one's going to take your things here, Noah. This is a safe place. It's where your mom would want you to be."

Miss Sarah was wrong about that. His mom was going to be so angry when she found out. If she found out. "Have...you heard if she's okay?"

She shook her head. "We'll call after breakfast. So, come on and let's get some food in you."

"Can you take me to see her?"

Her shoulders sagged. "Son, I wish I could, but I have to stay here at the shelter. I'll call Jason later. Maybe he can take you."

In the kitchen, the constant clanging from the dryer reassured him. They'd lived in a house once with a dryer, and when his mom put his jeans in it, the sound was the same. Logan and Lucas were already cleaning their plates. Lucas even eyed the three links of sausage on Noah's plate. "Don't even think about it," Noah muttered as he slid into his chair.

Miss Sarah piled scrambled eggs onto Noah's plate. "Want your biscuit buttered?"

"Yes, ma'am." Noah bit into one of the links.

"He didn't say the blessing."

Logan punched his brother. "Knock it off."

Noah kept eating. What was Lucas? The bless-ing boss?

"Now, Lucas," Miss Sarah said, patting Noah on the shoulder. "He may have said a silent one."

He shot the twin a ha-ha-ha smirk. Lucas would never be his friend, 'cause first chance Noah got, he was going to knock his block off.

Miss Sarah walked to the phone on the wall, her house shoes slapping against the floor. Noah held his breath as she dialed. *Let his mom be awake.* He repeated the prayer until she put the phone back in its cradle on the wall and turned to him.

"I'm sorry, Noah, but she's still…asleep."

Why didn't she just say it? His mom was in a coma. Like before. If he could just get to her, tell her he was sorry and that he never should've left her, she'd wake up. He pushed back his plate.

"Honey, you need to eat to keep your strength up."

"I don't want anything."

"Can I have your sausage, then?" Lucas reached toward his plate.

"No!" Noah snatched the remaining link and bit into it. The taste nearly gagged him, but chok-ing it down would be better than letting Lucas have it.

Miss Sarah placed another pan of biscuits on

the table and the twins grabbed two each. "Boys, I have work to do in the office. You three behave until Brittany gets here."

"Yes, ma'am," the twins said in unison. Noah kept chewing.

After Miss Sarah left, he turned to Logan. "Who's Brittany?"

"She helps Miss Sarah." Logan smeared strawberry jam on his biscuit.

"How long have you been here? I don't re-member seeing you in school."

"That's 'cause you always sit with your head down." Logan's lips pressed into a thin line.

"So?" Noah sort of remembered the twins from the cafeteria.

Lucas leaned forward. "We're not gonna be here much longer. Our dad's gonna come get us."

"I thought you said he was in jail."

Lucas shot him a look of disgust. "He's gonna break out. Boy, are you stupid."

Noah's hands curled into fists. Nobody was ever going to call him that again. "I'm not stu-pid. You're stupid if you believe that." He looked toward the door. "How are you gonna get out of here, anyway? Do you know the code?"

Lucas elbowed his brother. "Told you he was stupid. That ain't no lock. It's just something that tells when a door opens."

"You're kidding." Noah's mind raced. All he

had to do was get his clothes on and walk out the door? He crammed the last of the sausage in his mouth and hurried to get his clothes from the dryer. They were almost dry and he quickly changed out of his pajamas.

"What're you doin'?" Logan asked.

"What does it look like? Putting my clothes on."

"You're gonna run away." Lucas's voice raised a notch.

"Shut up." Noah slipped into his still-warm jacket and headed toward the door.

Logan grabbed his arm. "Where're you going?"

Noah shook his arm free and opened the door. Logan might not tell, but Lucas would rat him out in a heartbeat. A soft voice intoned a warning that the back door was open. His heart leaped into his throat. He darted through the door to the outside and didn't quit running until he came to a corner with a traffic light.

With his chest heaving, he tried to get his breath and his bearings. Which way was the hospital? He'd been there, his mom had taken him to the emergency room when he cut his hand. Noah bit his lip. Maybe he could ask someone. He looked around—a patrol car idled in the convenience store parking lot across the street. Swallowing hard, he took a second peek. Empty. The cop must be in the store. Noah ran against the light and kept going until he reached the next corner. Another convenience store. Maybe some-one inside would tell him how to get to the hos-pital.

ALLIE STARED AT the cell number Peter had given her last night. He'd said to call her if she changed her mind about having breakfast with him this morning. She dialed before second thoughts set in. He answered with his last name, sounding very businesslike.

"Uh, it's me, Allie. You said to—"

"Allie! Oh, good, you've changed your mind. Great. I'm staying at the Winthrop, and they serve an excellent brunch until one this af-ternoon. Would you like me to pick you up at Clint's?"

"No, I'll drive." She'd leave for Cedar Grove from the hotel. "I'll be there in twenty minutes."

Allie disconnected. She hadn't been able to forget the call Peter had received last night. In a town the size of Cedar Grove, she had to know the nine-year-old—more than likely he was one of her students. And after a restless night, she was pretty sure which one.

She arrived at the top floor of the Winthrop where the dining room overflowed into the mez-zanine. She spotted Peter over by a window and hesitated. This was not a good idea. What would they talk about? Last night, conversation revolved around dancing and lots of other people. Talking with children one-on-one—piece of cake. Not so much with a man as good-looking as Peter—being the introvert she was, she never felt she was interesting enough to hold an attractive man's attention. With her heart pounding, she took a step back, looking for an escape, but Peter spied her and waved her over. Allie smoothed the winter-white slacks she'd chosen and fastened a smile on her lips.

She accepted the chair Peter pulled out for her. From the window, she glimpsed a view of the Mississippi River as it rolled south. "I've never eaten here before."

A pleased smile spread across his face. Maybe this wouldn't be so bad.

"Good." He lifted his eyebrows. "Maybe there will be more 'firsts' in the future. And I've ordered for us."

"You've ordered for me?" She struggled to keep from giving him her detention glare.

"They were so busy, and I knew you wanted to leave for Cedar Grove as soon as you could."

He made sense, but still…

"Your first course, sir." The waiter placed identical bowls of tropical fruit before them.

As soon as they finished the fruit, the waiter

produced their main course. How much money had Peter given him to hover? She stared at her plate.

"It's a spanakopita omelet," Peter said. "I had the chef make it especially for you."

A Greek omelet. She took a hesitant bite, and as the contrasting flavors of spinach and feta cheese hit her taste buds, she smiled. "Very delicious."

"I didn't think you'd order one yourself, so I took the liberty."

She frowned. How well did he think he knew her? He might have a surprise or two. She eyed Peter's Belgian waffle and sausage. How in the world did he stay so trim? "Either you don't eat like this every day or you are a workout nut."

He laughed, his rich baritone warm to her ears. "Yes and no."

She glanced up, seeking clarification, and he chuckled again.

"Yes, I don't eat like this every day, and no, I don't exercise. At least not too strenuously or every day."

Some people got all the luck. Today Peter wore a black mock turtleneck that hugged his abs and he didn't show an ounce of fat.

He leaned toward Allie. "It's evident you work out."

"Thank you." At least Peter had noticed her

weight loss since college. The approval in his eyes was the payoff for her hours in the gym, and she took a moment to enjoy the compliment.

"I understand you're not seeing anyone right now."

Allie almost choked on her omelet. She patted her lips with the napkin. "I don't have time."

"I've heard that, too. I don't even know how you have time for the gym." Peter used his fingers to count. "Teacher, counselor and Sarah told me you mentor some of the children who come into the shelter. And now you've added foster parenting to the mix?"

Peter had been doing his homework on her. "I like working with kids—it's probably in my genes. Just like with Clint. Watching Mom and Dad take in foster kids influenced both of us. He works with kids at the Boys and Girls Club, and I do what I do. But, because I am busy, I've asked to be considered only for school-age children."

She paused as the waiter appeared at their table and whisked the empty plates away. "But that's enough talk about me," Allie said after he left. "How did you get into social work?"

Peter shrugged. "Dad wanted me to become a psychiatrist, and I wanted to be a musician." A wry grin spread across his lips. "We compromised."

She laughed. "And neither of you won."

"I don't know. It brought me back to Cedar Grove and you."

His pale blue eyes darkened, and she looked away.

"Actually, I never considered being a musician. I think that was just to irritate Dad. I did get a bachelor's in psychology then knocked around for a while."

"So, how did you get to be director of social services in Cedar Grove?"

He leaned back and folded his arms. "*That* is all your fault."

"My fault?"

"Yeah, all that time I was trying to figure out what I wanted to do with the rest of my life, something you said at graduation kept bouncing around in my head."

She cocked her head. "And that was?"

"You paraphrased John Kennedy, who paraphrased an old school master. 'Don't ask what our country can do for us—'"

"Ask what we can do for her." Allie grinned as she finished the sentence. "I was young and idealistic."

"You're still idealistic. I've wanted to tell you for some time that the impact of your words prompted me to apply for a job with the Department of Human Services in Washington, and it didn't take long to figure out I needed a master's in social work."

"Why did you come back to Cedar Grove?"

He took her hand and caressed her fingers. "Because of you."

Her face burning, she withdrew her hand. "Why are you suddenly interested in me?"

"It's not sudden. I've always been interested, but in high school and during college, you only had eyes for Matt. When I returned to Cedar Grove last year, friends told me not to waste my time. You were married to your job and your volunteer projects. I invented excuses to be at the shelter when I knew you would be there, but every time we met, you pulled into your shell and hung out the Do Not Disturb sign. That's why I resorted to practically begging your brother to invite me last night."

"Why didn't you just flat-out ask?"

Peter flashed a wicked grin. "Let's see if that will work." He cleared his throat and leaned toward her. "Miss Carson, I enjoyed dancing with you last night. There's a nice supper club in Cedar Grove. So what do you say? Dinner and dancing Friday night?"

Why not? Dancing with Peter had been fun, and today had been...different. Just because they went out, didn't mean she had to give him her heart. It was in too many pieces anyway. She tilted her head toward him. "I would love to."

"Good." He motioned to the waiter for another refill on their coffee. "Can I ask you a personal question?"

"You can ask. Don't know if you'll get an answer."

"What did you ever see in Matt Jefferies?"

"I can't believe you asked me that."

He shrugged. "I just never understood why you dated him. He wasn't good enough for you."

Suddenly Peter's interest in her became clearer. Allie blotted her mouth with her napkin. A memory from high school. Peter losing a math competition to Matt. Peter telling Matt he'd never be anything but the kid from the wrong side of town. Surely that wasn't what Peter referred to. But she had to know for sure.

Allie fingered the handle of the porcelain cup, and on cue, the waiter appeared and refilled it with coffee. After he left, she stirred cream into her cup. "You're not still competing with Matt, are you?"

"Compete with Matt? Of course not. I'm glad to see him doing well. I just always thought you belonged with someone more like me." He smiled, exposing perfectly even white teeth.

"And not the kid from Beaker Street?"

A red flush started at his neck and ended at

his ears. "That was a stupid remark I made a long time ago. I never should've said it. I didn't like that he always beat me in everything. Math, quarterback position, you."

She eyed him over the cup's rim.

"Honestly," he said, "I've always regretted saying that."

What was it she'd always heard about people using the word *honestly?*

Peter's cell phone rang, and he slid it from his belt. He frowned. "I can't believe I'm getting another call from the office. Excuse me."

He stepped away from the table. When he returned, his face was pinched and the muscle in his jaw twitched.

"That case from last night?" She'd been trying to figure out how to bring up the subject without being too obvious. Now the problem was solved.

"Yeah," he muttered. "The kid's run away."

"Last night you said the child was a nine-year-old boy. He may be in my reading class. Maybe I can help. It's possible I know the family, or where he might've gone."

"Oh, I know where he's gone. The hospital to check on his OD'd mother. Sarah at the shelter said that's all he talked about."

Protective son, overdosed mother. *Don't let it be—* "Is the mother's name Mariah Connors?"

He stared at her. "How do you know Mariah Connors?"

She swallowed the bile that rose up her throat. Poor Noah. "I've counseled the boy, had parent-teacher meetings with Mariah, so I know the situation. She's Matt Jefferies's sister."

MATT TOOK ONE last look at the diamond engagement ring and closed the box. He'd locked the wedding band away in his wall safe until the wedding. *Wedding.* He liked the sound of the word.

A tiny flicker of regret pierced his memory. He'd asked Allie to marry him once, and she'd turned him down. Looking back, it was probably for the best. Allie never approved of his bold plans to get ahead, and she wouldn't fit into his present lifestyle. Besides, she was his past. Jessica was his future. A future that was within his grasp, one he had worked hard to get. Jessica wanted the same things he did. But it was more than wanting the same things. She was kind and caring.

His heart tendered at a memory of Jessica in the park last summer. She'd set up her easel at the Memphis Zoo to sketch the snow leopards, and a small girl had wanted to "help." Without hesitation, Jessica flipped to a new sheet in her sketch pad and spent the next fifteen minutes letting the child try her hand at drawing.

The kitten mewed, and he glanced at the cardboard box. The kitten had surprised him when he returned home with it, lapping milk from a bowl. It mewed again. "Shh," he said as he knelt by the box. "You need to be quiet. Jessica will be here soon and if she hears you, she'll want to hold you and that will make her sneeze. Are you hungry?"

Matt had cleaned the closed eye, and now the kitten stared at him with two good eyes. It mewed again, and he frowned. He'd barely got ten a little more milk poured when the doorbell rang. He settled it gently on an old T-shirt in a corner of the box. "Be quiet," he said and closed the door to his bedroom.

"Happy New Year, love." Jessica swept into the room and wrapped her arms around his neck.

He tilted her face toward him and gently kissed her as the strains of "Clair de Lune" played softly in the background. Matt kissed her again, and she leaned into him, returning his kiss. "Happy New Year to you, too," he said when they broke apart. "Are you hungry?"

"Hmm, I don't know. This is nice." Her stomach growled, and she giggled. "I guess that ruined the mood."

"Right this way, m'lady."

"What's this?" She shifted her gaze from the table set with his best china and back to Matt.

"Just setting the mood," he replied. "You look great, as usual."

And she did, in boots and black leggings and a short, hunter-green dress that brought out the green in her hazel eyes.

"You're not so bad yourself." She stroked the red cashmere sweater he wore, a Christmas gift from her. "So, what have you made me?"

He pulled out her chair. "Eggs Benedict—I just have to cook the eggs, but we'll start off with fruit, and caramel coffee."

An hour later, Matt refreshed their cups. Everything had gone off without a hitch, even the eggs. Jessica smiled

"Thank you, Matthew. I don't know when I've ever had a better New Year's celebration. Last night and now this morning."

His heart thumped faster as he looked into her eyes. The velvet box was in his pocket, waiting for him to bring out at the right moment. He took her hand. "Jessica, we've talked about marriage before, and you know how much I—"

A yowl from his bedroom made him flinch.

"What was that?" She looked over his shoulder toward the bedroom.

The kitten. Not mewing, but sounding exactly

like it had in the parking lot. Loud. Pitiful. It was a noise that could not be ignored. "Uh…"

"Matthew, do I hear a cat?" She cocked her head. "It is. But…but you know I'm allergic."

"I know. It's a kitten, and I thought I ran over it. You stay here while I go check—"

The doorbell rang, and rang again. And again.

"I'll get the door." Jessica pointed toward the bedroom. "You see about that poor kitty."

The kitten howled again, and Matt huffed a sigh. It probably needed milk again, and he grabbed the carton. "Be right back. Entertain whoever it is."

The kitten stared plaintively at him when he opened the door and immediately hushed its crying. He picked up the bowl and refilled it. Voices came from the other room. Women's voices. Matt placed the bowl beside the kitten and guided it to the milk. "You're on your own, kiddo," he said and went to wash his hands.

Then he stepped into the living room and stopped. "Allie?"

Jessica's gaze went from Allie to him. "You didn't tell me Clint's sister was stopping by."

Something was wrong. Bad wrong. It was stamped in the way Allie stood, in the slump of her shoulders, in her face. "What's going on?"

"Matt, I don't know how to tell you… Mariah

is in the hospital. Your sister may not make it. And her son has run away from the shelter."

He didn't know why he felt so surprised.

"Sister?" Jessica turned to him. "You never said anything about a sister."

"Everybody, just sit down." He sank into the hard leather chair closest to him and looked at Allie. "What happened?"

"I'm not sure. All I know is she overdosed on heroin and her little boy has run away from the person who was looking after him temporarily," Allie said. "You'll have to ask Peter Elliott exactly what happened."

He missed whatever she said next. Peter Elliott? He was taken aback the great man hadn't already called to rub Matt's nose in the news. *Mariah. What have you done?* His sister might be two years older, but he'd always taken care of her until she ran off with that Connors thug. He realized Allie had asked him something. "I'm sorry, I didn't—"

"I have the hospital number, if you want it." She held a slip of paper out toward him.

Matt folded his arms across his chest. "I don't know what you expect me to do. I tried to talk to Mariah when she first started using—after Connors introduced her to drugs. She didn't listen then, and I doubt that anything has changed. I'm sorry, but she made her choice a long time ago."

And he had made his when he left Cedar Grove. He just never thought his past would choose today to catch up with him.

CHAPTER FOUR

NOAH WAITED FOR an opportunity to slip into the hospital entrance unnoticed. By now, the cops were sure to be looking for him, and they'd probably figure out where he'd gone. A man and woman with four boys walked toward the door. Maybe no one would notice if he tagged along. Noah fell in behind them, staying just close enough, but not so close the man or woman would notice him.

Noah almost bumped into the last boy when the man stopped and turned around.

"'Scuse me," Noah mumbled and bent over to untie his shoe and retie it.

The man clapped his hands once. "Okay, boys, listen up We're going down this hall to the ICU waiting room. I want you to be quiet. There's folks here that have really sick people in the hospital. You mind your manners now, you hear?"

Noah couldn't believe his luck. As soon as they started walking, he stood and tagged along. Once in the waiting room, he glanced around. Adults sat in little groups, but there was one area where kids watched cartoons on a wall TV. An empty chair next to a girl about his age beckoned to him. He sauntered over and sat in the vinyl wingback like he owned it. After a few minutes, he braved a glance around. People seemed to be lining up toward the silver double doors. "Where's everybody going?" he muttered under his breath.

"It's almost visiting time. But you're not old enough to go back."

Noah whipped his head around. He hadn't meant anyone to hear him. The girl never looked up from her book. "What do you know about how old I am?"

"Puh-leese." She eyed him over the book. "We're both in Miss Allie's reading class. *Hello?*"

Heat crawled up his neck and spread to the tip of his ears. *Ashley...something or other.* She always knew the answer to everything, and she never stumbled over her words. Noah dug his fingers into the hard vinyl. Maybe if he squeezed his eyes hard enough, when he opened them she'd be gone. Nope, she was still there.

She stared at him. "What are you doing? You look like you're going to be sick or something. Why are you here?"

"What're you doin' here?" he snapped.

"My granna's real sick."

Oh. He never had a grandmother. "Do you get to go back there to see her?"

"Of course, but with my mother."

She tilted her head up in that superior way girls had, and he quit feeling sorry for her. "Well, when those doors open, I'm going through 'em."

"They'll just make you come back if you don't have an adult with you."

He crossed his arms. "No, they won't."

She gave him a sour look and picked up her book again. "Whatever. But you'll see."

Noah spied the man he'd walked in with standing in line. He had one of the boys with him. "See ya," he said and nonchalantly strolled over to the boy. If Ashley told on him, he'd... He fisted his hands. She just better not.

The doors opened with a soft swish, and people streamed through them and down a hallway with glass enclosures. His heart pounded against his chest until he thought it'd pop out. He didn't see his mom in any of the first rooms. What if she'd died?

Then he noticed each room had a name on the door, and he kept walking even though his legs had turned to spaghetti, peering at each name. *Mariah Connors*. He inched inside the room and approached the person in the bed. Black hair fanned across the pillow, just like his mom's, but this couldn't be her. This person had tubes

and wires *everywhere*. And her face was so big.
Then he spied the little black mole next to her
lips. "Mom?"

He touched her hand that lay elevated on a pillow. "Mom. Wake up."

The rhythmic hissing in the room and the
steady *beep, beep, beep* over her head answered
him. He blinked back the tears that threatened
to flood his eyes. "Mom, please."

"I figured I'd find you here."

Noah recognized the cop's voice and whirled
around to face him. Jason didn't look too happy.

Suddenly, the beeping increased and just as
fast it stopped. One long beep scraped against
his eardrums. Alarms went off. Jason grabbed
him up and carried him into the hall as nurses
swarmed the room.

"Mommm!"

ALLIE'S HEART PLUMMETED. Who was this person
Matt had turned himself into? The man she had
loved would never turn his back on his family. But that was the reason they broke up. He'd
been so bent on shedding everything about his
life in Cedar Grove, including his values, that
she couldn't bear to watch.

He just proved she'd made the right choice,
and now every second in his presence picked at
the scab on her heart, reminding Allie that the

Matt she'd known was truly gone. Why had she even bothered? She should have just let Peter handle the whole matter.

For the first time, Allie noticed the closed blinds, the fancy dishes on the dining room table. *We're kind of talking about getting married.* Uh-oh. Heat crawled up her spine and across her face. Could the floor just open and swallow her right now? "I'm sorry—"

"Matthew…" Jessica's soft voice held a touch of steel. "Would you please explain about this sister you never told me about? And why you don't want to help her?"

Allie stared at him. Yeah, Matthew, why *didn't* you tell this woman you're about to propose to that you had a sister? Exactly what kind of relationship did they have?

A wince flitted across Matt's face. He sat a little straighter and rubbed his hands on his thighs. "She's not anyone you would want to know. She hasn't made the best decisions in life, and I rarely hear from her…I didn't even know she had a son until Allie told me last night."

Conflicting emotions crossed Jessica's face. Allie sensed Matt's fiancée was not happy. "Look, I'm kind of in the way here, and I need to get on the road home. Mariah is at Cedar Grove Memorial, if you change your mind."

"Would you leave the number, as well?" Jessica's gaze was on Matt.

Allie laid the paper on the coffee table. "Nice seeing you again, Jessica. Matt, I'll see myself out."

In the elevator, Allie hugged her jacket closer. Matt hadn't even tried to stop her. If she never saw him again, it'd be too soon. She'd rather walk through a pasture full of cow pies. Be easier. At least in the pasture, she only had to watch where she stepped. She couldn't wait to get away from Memphis.

As soon as Allie left the Memphis city limits and traffic behind, she voice-dialed the shelter's director. For the past year, Allie had volunteered at the children's shelter, helping several of the kids with their reading and writing skills. Friendship with Sarah had been a bonus. When she answered, Sarah sounded close to tears. "What's wrong?" Allie asked.

"It's this boy Jason brought in last—"

"Noah Connors? Has he been found?"

"You know?"

"Yes. Is he hurt?"

"No, he's okay. I don't know how the boy did it, but he made it to the hospital where his mom is. Jason found Noah in her room just about the time everything went bad. She stopped breathing, her heart stopped. Jason said it was terrible."

Allie swallowed. "Did she…"

"No, she didn't die. Well, she did, but they brought her back."

"Where's Noah now?"

"My helper, Brittany, is with him at the hospital. When Jason told me what happened, I just couldn't make him leave until she got better."

"I'm an hour away from Cedar Grove. I'll stop at the hospital and check on him."

"Does he have any other family?"

Allie hesitated. "His uncle is aware of the situation."

"Oh, good. That boy needs family around him."

Allie agreed. She ended the call and pulled over to the side of the road. Matt wouldn't listen to her, and she didn't have his phone number, anyway. Maybe he'd listen to her brother. She dialed Clint's number.

Her brother answered on the second ring. "What's up?"

"I need you to call Matt." Allie explained about Mariah and Noah.

"The poor kid." Clint's concern came through the phone. "I'll call Matt and see to it he gets his priorities in order."

She wished him luck and ended the call. If she pushed it, she'd make the hospital in forty-five minutes.

WHEN ALLIE ROUNDED the corner to the ICU waiting room, she spied Noah huddled in a chair with his eyes closed. He reminded her of a fledgling bird that'd fallen out of the nest. She nodded to Brittany in the next chair, and then knelt beside him.

"Miss Allie." He rubbed his eyes.

She brushed his blond hair back. "Are you doing okay?"

His chin quivered, but he nodded. "My mom. They won't let me see her."

"Maybe when she feels a little better…"

"But what if she doesn't get better?" he whispered, his blue eyes round.

Allie gulped. Why couldn't there be easy answers? Right now she could just about wring Mariah's neck for putting her son through this hurt. "Let's don't cross that bridge just yet." She squeezed his hand. "Let me see what I can find out."

At the desk, she identified herself and asked the receptionist about Mariah's condition.

"Are you family?"

"No. I'm a friend of the family." Allie leaned in closer so she could see the woman's name tag. "But, Melanie, I'm asking for a little boy who desperately needs to know how his mother is doing."

Melanie eyed her, then her gaze slid past Allie

toward the waiting room. "We have to ask," she said. Her mouth quirked down into a frown. "Let me call her nurse."

A minute later she nodded. "She's stabilized, and they've given her something to keep her knocked out for a while."

"Can I take him back, just so he can see that she's okay?"

The receptionist hesitated, visibly tensing.

"If you were in his mom's shape, wouldn't you want your child to know you were okay?"

Melanie's shoulders relaxed, and she nodded. "But you can only stay a few minutes."

Allie walked back to where Noah sat. "They said I could take you to see her. But, remember, she's sleeping—we can only stay a few minutes."

His eyes widened. "Really?"

"Really." He hopped from the chair and took her hand.

"Wait a minute." Noah grabbed a piece of paper. "I wrote her a letter. Can I take it back?"

"I don't see why not." She turned to Brittany. "I can take over from here. I'll get him back to the shelter."

"Will that be all right with Miss Sarah?" Brittany asked.

"I'm sure it will be. I'm a certified volunteer at the shelter, and I've taken the children on field trips. You can call and check with her while we visit his mother."

The double doors opened to let them through. When they reached Mariah's cubicle, Noah pulled at her hand. "Come on, they might change their minds."

Allie let him pull her inside the room. She hadn't expected Mariah to look so...corpselike. Noah dropped her hand and approached the bed as a monitor beeped an irregular rhythm. Allie didn't even recognize the woman lying in the hospital bed. Mariah lay unmoving, her bloated face as white as the sheet covering her.

"Mom," Noah said softly. He patted her distended hand. "I'm here."

The beeping sped up. Allie stepped toward him. "Noah, we can't stay."

He blinked fast, his eyes shiny. "Not yet." He turned back to his mom. "Please, Mom. Wake up."

A nurse appeared at the door. "You have to leave."

"No!" His desperate cry squeezed Allie's heart. "She'll get better if I talk to her."

As if on cue, Mariah's heart rate slowed to an even tempo. The nurse glanced at the monitor then back at Noah. "Five minutes," she said. Then she gave him a gentle smile. "She needs to rest."

"I think he'll be ready then," Allie said.

Noah patted Mariah's arm. "Mom, you've got to get better." He licked his lips. "You didn't finish teaching me how to dance."

As the boy talked to his mom, the back of Allie's throat ached. She dug in her jeans for a tissue and, not finding one, used the back of her hand to blot her eyes. The wall clock ticked the minutes by while she leaned against the wall and let her gaze travel around the room. On a white board, someone had written, *Good morning. I'm Becky and I'll be your nurse today.* That solved the question of who the nurse was. She glanced through the glass partition at the nurses' station. Becky tapped her watch, and Allie nodded. She turned to Noah. He'd found a wet cloth and wiped Mariah's forehead with it. How many times had he done that in the past?

"Noah." Her voice cracked. She pressed her lips together and took a breath and blew it out. "We have to go."

"Just one more minute."

"The nurse wants her to rest. Come on," she urged softly. "We'll come back."

He reached on his tiptoes and kissed his mother's pasty cheek, then ducked his head as he walked toward Allie.

She reached to take his hand, but he stopped short. "Wait! I didn't give her my letter." Noah slipped the paper from his pants pocket and folded it until it was small enough to tuck into Mariah's closed hand.

At the nurses' desk, Allie fished one of her business cards from her purse and gave it to Becky. "Would you call me if there's any change?"

"I'll put this with her chart," the nurse replied.

"And thanks for letting us stay longer than five minutes."

"I think your visit may do more good than all the medicine."

Noah flipped his bangs out of his eyes. "Will you read my note to her when she wakes up?"

Becky leaned over the desk. "I will, honey. Your mama's going to be all right. She's got some mighty fine doctors."

Don't tell him that. You don't know for sure. Allie bit the words back. The nurse meant well, but what if Mariah didn't make it?

Back in the waiting area, Allie called Sarah and gave her an update on Mariah. "The regular visiting time is at three. I'll bring him back to the shelter after that, unless something comes up. If it does, I'll call you."

Noah glanced up at her after she'd disconnected. "Do I have to go back?"

"You don't like it there?"

He shrugged. "Miss Sarah's nice. And Logan's okay. Lucas is a pain...."

"But?"

He shrank back into the chair and lifted his thin shoulder in a timid gesture. "Have you ever stayed in a place like the shelter before?"

Noah glanced toward the exit sign. She cupped his chin and turned his face back to her. "Where was it, Noah?"

He licked his lips. "In another state. Before we came to Cedar Grove. Mom was...sick, and this woman came and took me to this house."

"What happened?" She forced out the question, not sure she wanted to hear the answer.

"I ran away."

AFTER THE DOOR closed behind Allie, Matt pressed his fingers against his eyelids, then slid his hands to the side of his head and massaged his temples. If New Year's Day was any indication of how the rest of his year would be...he didn't want to go there.

"Matthew..." Jessica stood at the sliding door with her back to him. She turned to face him. "I think we need to talk."

He rose and went to her, taking her hands. "You're right."

"Why didn't you tell me about your sister? I mean, I realize you may not be all that proud, her being on drugs and all, but you could've told me. Did you think it would change the way I feel about you?"

He wanted to say he didn't know why he never mentioned Mariah to Jessica, but he did know. Just like he knew why he never mentioned anything else about his past, and it had nothing to do with Jessica. "I know you better than that. It's like I said before. Mariah and I have grown so far apart, it's almost like she wasn't there. I didn't even know about the kid." He rubbed the locked muscles in the back of his neck.

"But family is important. I think you should go."

Matt stiffened. Jessica didn't have a clue what she was asking him to do. He wasn't ready to go back to Cedar Grove, where everyone remembered him as the kid from Beaker Street. The kid who had said he'd own his own company by the time he turned thirty. Well, he was thirty and still working for someone else. It didn't matter that he pulled in six figures a year—he wasn't his own boss, and that's what everyone would remember.

His cell phone rang, and he glanced at the caller ID.

"It's Clint." Allie was calling in the big guns. "I'm not going," he said when he answered.

"Did you know her heart stopped? And she's in a coma."

Clint's blunt words startled Matt. He sank onto the couch. "I…had no idea. How about the boy? Has he been found?"

"Yes, he was at the hospital. Do you want me to go with you? You know, so you won't have to face this by yourself."

Or to make sure Matt went. "No. You have responsibilities here."

"You're going then?"

Matt sucked in a breath of air through his nose and exhaled. A memory of Mariah standing between him and their drunken father surfaced. Mariah taking the beating. He closed his eyes. "Yes, I'm going."

"I'll text you Allie's number so you can let her know," Clint said.

"Is she worse?" Jessica asked after he hung up.

"She's in a coma."

Jessica crossed the room and sat beside him, squeezing his hand. "I'm going with you."

"No!"

Jessica flinched.

"I'm sorry, I didn't mean to bite your head off, but I don't know how long I'll be there." No way was Jessica going to Cedar Grove. He could just see her in his mother's tiny frame house. No amount of paint or chrome and fancy furniture would transform it into something other than the four-room, white-clapboard dump that it was. And even though it wouldn't matter one way or the other to Jessica, he wasn't quite ready to show her how he'd grown up. "Not this time. There's the boy to consider, and I don't even know if Mariah will make it."

"Oh, Matthew." She put her arms around him. "That's all the more reason for me to go."

He stilled. Jessica could be quite stubborn when she wanted to be. "Maybe next time."

"But—"

A plaintive meow interrupted her. Matt had forgotten the kitten.

Jessica glanced toward his bedroom. "Where did you get that kitten? And what are you going to do with it?"

Good question. Jessica certainly couldn't take it, because of her allergies, not even for the two days until the animal shelter opened. "Maybe Clint will take it."

She tilted her head to the side. "Tell me about you and Allie. You two seem very close."

"We grew up together, went to the same college." His hometown wasn't the only thing Matt wasn't ready to tell Jessica about. "Sweetheart, I have a lot to do, and I need you to leave so I can do it. I'll call you tonight after I see Mariah."

She patted his cheek. "I could help you. You

know, clear the table, put the dishes in the dishwasher…"

"Thanks, but you would be a distraction."

"You mean, like this?" Jessica slipped her arms around his neck and pressed her lips to his.

He leaned into the kiss…until the kitten intruded again with another insistent meow. He eased his lips away from hers and he turned her to face the door. "Yes, like that."

After he closed the door behind Jessica, Matt leaned his head against the wood. How he dreaded returning to Cedar Grove.

JUST OUTSIDE OF MEMPHIS, a black sports car with its top down passed Matt on the four-lane highway. Unthinkable for it to be warm enough to lower the top on New Year's Day, and if it hadn't been for the kitten he'd been forced to bring along, he'd be enjoying the fresh air.

"Thanks, Kiddo," Matt muttered to the kitten curled up in the pet carrier he'd stopped to buy after Clint had been unable to come for it. Something about his apartment lease. Maybe Cedar Grove had a good animal shelter. At least he'd been able to reach the real estate agent who managed his mother's house for him. The last renters had moved out before Christmas, and it hadn't been rented yet. The agent assured Matt that linens and a few basic items would be waiting for him. He'd forgotten that aspect of a small town —the willingness to accommodate.

His cell phone chirped, and he glanced at the ID. A Cedar Grove number, but not Allie's. That one he knew by heart after trying to reach her for the better part of two hours. He'd finally given up and left her a voice mail that he was on his way and should be there by four-thirty.

"Hello?"

"Peter Elliott here. Clint gave me your number."

"Hello, Peter." Matt deadpanned his voice. "If you're calling about Mariah and her son, I'm on my way to Cedar Grove. I understand the boy has been found."

"Yes. Noah will be returning to the shelter, and that's where he will remain until Tuesday's youth court hearing. I'm looking for a foster home to place him in until it can be determined that Mariah can care for him."

Matt gripped the phone. Who did Peter think he was, making decisions for his nephew? A car whizzed past him, the horn blowing, and Matt glanced at the speedometer. Fifty miles an hour. Time to pull over and focus on one thing. "No. He'll be staying with me. I'm his uncle," he said as he maneuvered the car onto the shoulder of the road.

"He's a ward of the state, Matt."

"He can't be. Not legally. It's New Year's Day, and there's no way that you've been able to file the paperwork. And when Mariah regains consciousness, I'm sure she will agree."

"It's not that simple, Matthew."

His phone beeped, and he glanced at it. A text from Allie. Noah and I are at the hospital. ICU waiting room. "I'll contact you when I reach Cedar Grove, Peter." Matt broke the connection. In a pig's eye he would.

Maybe he should call his attorney. He hated to on New Year's Day, but on the other hand, Matt needed to know his rights. He scrolled through his contacts and found his attorney's cell phone number. Ten minutes later, he disconnected, satisfied that all he needed to do was get a notarized statement from Mariah giving him temporary custody. And one of the attorneys in the office would be available to attend Tuesday's hearing if he needed one.

An hour later, Matt turned off the highway onto the street to the hospital as dusk edged toward night. He hadn't planned to stop there first, but he wanted to take custody of the boy before Peter got to him. He parked near the door and glanced at the kitten. Check on Mariah, get Noah. Shouldn't take fifteen minutes. Kiddo should be fine.

He hurried to the waiting room. Allie sat on

a small sofa in a corner of the room, cocooning a sleeping boy in her arms, and it hit him—this was a living, breathing nine-year-old boy. With needs. What was he thinking? He clenched his jaw. Peter Elliott had him cornered. No. Truth smacked him in the face. Nothing but his pride had painted himself into this corner.

Allie saw him and held her finger to her lips. Matt nodded. It was better if he visited Mariah first, anyway. He pointed to himself and then to the double doors. Allie nodded she understood and Matt approached the reception desk. "I'm Mariah Connors's brother. I live out of state and just found out she was here. Is there any way I can go back and see her now?"

The receptionist frowned.

Before she could give him a no, he pointed toward Allie and Noah. "My sister's son is really worn out, and I'd like to get him home. If I could just go back for a couple of minutes, see for myself how she is, it'd be great."

She waved him back. "But just this once… since you've come from out of town. Room twelve."

Inside the steel doors, his muscles tensed as he counted the glass-encased rooms. Near the end his mother had been in one of these very rooms, struggling for each breath. He stopped outside the door of room twelve to collect himself. Somehow he hadn't gotten here in his mind. Matt sucked in a deep breath and squared his shoulders, but nothing could've prepared him for what waited inside the cubicle.

The woman in the bed could not be his sister. And for a second, she wasn't. Instead his mom lay in the bed, a tube sending a steady stream of oxygen in her nose. Matt shook his head hard, and the image of his mother cleared. But not the deep pain in his heart. This slip of a girl looked nothing like the Mariah he remembered, even taking into account the swelling in her face and hands.

His Mariah sang and danced and filled a room with her lively spirit. Matt's hands curled into two fists as he tried to hold on to the Mariah in his memories. He fixed his gaze on the rise and fall of her chest then leaned over and stroked her arm. He'd give anything if she'd just open her blue eyes and laugh at his tears. "Oh, Mariah... what happened?"

He pulled a chair beside the bed and sat beside her, stroking her arm. "I haven't met your son, yet. Why didn't you tell me about him? I'm going to take him home with me. He'll like it in Memphis. Then when you get better, you can come live with us."

He had no idea where the words came from. Of if he even meant them. But it seemed important to say them. A piece of paper lay under her hand. Matt pulled it out and unfolded it. Some sort of note. The words he read seared his heart. "I don't know if you can hear me, Mariah, but I want to read you something.... 'Dear Mom, I'm sorry I went to find something to eat. Maybe if I had stayed you'd be all right. You have to get better. I love you. Noah.'" Matt cleared his throat. "Sis, don't leave your son. Not like this."

Shoes squeaked behind Matt, and he looked around. A nurse charted her vitals. "Can you tell me how she's doing?"

"She's...actually improving. I know right now it doesn't appear that way, but the doctors have her sedated. Her heart has really calmed down." The nurse put Mariah's chart back in the holder on the wall. "I'm sorry, but I need you to return to the waiting room."

He nodded and stood. "When is the next visiting time?"

"Not until eight."

Three hours. Matt glanced at the monitor over Mariah's head like he had so many times before with his mom. Her heart rate beeped a steady eighty-two times a minute. A good sign.

Back in the waiting room, Allie's arms were still wrapped around the sleeping boy.

"He's exhausted," she whispered when he sat

in the chair across from them. "I'm glad you came."

Noah stirred, and she shifted his weight. Slowly his eyes opened, revealing blue eyes just like Mariah's. When he saw Matt, he jerked upright and pulled away from Allie.

"Noah, this is your Uncle Matt." Allie brushed his blond hair out of his eyes.

The boy needed a haircut, and he didn't seem at all pleased to see him. Matt stuck out his hand. "It's good to finally meet you."

Noah ignored it and wrapped his arms across his chest. Allie leaned over and whispered in his ear. The boy shook his head.

"Noah, I'd really like for us to be friends," Matt said. "I'd like for you to stay with me until your mom gets better."

"No!"

"Why not?"

Noah jutted his jaw. "Mom said not to trust you."

CHAPTER FIVE

HIS UNCLE ROCKED back in the chair, looking at Noah as if he didn't know what to do next, but Noah wasn't about to be friends with this guy. His mom didn't trust him. Neither would he. He glanced up at Miss Allie. Even she looked at him funny.

"I'd like a chance to get to know you," Matt said.

"Why?"

"Uh…" His uncle scratched his head. "You're my nephew? I know I haven't been around, but that's not entirely my fault. Your mom never told me about you."

"Give him time, Matt." Noah blinked as Miss Allie smiled warmly at him. "Your Uncle Matt really didn't know."

Matt leaned forward. "I really do want you to live with me until your mom gets better."

"No, you don't. Mom said you didn't want to be bothered with us, that you were too busy getting rich."

His uncle looked like he'd eaten a lemon, but

Miss Allie seemed to think what Noah said was funny.

"Well, your mom had it wrong, but if you'd rather stay at the shelter than to trust me…" Matt shrugged. "I'll just return to Memphis so I can go back to getting rich."

The shelter. Noah hadn't thought about that. His stomach growled. He was hungry—really hungry.

"Tell you what," Matt said. "I haven't eaten since lunch, and it's kind of hard to think when I'm hungry. What do you say we go get a burger? Then we'll sort all this out."

He wasn't going anywhere with this guy by himself. "Can Miss Allie go?"

Matt shrugged. "If she wants to."

Miss Allie didn't look like she thought it was a good idea at all. His stomach growled again, and both of them looked at him. "You are hungry," Miss Allie said. "Tell you what. Matt, you can follow us in your car to this great burger place over on Second Street."

Suddenly his uncle gasped like he had a pain. "I have something in my car I need to check on. Are you ready to go?"

"Can we come back here later?" Noah asked.

Miss Allie and Matt looked at each other, and then Matt checked his watch. "I don't see why not. There's one more visiting hour tonight at eight. We can come back for that."

They followed Matt as he hurried out of the hospital. It was already dark, but still not too cold. Miss Allie told him to zip up his jacket, though, and Noah did. He wished his mom would wake up so he could ask her about Matt. Noah kind of liked him. His uncle didn't talk to him like he was a baby.

"I'm parked over here." Miss Allie pointed to the left.

"Me, too." Matt jogged to a small black car parked beneath the security light and opened the passenger door. A loud wail spilled out into the night air, sounding almost as scary as the siren Noah had heard earlier.

"What in the world…" Miss Allie peered over Matt's shoulder as Noah drew closer to her.

"I'm sorry, Kiddo," Matt said as he turned around, cradling a small ball of white and black and orange fur.

"Matthew Jefferies, did you leave that kitten in your car all this time?"

His uncle stared at Miss Allie. "Where was I supposed to leave it? It's not that cold, and Kiddo has a fur coat and an old T-shirt."

Noah edged closer to Matt. The kitten fixed its dark eyes on him and wailed again, but not as loud. Noah held out his hand, and the kitten rubbed his finger with the side of its face.

"Want to hold Kiddo?"

Noah nodded and Matt placed the kitten in his arms. Kiddo nudged his chest. "I think she's hungry."

"You think so?" his uncle asked. "And how do you know it's a she?"

Noah rolled his eyes. "It's a calico." Boy, his uncle was dumb. *Everyone* knew a calico was a girl kitten. He looked up. "Do you have anything to feed her?"

Matt was looking at him with a funny expression in his eyes. The kitten nudged him again and meowed just as loud as before. "When I bought the pet carrier, I picked up a couple of cans of kitten formula and some solid food. Why don't we go to my house and feed this kitten before we go eat?"

His uncle had a house in Cedar Grove? He bit his lip. Maybe he'd go with him long enough to feed Kiddo.

"I have an idea," Miss Allie said. "Why don't you two go to the house while I pick up the burgers? If there's a table and plates and stuff, we can eat there." She looked at Noah. "You okay with that?"

He cut his eyes up at Matt, then back to the kitten. His uncle didn't know much about kittens. He rubbed the top of Kiddo's head, and she tried to find his fingers, looking for something to eat. "I guess I better. You'd probably feed her too much and then she'd get sick. But I'm not calling her Kiddo. That's a stupid name."

ONE SMALL VICTORY. Matt felt like cheering, and he really didn't blame his nephew for being suspicious. His conscience pricked him. He should've stayed in touch with Mariah. He should've known about Noah. Allie left him to get her car while he buckled Noah in the passenger side of his convertible then hurried around to the driver's side.

"Wait!" Allie flagged him down before he got out of the parking lot. "You didn't put him in the backseat!"

Matt lowered his window. "What?"

"It's dangerous for a child Noah's size to ride in the front seat."

Mentally he kicked himself. He didn't know anything about raising cats or kids. A quick glance over his shoulder told him what he already knew. No way would the kid fit in the back with all his stuff. "We're just going a few blocks."

"Matthew! It only takes one accident." She looked past him to the backseat. "Oh, I see your problem. Why don't I drop him off then go get the burgers? Cedar Grove isn't that big and it won't take ten minutes longer."

After transferring Noah and the kitten, Matt led the way, passing by the housing projects on Beaker Street. Allie had said Noah and his sister lived somewhere around here. The boy would need clothes no matter where he stayed, and maybe they could stop by their house and pick up something for him to wear. A mile later, dread leached its way into his stomach. Maybe staying in his mom's old house wasn't the best idea. He pulled into the drive and shut off the ignition, waiting for Allie to pull in behind him.

A light shone from the front stoop, illuminating the tiny gray slab that served as a porch. The four-room white-frame house would fit into his top-floor apartment with room to spare. Matt had come full circle, and he didn't know if he could do it. Maybe they could stay in a hotel. Lights flashed behind him, blocking his car in.

With a sigh, he grabbed the kitten supplies and climbed out of the car, almost bumping into Noah, who had the kitten still clutched in his arms. "Is she still hungry?" Matt asked. The boy nodded. "Then let's get her inside and fed." He half turned as Allie backed out of the drive. He almost wished... He summoned his courage. He didn't need a nursemaid to walk through that door again.

"I think this is where Mom and I came one day," Noah said.

Mariah had brought Noah here? That surprised him. She'd hated this house even more than Matt. Beaker Street wasn't where the popular kids lived. "Why did you and your mom move to Cedar Grove?"

He shifted the kitten to the other arm. "I dunno."

Matt unlocked the door and shoved it open, letting Noah walk in first. The smell of old wood and years of renters met Matt as he crossed the threshold. Then he shook his head and blinked. How did the property managers get all this furniture in the house today? Or did the last renters move and leave it?

"Wow." Noah walked around the tiny living room. "This is nice."

Matt stared at Noah. What kind of places had the poor kid lived in? He tried to look at the room from Noah's perspective. A tired plaid sofa rested along one wall, a wooden rocker and another chair that matched the sofa sat in the corners. Several different scenes of old barns hung on the wall. Not a lot different than when he lived here.

"Glad you like it," he said. "Come on back to the kitchen, and we'll feed Kiddo."

"We'll feed Patches," Noah said as he followed.

"So, it's going to be Patches, is it?" Matt pushed through the swinging wooden door to the kitchen, and time flipped back twenty years.

Mom, I'm home.

Shut the door, son. This isn't a barn. How she always knew he left it open mystified him. He tried to shrug off the memories, but they bombarded him. Coming into the kitchen to the aroma of cookies baking in the oven, or spaghetti simmering on the stove…his mom, deep creases lining her face. Most days she beat him home from school after working eight hours at the Elliotts' house. While Matt had been embarrassed that she worked as a housekeeper, his mom had worn the title with pride. *The job title doesn't matter, Matthew. You bring dignity to the job, not the other way around.* Too bad his dad hadn't felt the same way.

Noah tugged at his arm. "Do you have a bowl?"

"Well, let's see." Matt rummaged through the cabinet until he found a saucer. "How about this?"

Noah scooped in a small amount of kitten food and set the saucer on the floor. "She likes it."

They'd barely gotten the kitty fed when Allie

returned with burgers. "Where'd you get the furniture?"

"No idea," he replied. He opened the bag of
paper plates the property manager had left and
placed three around the table. "Guess the last
renters went off and left it."

He didn't need the frown she shot him. Yeah,
he ought to know, just like he should've known
about Mariah and the trouble she was in. But
he'd done a good job of separating his life in
Memphis from anything to do with his family
or Cedar Grove. Maybe too good.

"Good thing you didn't sell the house." Allie
set a burger on each plate then pulled out a chair
for Noah.

"Yeah."

Allie fixed Noah's plate then concentrated on
her sandwich as his nephew took the top bun off
his burger and removed the pickles.

"You don't like pickles?" Matt asked.

His nephew shook his head, and Matt forked
the dill slices from his nephew's plate.

"Can we keep Patches?"

Keep the cat? Matt hadn't planned on it.

Allie set her sandwich on the plate and wiped
her mouth with a napkin. "How did you come to
have a kitten in the first place?"

"I thought I had hit it with my tire when I
parked at Starbucks this morning. Then he—I

mean she—looked so pitiful, I couldn't leave her there all by herself."

"You're a good man, Charlie Brown."

He jerked his gaze from the kitten. "I haven't heard that phrase since…" He gulped as their eyes met, and he quickly averted his gaze.

"Yeah."

"Uncle Matt, can we keep her?"

Uncle Matt. He turned to his nephew. Noah had finished his sandwich and cuddled Patches against his small chest. The yearning in the boy's face melted the *no* on Matt's lips. How much trouble could a kitten be, anyway? "I suppose."

"Thank you! Thank you!" Noah danced around the room.

Allie's eyes followed the boy around the kitchen. "I wish your mom had lived to meet him," she murmured to Matt.

"Me, too." It was all he could get out. He wrapped his half-eaten burger in the foil wrapper.

"I love this house, this kitchen. Do you remember the cookies your mom baked?" She laughed. "Of course you do. Your mom was a great cook. She could take almost nothing and make a meal out of it."

He stared at Allie, having trouble getting past the house part. While he'd hated, not just the house, but the neighborhood, Allie had turned a blind eye to his circumstances. Allie Carson, whose dad owned the largest horse farm in the county, had always been his champion, even when he'd hated anyone knowing where he lived. "My mom never seemed to belong here. When I was a kid, I wondered if she was someone else."

"What do you mean?"

"You knew her. Did it ever strike you as odd that she seemed so cultured? And her word choices—no one else in this neighborhood spoke the way she did. And you saw the set of rings that came from her mother." Matt gulped, wishing he could take back the last words. He glanced at Allie, and the red crawling up her neck pinched his heart.

Allie leaned away from him. "I do remember them, and you're right. Neither your mother nor the rings belonged in this neighborhood." She glanced around the kitchen. "We need to clean up your kitchen and get back to the hospital."

"Wait, what I said was insensitive. I'm sorry."

She brushed him off with a shrug. "Nothing to be sorry about. Things didn't work out between us. We've both moved on."

Moved on, indeed. Allie to Peter, and him to Jessica. *Jessica.* He'd forgotten to call her. He dug out his cell. "I need to make a call."

BREATHE. AS MATT used his phone, Allie released the tension that'd been building in her since she'd made the Charlie Brown remark. What had she been thinking? But for a few minutes, he'd been the old Matt. Why couldn't he just keep on being the Matt on a fast track to success and wealth with a girlfriend who would help him get it? The Matt who'd shattered her heart.

Allie needed to remember she was here because she cared about her student and what was best for him. She knew the system—both from experience in her school counseling job and watching her parents take in children from the foster care program for the past ten years. Children in Noah's predicament were usually placed with family if possible. However, she wasn't certain Noah would be better off with his uncle, not until she knew the reason Matt went from hands-off to suddenly caring. And she couldn't very well ask him in front of the boy.

She tried not to listen to his conversation, a hard thing to do since he didn't leave the room.

"Sorry I didn't call earlier. Mariah is still unconscious." Matt was silent for a minute. "Yeah, the kitten made it fine. Turns out he's a she, and yes, I plan to check out the animal shelter here in Cedar Grove on Tuesday."

Noah's head jerked up. Panic pinched his small face. "Miss Allie—"

"We'll talk to him about it," she whispered.

Matt rubbed his brow. "Hopefully by Tuesday evening. Bradford is awarding the contract Wednesday morning, and I want to be in town." He listened once again, and a blush crept up his neck. He glanced their way then turned toward the door. "You, too."

He ended the call and turned to them.

"You're taking Patches to the shelter." Noah's voice trembled.

"I, ah…"

"You promised. You said I could keep her."

Matt raised his hands. "I don't know yet. It's complicated, Noah."

Allie folded her arms across her chest. It hadn't been complicated before he talked to Jessica.

"Look, right now I'm taking this situation one hour at a time." He checked his watch. "And it's almost eight. If we're going to be at the hospital by visiting time, we need to leave."

Noah picked up the kitten. "What about—"

"She can stay here in the kitchen." Matt took Patches and placed her in the pet carrier and started to shut the crate door.

"Don't close her up."

He rolled his eyes, but left the door open.

"Noah and I will meet you at the hospital," Allie said. "Unless you want to get your things from the backseat now."

Noah tugged on her arm. "I want to ride with you."

Matt squatted in front of the boy. "Look, I know this is hard for you. It's hard for me. I feel real bad that your mom is in the hospital, and that I didn't know about you."

"But you're going to leave Patches at that rescue place. She's too little. She'll die there."

Allie gripped the table edge as the boy dropped his head and hunched his shoulders. Noah wasn't talking about just the kitten. "Patches isn't going to the shelter. *I* promise you that," she told them.

His head shot up, and hope leapt into his eyes. "You promise?"

If Matt made her take this kitten, she'd kill him. She didn't have time for it. She heaved a sigh. "I promise." She directed her gaze to Matt. "But it won't come to that, *will* it?"

As Noah dropped beside the carrier to pet Patches, Matt stood. "I hope not." Then he turned to Noah. "Are you coming back here with me when we leave the hospital?"

Noah's eyes pleaded with her. "I want to stay with Miss Allie."

Her chest tightened. As a mentor at the shelter, she was authorized to take children for short day trips, and had pushed the limits of her authority when she brought him here. She knelt beside him. "I'm afraid that might not be possible. I don't have permission to keep you overnight."

Allie glanced up at Matt. "Legally, he probably needs to go back to the shelter. It's a nice place."

He shook his head. "Not happening. Noah is my nephew and he's staying here. I'll get a TV so he'll have something to do while I work. Maybe some video games, too."

She stared at him, wanting to ask why he'd changed his tune. "Are TV and video games your idea of how to entertain a child?"

"Mom won't let me play video games."

"Good for her," Allie said.

Matt checked his watch. "Can we figure this out later? We need to leave."

ONLY TWO AT a time were let into ICU, so Allie waited while Matt and Noah visited Mariah. The waiting room had a small kitchen area, and she poured herself a cup of decaf. When she turned around she almost bumped into Peter. They spoke simultaneously.

"I thought I'd find you here—"

"Are you inventing excuses—"

"You first," Allie said.

He shrugged. "No, I'm not inventing excuses this time. I checked with the shelter, and Sarah said Noah was with you. You didn't answer your cell phone, but I figured you two were here."

She pulled out her phone. Still on silent and a message Peter had called. She cocked her head. "Why are you here? It's New Year's Day, and you don't normally handle these cases. Why this one?"

He stiffened. "For the same reason you're here. Mariah's mother worked for us. She was a fine woman, and she'd want me to help her grandson. Where is he, anyway?"

"Visiting his mom."

"By himself?"

"No, Matt's with him."

Peter lifted his chin. "I told him he's not getting the boy. At least not until a judge says so, and that won't happen until Tuesday since Monday is the legal holiday for New Year's."

That answered the question of why Matt suddenly wanted Noah. Movement behind Peter caught her eye. Matt and Noah had returned from their visit. Noah ran toward her. "Mom's nurse said she was better. That maybe she'd wake up tomorrow."

He stopped short when he saw Peter. He sidled next to Allie, and she wrapped her arm across his shoulders. "Good. Noah, I'd like you to meet Peter Elliott."

Peter knelt down and stuck out his hand. "Hello, Noah. I'm here to help you."

Noah tried to bury himself in Allie's side when Peter held out his hand. "He's a little shy," she said.

Matt cleared his throat. "He doesn't need your help. He has family here to help him."

Peter rose and turned around. "Hello again, Matthew. Hadn't seen you in years, and now twice."

"Your lucky weekend, I guess. Did Allie tell you Noah's going home with me?"

"No, he's not. That's why I'm here. He's a ward of the state. He'll be going back to the shelter."

Noah looked up at Allie, his face the color of flour. "Miss Allie…" He sniffed. "I want to go see Patches."

Allie looked from Matt to Peter. They reminded her of two bulldogs eying each other over a bone. "This isn't the place or the time. But legally, doesn't the family's right supersede the state's?"

Peter's expression softened as he turned to Allie. He shook his head. "Not until it goes before a judge."

CHAPTER SIX

"NOAH IS MY nephew and you're not taking him back to that shelter." Matt reached for the boy's hand. "Let's go home and see Patches."

Peter stepped between them. "I'm afraid not. When the state took custody of Noah last night after his mother overdosed, he became a ward of the state. My responsibility. And—"

"Have you filed the paperwork?" Matt shifted his feet, planting them wide.

Peter's lips thinned. "In emergency situations, paperwork can wait until the hearing, which will be Tuesday. As a representative of the state, it is my opinion that the child will be better off at the shelter, at least until the hearing, when a solution can be found."

Peter planned to take Noah away from Mariah. Matt could read it in his face. His hands curled into tight fists. As director of social services, Peter had the power to do it. And maybe his sister hadn't been the best mother, but she deserved a chance to do better. If she went into rehab and got her act straight, no one should take her son away. "Just what do you base your opinion on?"

"We don't need to discuss this in front of the boy here," Peter said.

"You're right." Allie lowered her voice. "Why don't you two grow up? This isn't a math competition or a quarterback position you're fighting over. It's a child."

Matt flinched when Allie snapped her gaze to him.

"This is not something that should be discussed in front of him, or here in the ICU waiting room."

"Tell *him* that." Matt jerked his head toward Peter. Just once, he'd like to wipe that superior smirk from his face.

Peter blanched, and then bent over until he was eye level with Noah. "I apologize for talking about you like you weren't here. You liked the shelter, didn't you?"

Noah gave a half shrug.

Matt cleared his throat. "But you would rather stay with me, right?"

"I want to stay with Miss Allie."

Peter sighed. "And you could if Miss Allie were legally a foster parent."

"I might have a solution," Allie said. "My folks have been foster parents for years. If they are willing, can he be placed with them until the hearing Tuesday?"

Peter scratched his jaw. "Are they fostering anyone presently?"

"No." Noah tugged at her arm and she looked down at him.

"But, Miss Allie, I want to stay with you."

"In a way, you will. I'll spend the weekend there." She took out her phone. "Let me call them."

Matt opened his mouth to protest, and Allie stared him down. He shoved his hands in his pockets as she dialed her parents and spoke with them. He couldn't deny the relief he felt when she nodded an okay to Peter—her parents were the perfect answer, but he didn't like losing, not even to Allie.

At least Peter wasn't taking Noah to the shelter this weekend. Matt's old rival apparently didn't like this turn any more than he did, and history told him the determined social services director would try to do something about it the first day he could. Matt jingled the change in his pocket. Peter Elliott didn't know the meaning of the word *determination,* but he would when Matt got through with him.

"They're waiting for us." Allie knelt and lifted Noah's chin. "Is spending the night at my parents' house good with you? We'll stop and get

you something to sleep in, and then I'll bring you
back to see your mom for the ten o'clock visiting time in the morning."

"Can we go get Patches?"

"Honey, she's probably asleep. Why don't we
leave her at your Uncle Matt's tonight and tomorrow we'll decide what to do."

Matt tousled Noah's hair. "I'll see you tomorrow, okay?"

Noah pulled back, his eyes darting toward
the exit. What had happened? Matt thought they
were making progress.

"Give him a little space," Allie said softly.
"I don't think he's had a lot of positive male
role models, and what just happened here didn't
help."

Matt riveted his eyes on Noah. "I won't hurt
you, son. And I won't let them take you away
from your mom. I guarantee it."

Noah shrugged again, and hurt emanated from
his small frame like a blazing neon sign. Matt
knew that hurt, the frustration of being part of
the Jefferies family in Cedar Grove. He might
have to wait until the hearing, but come Tuesday
afternoon, he and Noah would shake the dust of
Cedar Grove from their coattails. Matt squeezed
Noah's shoulder. "It's going to be okay."

The distrust in Noah's eyes softened a little.
The boy glanced up at Allie, and she gave him

a short nod before she turned to Matt and Peter. "I'll be in touch with each of you tomorrow, but I'd like you both to go along with letting Noah stay at my parents' until after the hearing Tuesday."

Without waiting for either of them to answer, she led Noah toward the exit. Halfway there, Noah tugged at her arm and said something Matt couldn't hear. She seemed to consider whatever he said then nodded. "Matt," Allie called. "We want to visit with Patches sometime tomorrow."

"You bet," he replied. "Just let me know when."

When the door closed behind Allie and Noah, Peter folded his arms. "You haven't won yet. So you can wipe that grin off your face."

"There's no reason why I won't get custody of Noah," Matt retorted.

"Really? You're single, you have no relationship with the kid or his mother, and you have no place to live in Cedar Grove other than that tiny house on Beaker Street. You do realize, if you get custody, you'll have him until his mother finishes rehab. Because no way is that boy going back into her care until she shows she'll stay off of drugs."

"His name is Noah," Matt growled through gritted teeth. "And my sister will beat the drugs." His cell beeped, and he slipped his phone from his pocket and glanced at it. A text from J. Phillip Bradford. That was about the last thing he wanted to see right now. He eyed Peter. "If you'll excuse me, I have work to do. Hopefully, we won't meet again until the hearing." Matt didn't wait around for a reply.

"That boy is going to interfere with your work," Peter called behind him.

At his car, Matt read the text and groaned. Bradford wanted a meeting tomorrow. Sunday. Did the man never take a day off? He speed-dialed the CEO's number. "Mr. Bradford, just received your text. Is there a problem?"

"I'd like your advice on entertainment for the banquet." Bradford's gravelly voice raked Matt's ears.

"I'm afraid I'm out of town until Tuesday evening. Can we handle this over the phone?" He turned the ignition and let the car idle.

"You didn't mention leaving town this morning."

"A family emergency came up."

"Oh? Is someone ill?"

"Uh, yes, sir." That surely wasn't a note of concern he detected in Bradford's voice. "My sister."

"Will she be all right?"

Definitely a note of concern. "I haven't seen a doctor, but the nurses seem to think so." Matt stared at the BMW insignia above the speedometer. "She has a son, though, and there's no one to care for him."

"Yes, with your mother dead, I suppose you are the only one."

How did Bradford know his mom had died? Matt rubbed the bridge of his nose. Of course. Bradford must have run a background check on Matt. A bit over-the-top perhaps, but not entirely unexpected. "Yes, sir. There's a court hearing on Tuesday to determine where the boy will stay. I should have the paperwork wrapped up by noon and be back in Memphis by evening with my nephew. And about the entertainment, may I think about that tonight and get back to you in the morning?" Before he suggested anyone, he wanted to make sure they were available for a Valentine's Day gig this close to the date.

"Of course. And let me know how your sister progresses."

So the old curmudgeon had a heart, after all. "Yes, sir." Matt had barely disconnected from the call when his cell rang again. Allie. "Is everything okay?"

"Yes. We're at the store now, getting him some clothes."

"I had planned for us to go by his house when we left the hospital and pick up a few things."

"That's why I called—to see if you wanted to

meet us there tomorrow, and then we can swing by your house, and he can see Patches for a few minutes before we go to the hospital."

"How about I pick you two up at eight and take you to breakfast?"

She laughed. "In that tiny thing you call a car? No. Besides, my mom will want to make breakfast before she goes to church."

The memory of Mrs. Carson's biscuits made his mouth water. "Any way I can get an invite to that breakfast?"

Silence answered him.

"That's okay. I'll just meet you at my house."

"No, Mom and Dad will want to see you. But you better be there by eight or there won't be anything left."

"I'll be there on time. See you tomorrow."

"I hope you sleep well tonight, Matt."

He rubbed his thumb against the wood-grained steering wheel. It would probably be a long night. "I hear sleep is highly overrated."

"I wouldn't know. I'm always glad if I get six hours," she said with a soft chuckle.

Matt disconnected and inched out of the parking lot. He could see the full moon through the bare trees. He swallowed. Same moon as in Memphis, but somehow in Cedar Grove the cold beauty pricked his soul and filled him with regret.

At the road, he turned left, leaving the image behind. No doubt about it. He needed to finish his business and get out of Cedar Grove.

"HURRY, IT'S COLD out here." Ruth Carson held the back door open. "Let me help you with those packages."

"Thanks." Allie handed her two of the bags, and she and Noah followed her mother into the farmhouse. Inside the warm kitchen, the sweet scent of chocolate welcomed them.

"Noah, meet my mom, Mrs. Carson." He hesitated before ducking his head in a nod, and she tried to see her mom from his eyes. Shorter than Allie's five foot six, her mom wore jeans and a plaid shirt and a baker's apron that had gingerbread men on it. Allie leaned over and whispered in his ear. "She won't bite."

He smiled. Barely. But he kept staring at his feet. Allie followed her nose to a platter of brownies on the island. "Mom, you're sabotaging my diet," she said, taking the thin jacket Noah shrugged out of. She made a mental note to get him a heavier coat.

"These aren't for you." Ruth placed two brownies on a saucer and held them out to Noah. "Would you like milk to go with them?"

He raised his head, caution flitting across his eyes. "Yes, ma'am, Mrs. Carson."

She tousled his hair. "All the kids call me Mrs. C. I hope you will, too."

Allie broke a brownie in half. "Where's Dad?"

"At the barn. He's expecting a mare to foal tonight."

"In January?"

"You tell the mare her cycle was wrong."

Noah stared at them, his mouth forming a small *O*. "You have horses here?"

"We do. And in the morning, perhaps we'll have a baby for you to meet." Ruth removed her apron and hung it on a peg by the door. "As soon as you finish your snack, we'll get your bath, and then you won't have that to do before you go out to the barn tomorrow."

Allie rinsed Noah's new pajamas and threw them in the dryer while he took a bath. Later as he curled beside her on the leather couch that had been in her parents den since she was a teenager, she tried to relax, but her mind was having none of it.

The day had been like a ride on a Tilt-A-Whirl at the carnival. She didn't know which was harder to process—Peter's interest in her, or Matt's change of heart with his family. She doubted both. And she couldn't deny that being around Matt unsettled her and stirred up memories of the good times they had shared. They played in her head like a slide show. *Stop it*.

"Did I do something wrong, Miss Allie?"

She hadn't realized she said the words out loud. "No, Noah, I was just talking to myself."

"I do that sometimes. The kids at school think I'm weird."

She shifted on the soft leather couch and put her arm around his thin shoulders. "Then we both are."

For a minute neither of them said anything. A log shifted in the fireplace, sending sparks up the chimney. She loved this room, the two recliners her mom and dad sat in, the current book her dad was reading on the table between them and her mom's knitting in a basket on the floor. A grouping of prints adorned one wall, pictures she'd painted of the farm. On another wall was Clint's first metal sculpture.

The room reflected her family's personality. For some reason, she thought of Matt's apartment and realized her problem with his decor. It had been wiped clean of his personality.

Noah pointed to the picture of a running horse. "I like that. I wish I had a horse."

"That was mine when I was a little girl."

"Cool." His nose wrinkled in a frown. "Did someone paint that for you?"

"Me," she said, pleased he liked it. Painting was her relief valve. A case like Noah's would definitely send her searching for her oils and brushes. She rose from the couch and took down the painting so he could see it better.

Noah touched the canvas, brushing his finger over the horse's nose. "What's his name? Do you still have him?"

His questions tumbled together. Other than when he'd held the kitten, Allie hadn't seen him this animated. "His name is Bridger, and he's still here at the farm."

"Do you think I can ride him sometime?"

"I don't see why not." Maybe Bridger could be his relief valve.

Noah yawned, and she said, "Let's get you into bed, young man."

Allie led the way to Clint's old room. "You're sleeping in my brother's room."

Noah climbed in bed, and she tucked him in. The bed dwarfed his small frame. "I'm just across the hall, so if you need anything, wake me up."

He nodded. Sadness had settled in his face again.

"It's going to be okay, Noah."

He traced the plaid pattern on his sheet. A sigh settled in his shoulders. She waited, not wanting to push him.

Finally he looked up, his brows pinched. "Are we going to my house tomorrow?"

"After breakfast."

"Our stuff may be sittin' on the road."

She looked at him. "What?"

"Mom hasn't paid the rent, and today's the first."

So that's what was bothering him. And how many kids knew when the first of the month rolled around, anyway? "Has it happened before?"

He nodded. "Before we came to Cedar Grove. It's been better here. Mom gets to work more. And she hasn't been getting...sick. Until last night."

A viselike band gripped her chest. Somehow she had to make Mariah understand what she was doing to her son. If Mariah lived. "Where do you stay when your mom works?"

"Home."

Alone. While Mariah worked nights at a local bar. "I think you'll like staying here."

"But what if Uncle Matt wants me to go with him?"

Tuesday that could be a real possibility. She chewed the inside of her lip. "The court may let him take care of you until your mom is better, but if that happens, it'll be because the judge knows your uncle wants you."

"But he doesn't want me—he didn't even know about me."

Allie searched for an answer. "I don't think

that's entirely his fault. Grown-ups get messed up in their thinking sometimes, and they lose touch with their families. I'm not saying it's right, just that it happens, and I think that's what happened with Matt and your mom."

Noah folded his arms across his chest. "Mom says we don't need anybody."

She sighed. "Let's look at it from a different direction. Your mom's in the hospital and you have to stay somewhere. Which would you prefer? Being with your Uncle Matt or the shelter?"

He pierced her with his blue eyes. "Why can't I stay here?"

"This is just temporary. Most of the time, courts want to keep families together." She tried to remember whether a nine-year-old had any say so in court. "It's complicated. I want you to be prepared in case the judge awards custody to your Uncle Matt."

"But he wants to take Patches to the animal rescue because she's too much trouble. She's too little. She'll die there."

Would he do the same thing with him, if Noah became a problem? That was his unspoken question. "Oh, I think once he has time to think about it, he won't. After all, Matt saved Patches." She had to have a talk with Matt. "All I'm saying is, maybe you need to give your uncle a chance."

When Noah didn't answer, she hugged him. "Just think about it."

She would have to do the same thing.

WHEN SHE RETURNED to the den, Allie automatically started straightening the room, picking up magazines and stacking them neatly on the coffee table.

"Now I'll have to sort through those to find the article I was reading."

She jerked her head toward the door. "Dad. I thought you were at the barn."

"Just left. The mom and her new son needed bonding time." He glanced at the magazines. "What's with this tidying up of my magazines? Are we feeling a need to restore order somewhere?"

Busted. How did he do that? How did he read her emotions from the doorway? "Maybe."

He walked to her and put his arm around her shoulders. "Anything you want to talk about?"

She leaned into his embrace. Her dad remained as solid in size as he was in heart. His calloused hands could heft a bale of hay onto a flatbed trailer or gentle a terrified mare in the throes of a breech birth.

"When you were straightening, did you see a spiral notebook?"

She pulled a red composition book from the bottom of the stack.

"Oh, good. I need to give that to Clint in the morning."

"Clint's coming?"

Her dad nodded. "I told you last week we're going to your grandmother's for a few days. Clint is taking care of some of the horse matters."

She'd forgotten her parents were leaving town next weekend. "I could've done that, and Clint wouldn't have to drive over from Memphis."

He chuckled. "Clint doesn't mind taking a few vacation days to help the old man. And I have several visits scheduled for the vet, and he comes during the day. Didn't figure you'd want to take time off from school to run out here."

"Oh. I'll let Clint handle that." Allie lined the magazines up again and looked around for something else to straighten.

"I heard Matthew is back in town."

"Yeah." She breathed the word out. He squeezed her shoulder.

"Do you wish you'd made a different choice seven years ago? Back then you didn't want to leave Cedar Grove."

"I still don't want to leave Cedar Grove," she said. "But that isn't why we broke up. That last year of college Matt changed. He became so focused on leaving his past behind that he became someone I didn't know. Besides, that's past history. He's practically engaged to somebody else now. She's better suited to the new Matt."

Her dad lifted her chin. "Honey, you can hold your own with anyone. And don't you ever forget it."

She curved her lips into a tenuous smile. "Thanks. I needed that."

STEPPING THROUGH THE Carsons' back door Sunday morning was like stepping back seven years. Little had been changed in a kitchen that reflected its owners. Nothing fancy, just oak cabinets and butcher-block countertops that carried the rustic theme to the terra-cotta floor. Even the blue-and-white checkered curtains looked the same, giving the room warmth that he wanted to wrap around him. So different from his shiny silver-and-black kitchen in the city.

But it wasn't the homespun charm that made the kitchen special. That came from the people in it. Stan Carson stood at the stove, wearing a white apron that proclaimed The Chef Is In. He waved a spatula in his left hand and held out the other. "Good to see you again, Matthew."

"Thank you, sir." Matt hadn't been eager to meet Allie's dad again. Hadn't been too sure of the kind of reception he'd receive. Mr. C's grip was firm, but not bone-crushing. Encouraging.

Mrs. Carson patted his shoulder as she carried a platter of bacon to the table. "Take a seat, Matt. Allie is cleaning Noah's shoes. Would you like a couple of pancakes? Stan's making his famous chocolate-chip ones."

"Uncle Matt, did you ever see a baby horse before? Mr. C has one in the barn. And he's not as tall as me."

Explained the shoes. And Stan already had the boy calling him by his special name. Matt pulled the chair beside Noah from the table. "Yep, I've seen a foal before. And pancakes would be fine, Mrs. C."

"Miss Allie is sitting there."

"Take the end seat, Matthew," Stan said as he flipped a pancake in the air.

Allie entered the kitchen from the hallway and set Noah's shoes beside the door. "Watch where you walk the next time, mister."

"Yes, ma'am."

She glanced briefly at Matt and nodded before turning to her mother. "Did I hear you talking to Clint earlier?"

"You did. He said he'd be here before we finish breakfast."

He barely heard their words. Allie looked… different this morning. It was her hair. It was straight instead of curly, and it must be the navy sweater that made her eyes so blue. He reined in his thoughts as Mr. C set a plate of pancakes on the table, and Allie joined them at the table.

Conversation slowed as everyone ate. Matt didn't know when he'd last had chocolate-chip pancakes. Yes, he did. Right here in this kitchen.

Noah leaned toward him. "Did you feed Patches this morning?"

"Nope. She's too fat. I think she needs to go on a diet."

Noah's gasp startled him. "But—but…"

Allie patted his hand. "He's teasing you. I'm sure he fed the kitten."

"No, he isn't. He wants to give Patches away."

"Oh-hh." Matt made two syllables of the word. "If I planned to give Patches away, would I go out this morning and buy a bed for her?"

"You're going to keep her?" Noah wrinkled his nose. "But you said last night—"

"I was tired last night. When I was feeding Patches this morning, she said she was tired of sleeping in that carrier. And she wanted to know what I was going to do about it."

Noah narrowed his eyes. "Patches didn't talk to you."

"Then why did I go and buy her a kitty bed?" When Noah kept staring at him, Matt shrugged. "Okay, maybe not with words, but believe me, she can meow. We'll take it by the house and see how she likes it after we go to the hospital."

The frown lines eased in the small boy's face, and his shoulders relaxed. "Okay."

The back door opened and Clint hustled in. "It's cold out there this morning," he said, rubbing his hands together. "I hope y'all saved me something to eat."

The kitchen erupted in a flurry of activity once more as Mrs. C embraced her son.

"Your pancakes will be ready in a minute, son."

"Matt, good to see you again. Great New Year's Eve party." He gripped Matt's hand. "And you must be Noah," he said, turning to the boy. "Did you know your uncle was one of the best quarterbacks Cedar Grove High ever had? And he was pretty fair at basketball, too."

"I don't know about that. You were pretty good yourself."

Clint waved off Matt and hugged his sister before launching into a conversation with his dad about the current state of the high school basketball team. Unrest started in his heart and spread through his body. He checked his watch. "Uh, if we leave now, we have just enough time to run by Mariah's house before we go to the hospital. That way we can get Noah's clothes and look for something that Mariah can wear when she gets out of ICU. Once visiting time is over, we'll go check on Patches."

Noah scrambled out of his chair. "Can we bring Patches here?"

Matt hesitated. "Why don't we leave Patches where she is until we know what the judge is going to do Tuesday?"

Noah turned to Allie, clearly looking for an ally, but she shook her head, for once agreeing with Matt. Suddenly it hit him. Come Tuesday, if the judge awarded him temporary custody, he would be responsible for Noah. And he didn't know the first thing about raising a nine-year-old boy.

It was a long shot, but hopefully Jessica did.

THE CLOSER THEY got to the house, the more Noah thought he was going to throw up. What if all their stuff was on the street? It'd happened before when his mom couldn't pay the rent. He squeezed his eyes shut. *Don't be anything there.* He swayed as the car turned the corner, then he sneaked a peek out of one eye. Empty. The curb was empty. His body relaxed and the lump in his throat melted. He sucked in air. It was okay. Today, at least.

"Do you have a key?" Miss Allie asked.

He shook his head. Who would steal what they had? "The back door isn't locked."

Uncle Matt pulled in behind them as they stood beside Miss Allie's car. Matt's face looked all sad, and suddenly, Noah didn't want his uncle and Miss Allie seeing inside the house. "You wait here, and I'll go get my stuff."

His uncle patted Noah's shoulder. "No, we'll go with you."

Noah walked as slow as he could to the back door. He'd never let any of the kids at school come home with him, and he'd never wanted Miss Allie to see inside his house. The outside was bad enough with paint coming off the boards.

With a sigh, he pushed it open, and bleach stung his nose. He'd forgotten to take the clothes out of the pot on the stove. His uncle and Miss Allie followed him through the kitchen to his tiny room that contained only a twin bed. He ducked his head, refusing to look at them.

Miss Allie cleared her throat. "Uh, where are your clothes, Noah?"

He dragged a black plastic bag from under the bed and pulled out a pair of jeans and three shirts.

"Is…is this all?" Matt said.

"Mom usually washed my jeans at night." His cheeks burned. His underwear, too. "My socks and uh, you know…they're on the stove in bleach. That's what you smelled when you came through the door."

His uncle looked like he wanted to cry. Noah

narrowed his eyes and lifted his chin. "This place is okay, and we got each other. That's all that matters."

Miss Allie hugged him. "You're right, Noah. I'll go get your socks and other things."

"No! That's my job." He ran past them to the kitchen and grabbed the long fork he always used to dip his clothes out.

Matt followed him. "Let me pour the water out," he said, and carried the pot to the sink. "Do you have a plastic bag to put these in?"

Noah glanced around the kitchen. Did his uncle see any food here? Where would he get a plastic bag? Boy, kittens weren't the only thing he was clueless about.

"I should have one in my car," Miss Allie said. "I'll take care of this, and you two find some clothes for Mariah."

Noah led the way to his mother's bedroom.

"She doesn't have a bed?" Matt asked.

Noah straightened the wrinkled sheets on the mattress that was on the floor. "She said it was easier to move this way."

"I see. Have you two been here long?"

Noah stuck his tongue in his cheek, trying to remember when they'd moved into this place. "Before school started."

His uncle's face got all red.

"It's nicer than where we lived before."

Matt cleared his throat then looked around the room. "I see. Does your mom have any clothes we can take to the hospital?"

"If she does, it'll be there." Noah pointed toward the chest his mom had found at the city dump. "She always just wears jeans."

Matt started going through the drawers, his face getting redder all the time. Then he frowned. "What's this?" he asked and held up the pawn ticket the man had given his mom.

"Mom sold something to pay last month's rent."

"What'd she have that'd bring three hundred dollars?"

Noah pinched his brows together. His teeth had found the ridge inside his mouth, and he chewed on it. His mom did the best she could.

"Noah? Do you know?"

"Same thing she always pawns. A necklace."

His uncle turned so white, Noah thought he was gonna faint.

"Pearls?" It was barely a whisper.

Noah nodded. "She always got them back before."

Uncle Matt stared at the ticket. "Do you know where this place is?"

Again he nodded.

"What do you say we go get your mom's necklace?"

NOAH'S SHOE DUG at a hole in the carpet. "What about this month?"

This month? Matt frowned. "What about it?"

"The rent. It's due. If we don't pay it, Mr. Wilson's gonna put our stuff on the road. He said so."

"How much are we talking about? Three hundred, like you said?"

Noah nodded, and he stared at the floor.

Matt was glad his barely whispered expletive hadn't made it to Noah's ears. Like Noah, he'd ached to help his mother pay the rent and keep food on the table. He cleared his throat. "And where do we find this Mr. Wilson?"

As a businessman, Matt understood a landlord couldn't let a nonpaying renter stay indefinitely, but to put them out on the first day they were late?

"Down the street."

Matt glanced around the room. It wouldn't take an hour to load everything Mariah owned in a truck. If he moved their stuff today, it'd be one less thing to take care of Tuesday if the court awarded him custody of Noah. That way, as soon as the judge signed the papers, they could be on the road to Memphis. "What do you think about moving all your things to my house this afternoon?"

Noah's eyes widened. "Mom won't like that."

"You let me worry about your mom. Now, let's go see what Miss Allie is up to."

In the kitchen they found Allie holding up one of Noah's T-shirts. Or what was left of it. "What happened?" Matt asked.

"Stayed in the bleach too long. All of his underclothes are ruined." She dropped the shirt in the sink. "Looks like another trip to the store."

"I'll take him after we visit Mariah. Do you know where I can rent a truck today?"

"A truck?" She put her hands on her hips. "So, you're finally admitting that toy you call a car is useless."

"It's not useless, just not too practical for moving." He swept his arm around the kitchen.

"Oh." Understanding lit her eyes. "Dad will let you use his farm truck. Probably even help, if you ask."

Matt swallowed. Yeah, Mr. C would help— Clint, too. "I don't have his number. Could you give—"

"I'll do even better." A smile teased the corners of her mouth. "I'll call and ask for you."

"Thanks." Once again, Matt had underestimated the generosity of the Carson family.

CHAPTER SEVEN

Noah tugged at Matt's arm. "Don't forget my mom's necklace."

"I won't." Allie examined the ticket, which Matt produced. "Oh, I remember seeing this place—it's off the south end of Main. Remember the old cobbler's shop? It's right next door."

He pocketed the ticket. "I'll meet you two at the hospital. Unless you have things you need to do, and you want to let Noah go with me. After we take care of the pawn ticket, I can take him to see Mariah, and if you'll give me your address, I'll bring him to your house when we leave the hospital."

Allie hesitated. "I really do need to get ready for school Tuesday. I'd planned to work this afternoon, but I want to help you move." She tapped her fingers together. "Okay, take Noah with you, and I'll get my work done this morning. I'll text you my address."

"You sure? What if Peter finds out? He might not be happy with your decision."

"Well, Noah's status is technically undecided,

and still, you are his uncle. Nothing wrong with you spending time alone with your nephew."

A few minutes later, Matt found the last parking spot in front of Joe's Pawn Shop. A sign proclaimed the store was open seven days a week. Iron bars covered the two windows, and the door could use a coat of paint. This part of Cedar Grove had changed and not for the better. Sometime in the past, fire had left the cobbler's shop a burned-out shell. As for the other storefronts, fire would be an improvement.

A bell jingled overhead as he entered the pawn shop, and an older man turned from the customer at the counter. "Be with you in a minute."

Matt walked around the shop, stopping in front of a locked display of Case knives. He'd had a Case knife once. One his mom had taken away from him.

"May I help you?"

He turned to the clerk and showed him the ticket. "I'd like to redeem this."

A relieved smile creased his face. "Oh, good. I worried when she was late that I might have to eat this one."

Matt frowned. "What do you mean?"

"Pearls. No way could I get the three hundred dollars back I let her have for those pearls. Now gold, I could sell easy." He jerked his head toward Noah. "Only reason I let her have the money was the kid."

A pawn shop dealer with a heart. Matt didn't know such a person existed. "I appreciate that. Now I want to get them back. How much does she owe?"

"Three hundred and fifty dollars."

There went the heart. "Will you take a check?"

"As long as you have two forms of ID."

Matt made the check out while the older man went to the back room and retrieved a small brown envelope. After he handed it to him, Matt pulled out a black velvet pouch. Mariah still had the bag they were in when their mother gave her the pearls. His sister continued to surprise him. Maybe if Mariah understood he'd redeemed the pawn ticket, it would bring her around.

He removed the necklace and laid the thumb-sized pearls against the velvet. Eighteen inches of shimmering luster. How his mother had kept them hidden from his dad on his drunken rampages still remained a mystery to him. But a bigger mystery was why his mother had the pearls in the first place.

As a kid Matt had believed the necklace and the diamond rings he found hidden in the pantry were worth thousands of dollars, and he suggested that his mother sell them so they would be rich. She'd scolded him, and he'd argued with her, telling her that one day, he would be rich and successful.

"Be careful, Matthew," she'd said. "Wealth brings its own set of problems. And you may have to make a choice one day between what you believe in and that success and wealth you want so badly. Just remember that happiness and contentment are not for sale."

Matt hadn't agreed with her then, and he still didn't.

"MOM, WAKE UP!" Noah stood on the other side of the bed, stroking Mariah's arm. Matt glanced at the monitor where the rhythmic beeping didn't change. His nephew focused on him. "Why doesn't Mom open her eyes? The nurse said they were trying to wake her up."

"I don't know." Matt rubbed the bridge of his nose. Only the beeping broke the silence in the room. Evidently, Noah had heard him talking to the nurse. He took a deep breath and slipped the necklace from the velvet bag, imagining how desperate Mariah had been to pawn their mother's jewelry. He laid the necklace in his sister's open hand. "Mariah, I got Mom's pearls back."

Matt pushed down the desperation that crept up his spine as the monitor droned on. He'd all but promised Noah the pearls would bring his mom out of the coma, and if they didn't…

"I know you can hear me." Matt squeezed his sister's fingers. "We need you to wake up."

"Mom, please."

Her eyelid twitched. The heart monitor kicked a little higher. Matt rocked back on his heels. *Yes!*

A half groan, half sigh rumbled in her chest and Noah looked stunned, his eyes shinny. "You did it, Uncle Matt!"

Matt held his breath, waiting, but the monitor returned to the slow, steady beat of before. She'd slipped away from them again. With a firm nod, he returned the pearls to their velvet bag and put his arm around his nephew's sagging shoulders. "She's trying, Noah. Maybe by the time we come back she'll be wake."

ALLIE USED HER little finger to smudge a shadow under Noah's eye before she leaned back and viewed the sketch. Even as she'd collected her supplies for school, her fingers itched to draw the child. Her gaze shifted to Matt's image. She hadn't intended to sketch *him,* but as usual, once she picked up the charcoal, she couldn't resist.

The resemblance between Noah's and Matt's bone structure was strong, something she hadn't noticed until she started sketching Matt's face. She wiped the dust from her fingers and sprayed a fixative on the paper. Tomorrow she'd use pastels to bring the drawings to life. Although she rather liked the charcoal rendering. The doorbell rang. Matt and Noah already? She checked her watch—two o'clock. Time had flown. She closed off her studio and hurried down the stairs and whipped open the door. "Sorry it took me so long…" Her voice trailed off. "Peter?"

"I'm obviously not who you were expecting." His blue eyes twinkled. He appeared relaxed in his nubby sweater and jeans, and yet as he slipped his hands in his pockets, she sensed nervousness.

"Actually, you're not." Her heart sank. He would not be happy to know Noah was with Matt. "But come in."

Allie stepped back, and after he'd walked past her, she scanned the street for Matt. It'd be just her luck for them to drive up. Maybe Peter wouldn't stay long. "I'm surprised to see you."

He smiled at her and glanced around the room, his gaze stopping at the painting of the pier at the lake on her dad's farm. He walked closer to it, examining the signature. "You painted this?"

The frame tilted downward on one side a fraction of an inch, and she straightened it, noticing the black that rimmed her cuticles. Charcoal. She rubbed her fingers on her black jeans. "I did."

He nodded toward the other paintings in the room. "Those as well?"

"The sunset and the four seasons, but not the Monet."

He smiled at her little joke. "Do you ever sell your work? I'd be interested."

"No. It's not that good, just something I do to work out frustration." Her face burned. "But you didn't come to look at my paintings."

"You're right, I didn't. I tried to call, but your phone went immediately to voice mail. I wanted to see if you would like to have dinner with me tonight."

"Dinner?" If she said yes, maybe he would leave. "But I thought we were going out next Friday night. You know, dinner and dancing?"

"I thought tonight we might pick Noah up at your parents and take him with us. We could go to the pizza place."

She swallowed. What if Peter asked Noah how he spent his afternoon? She hated deception. "Noah's with Matt." The words fell out of her mouth, but she was glad the situation was out in the open.

Peter pressed his lips together in a thin line. "I see."

"I needed to get ready for school Tuesday, and Noah didn't have any clothes so they were going by the store and then to the hospital." She sounded frantic.

He held his hand up. "It's okay. Matt *is* taking the boy back to your parents this afternoon?"

She nodded. "Of course. They should be here any minute—we're taking my dad's truck and moving Mariah's furniture into Matt's shed."

"Oh…I see." Peter cleared his throat. "I, uh…" His shoulders lifted as he sucked in a deep breath. "I meant to do this tonight if you agreed to go to dinner, but it looks like you're going to be busy. I'm sorry about how I acted last night. It was totally unprofessional."

Her jaw dropped open and she blinked. "You're apologizing?"

He nodded. "I let my irritation at Matt get the best of me. But, look at it from my perspective. The boy doesn't know his uncle, and I personally believe he'd be better off with your parents or even at the shelter than to be taken out of school and moved to Memphis."

"Matt's not taking Noah to Memphis."

"Do you think he's going to stay in Cedar Grove? His job is in Memphis—he can't stay here until Mariah gets her act together. Besides, you know you can't depend on Matt Jefferies."

Allie's brows knit together. Of course Matt couldn't stay here. The life he'd carved out for himself was in Memphis, along with his fiancée.

"I didn't mean to upset you." He took her hand and uncurled her fingers. "You trust too much,

Allie Carson. But that's one of the things I like best about you." He leaned forward and kissed her lightly on the lips.

The front door banged open, and before she could react, Noah burst into the room. "Miss Allie! Mom—"

He stopped abruptly as soon as he saw her and Peter.

"Oh—" Noah stared at them. He stepped back, bumping into Matt.

"Did Noah tell—" Matt blinked. "Peter? What are you doing here?"

"Nothing that concerns you. I'm just leaving, anyway." He cocked his head toward Allie. "I'll call you later about Friday night."

"Sure."

He nodded. "I know my way out."

Allie rubbed her thumb against her palm. How was she going to explain Peter's visit? Wait a minute. She didn't owe Matt an explanation. And he better not ask for one. She straightened her shoulders and glanced at him. "Is Mariah better?"

Noah answered her, not Matt. "Yes, ma'am. She almost opened her eyes. Uncle Matt says she'll be awake when we go back."

Allie suppressed a groan. Matt shouldn't have told him that. "But she may not."

"But she will, Miss Allie. Uncle Matt said so." He looked up at his uncle. "Didn't you?"

She shot Matt a fix-this-problem look. He knelt to eye level with Noah. "I believe she will…if not this afternoon, by morning for sure."

She wanted to shake Matt. Never promise a child something you may not be able to deliver. But there was nothing she could say without undermining him. She just hoped Mariah was awake by morning.

Matt straightened up. "Did you call your dad?"

"I did. He said he'd have the truck gassed up and ready He and Clint both are going to help."

"Great."

MATT LEANED IN the doorway of the shed behind his mom's house. It'd been a while since he'd been this tired. With all the help, the move had gone smoothly, and every last item Mariah owned was stored in a small corner of the building.

"Man," Clint said, "I wish my stuff was organized like this."

Matt surveyed the room. Boxes lined one wall with labels identifying the contents. A bicycle hung from the ceiling, the fenders dusty, and at the opposite end, boxes labeled with Mariah's name waited to be claimed. Maybe he'd take some of his sister's boxes into the house later and go through them with Noah.

"Yeah. They are in alphabetical order, too." Matt scanned the labels on his boxes, glad now for his mom's almost compulsive insistence that every box have a full description of the contents.

Clint opened a box with Matt's name on it and held up a football. "Look what I found."

He caught the ball when Clint tossed it to him and ran his finger over the signatures of all the players. With three touchdowns, the game had been the highlight of his high school career and had taken them into the state finals his senior year. There'd been some aspects of living in Cedar Grove that hadn't been all bad.

Clint grinned at him. "You used to be pretty good. Think you can still throw the long one?

"The question is can you catch it?"

"Only one way to find out." Clint trotted out into the yard.

Matt put his phone in his jacket and laid it on the ground before wrapping his fingers around the pigskin. The ball felt natural in his hands. As he spiraled the ball toward Clint, he caught a glimpse of Allie rounding the corner of the house with Noah.

Clint snagged the throw, and hesitated, then pointed at a tree behind Matt. "See if you can keep the ball from getting there."

"You're on!" Matt trotted toward him as Clint motioned for Allie to join them.

Clint dropped back and lobbed the ball to Allie. She caught it and ran to the tree.

"Yay! Miss Allie!"

"No fair!" Matt crossed his hands in the air as she spiked the ball. He turned, looking for their dad. "Hey, Mr. C, come help me out," he yelled when he spied him near his truck. The older man obliged him, warning Matt he was out of shape. They swapped places with Clint and Allie and fifteen minutes later, Matt and Mr. C were behind by one touchdown. Matt fell back to throw the ball and Allie sacked him. He struggled to get up, and briefly their eyes locked. For a heartbeat, the years melted away, and he couldn't breathe. Then she scrambled up.

"Game's over! And we won!" Allie stomped her feet and pumped her fist, then high-fived Clint. Noah joined in the fun as Mr. C high-fived him then Allie.

"Hey! You're rooting for the wrong team," Matt called out as he climbed to his feet, rubbing his hip. He'd forgotten how Allie played for keeps.

The three walked toward him with Mr. C in the middle, his arms draped across his children's shoulders. Noah ran ahead of them. Matt's chest tightened. He could have been a part of this if—

"You tried, Matt," Clint said, slapping him on the back. "You still play a mean game."

"You're not so bad yourself." Matt picked up his jacket.

"Wow, Uncle Matt. You let a girl sack you."

The distinctive ringtone he'd assigned to the hospital shrieked from his pocket. He quickly answered. "Hello?"

"Mr. Matthew Jefferies?"

"Yes. Is...is my sister all right?"

"She's awake and is asking for her son."

Matt heaved a sigh. Mariah was going to make it. He hadn't realized how much he'd feared she wouldn't until now. He was grateful they would have a chance to start fresh. "We'll be there in ten minutes."

He pocketed the phone and hugged Noah. "Let's go see your mom."

MATT WAITED FOR the ICU doors to open. Noah stood beside him, chewing his thumbnail.

"Why doesn't Miss Allie come with us?"

"She wants to give us time alone with your mom."

The boy sighed, and Matt squeezed his shoulder. "Your mom's going to be okay."

"What if she's asleep again?"

"Then we'll wake her up." He imagined Noah's insides were like his own—quivering like jelly. What if Mariah had brain damage? He pushed the thought away as the doors opened, but it persisted down the hall and followed him inside the room. The nurses had elevated Mariah's head, but she lay with her eyes closed, her face the color of the sheets. Noah hesitated at the foot of the bed, and Matt nudged him forward.

Noah touched her arm. "Mom?"

"Noah?" Her eyes fluttered open.

Matt couldn't speak as Mariah stretched out her arms, and Noah threw himself into them. "Mom!"

Time seemed suspended as Mariah held her son close, stroking his back. "I'm so sorry, Noah."

"I shouldn't have left that night. When I came back, I thought you were…" He took a shuddering breath.

She lifted his chin and wiped the tears from his cheeks. "Honey, what happened wasn't your fault. You hear me?"

He nodded. "That's what Uncle Matt said."

"Matt?" She jerked her head up, and her eyes widened when she saw him.

He tweaked her toe under the sheet. "Hi, sis."

She sank back onto the bed, her face even paler than before. "How did you know?"

When Matt hesitated, Noah spoke up. "Miss

Allie told him. And she kept me from going back to the shelter. I'm staying at her parents' house."

Her hand flew to her mouth as tears rimmed her eyes again. "Oh, Noah. What have I done?"

Noah's eyes widened. "Mom, don't cry."

The boy blinked hard and his chin quivered, piercing Matt's heart. "Mariah, stop crying. You're scaring your son."

"I've made such a mess of things," she said through her tears.

Now was not the time to agree with her. He sat on the side of the bed. "We'll deal with that later. Right now I need your help. There's a hearing Tuesday to decide whether Noah goes into state care or not. It'd really help if I had a statement from you, giving me temporary custody."

She gave them a weak smile and struggled to sit up in the bed. "Why? You don't have time for him. Let him stay with the Carsons."

The words stung. Maybe he hadn't been the best brother. She certainly hadn't been the best mother. He hesitated. Here was his chance to step out of the picture. To go back to Memphis and his life. His blood pounded through his ears. *Run.*

Matt licked his lips. The only family he had was in this room. He shifted his gaze to Noah. The little bugger had dug his way under his skin. "Come on, Mariah. I want to help. Do you want

Noah placed in foster care with the state or with me? What if the family he's placed in decides they want to keep him permanently? Are you up to going through that?"

Mariah sank into the bed and closed her eyes, the lashes black against her pasty skin. Maybe he should leave her alone.

"Bring a paper, and I'll sign it."

"I'll see if Allie can find a computer we can use."

"Allie is here at the hospital?"

"She's in the waiting room."

"Thank her for me. I don't feel up to seeing anyone else."

He nodded. "I'll leave Noah with you while I get this done." He stopped at the door. "Mariah, everything is going to be okay."

She gave him a wan smile. "Not sure it's gonna happen this time, little brother."

CHAPTER EIGHT

"COFFEE OR HOT TEA?" Allie raised her eyebrows, waiting for Peter's answer. He had called earlier in the day, saying he didn't want to wait until their date Friday to see her again. Rather than going out with him, she offered to make sandwiches instead. She'd brought Noah to her house for a couple of hours while her parents went out to eat. Allie thought it was cute that they still had a "date night" every so often, and this one had been planned for a couple of weeks.

She also thought her home would provide less pressure for Noah than a restaurant. For her, too. She had him settled out of earshot in front of the TV with a pad and pencil and a plate of chocolate brownies.

"Are you having coffee?" Peter helped himself to a brownie.

"No, but that doesn't matter. I have a coffeemaker that makes one cup at a time."

"Coffee, then. It'll go with one of these." He waved the brownie. "Did you make them?"

"Mom did." Allie ran her fingers over the

different labels. Hazelnut, French vanilla, Columbian dark roast, decaf… Peter looked like a dark-roast type of man so she pulled out the bag. "I'd like to be at the hearing tomorrow if possible."

"Don't you have school?"

"It's a teacher workday. I can do most of my paperwork at home in the morning, but I do have appointments with a couple of parents after four to go over their children's progress reports. What time do you think we'll be in front of the judge?"

"There were three cases on the docket last Thursday, but I'll ask if Noah's case can be heard first. Did you ask Matt where he planned on living if he gets temporary custody?"

Allie shook her head and concentrated on measuring the coffee. The opportunity never showed itself. Matt had been consumed with getting a temporary custody agreement written for Mariah to sign, then they'd been whisked out of ICU and immediately Matt had received a phone call from some client.

She had overheard him say he could do whatever the client needed from Cedar Grove, so apparently he didn't have to show up at an office each day. Surely Matt realized how important it was for Noah to stay in familiar surroundings right now. She set Peter's cup of coffee on the table. "Mariah signed a temporary custody agreement last night."

"Oh?" Peter sipped the coffee. "We'll see what Judge Stafford says tomorrow. My main concern is the boy. I'm just not convinced he'd be better off with Matt, especially if he plans to yank him out of school and take him to Memphis."

"Matt won't do that." Even as she said the words, Allie knew Matt couldn't stay in Cedar Grove. The thought of Noah having to change schools, and then change again when Mariah recovered...there had to be another answer.

"I hope you're right." He took a bite of the brownie. "Mmm, good. So, is Friday night still looking good for me to take you dancing?"

"Dancing. After New Year's Eve, are you certain you want to risk your toes again?"

He winked at her. "I knew what I was getting into when we talked about it at breakfast the other morning. And you even agreed to go."

Feeling slightly embarrassed, she tried to change the subject.

"Let me get you another cup of coffee." She snatched up his cup and carried it to the coffeemaker.

He followed her. "I'd like to actually finish that first one," he said as he took the cup from her hands.

"Can't we just go out to dinner? You danced with me. I'm terrible."

"Just out of practice, and I know the perfect remedy. Come on, let's go into the living room."

She followed him around the wall that separated the kitchen from the rest of the room. Peter set his cup on a table and turned to Noah. "May I change the TV channel? I'd like to dance with Miss Allie. Would that be okay with you?"

Color drained from Noah's face. "No!" He jumped up, his hands clenched. "Please, don't!"

"Noah, what's wrong?" Allie rushed to him.

Noah jerked, and his back arched as his eyes rolled back. She grabbed him before he pitched to the floor. "Call 911. He's having a seizure."

ALLIE SHIFTED THE hospital pillow under Noah's head as he slept. The doctor had come and gone, and Peter had left in search of something for them to drink. The door jerked open, and Matt charged into the small cubicle. She raised her finger to her lips, and he skidded to a stop. She led him back into the hallway.

Matt paced in front of her. "What happened?"

"I don't know. Like I said when I called you, we were at my house. We'd eaten and…suddenly he had a seizure."

"What did the doctor say?"

She shrugged. "Not much. The EEG showed

a normal pattern, but it would since the seizure had passed. He thinks it may be a onetime thing. My personal opinion is that stress has finally caught up with Noah."

Matt raked his fingers through his hair. "Did anything in particular trigger it?"

She'd replayed the scene in her mind at least twenty times. "Peter asked me to dance. He—"

"What was Peter doing there?"

She narrowed her eyes. "I don't think that's any of your business. Anyway, that's when Noah went into a seizure. Since we've been here in E.R., he's been drowsy so I haven't questioned him about it."

Matt stopped pacing at the doorway. He stared toward the bed. "What do we do next?"

"Wait and see if he has another one. Onetime seizures are not uncommon in children. And try to keep his stress level down." Allie turned as a nurse approached.

"I have your discharge papers," she said. "Would you like to go over them out here?"

"Please." After the nurse went over the doctor's instructions, Allie signed at the bottom of the page. She turned to Matt. "I guess we can take him to Mom and Dad's now."

He rocked back on his feet. "Is that all?"

"According to the doctor, Noah should be back

to normal tomorrow. Of course, if he has another seizure, tests will have to be run."

They stepped inside the cubicle and Matt stood over the bed. "He looks okay…. I'm just not used to him being asleep."

"I know. I hate to wake him."

The nurse rolled a wheelchair into the room. "Can't I just carry him?" he said.

Allie looked from Matt to the nurse. "Any reason he can't do that?"

"Perfectly fine with me."

When Matt scooped Noah up, the boy curled an arm around his neck and put his head on Matt's shoulder. Allie followed behind and dialed Peter's cell number. "We're ready. We'll meet you at your car," she said when he answered.

Now to tell Matt. She caught him before he reached the E.R. doors. "We'll have to wait for Peter."

He stopped and turned around. Noah's arms and legs wrapped around Matt's body like a monkey. "What? Why?"

"Two reasons, maybe? We won't fit in your car, and my car isn't here."

"Oh. Well, where is he?"

"I'm right behind you," Peter said from the entrance. "And my car is waiting in the circle."

Allie scooted to the middle of the backseat

and buckled Noah in beside her. When they reached the farm, Peter carried the boy in, and Allie helped her mom get him into pajamas.

"I think I'll sit here with him a bit." Ruth tucked the blanket under Noah's chin and smoothed back his hair. "Such a sweet boy. I'll hate to see him leave here."

An ache filled Allie's chest. Noah had so much potential, and she wanted so badly to help him live up to it. A soft snore escaped his lips. "I wish there was a way he could stay here until Mariah is well."

Her mom sighed. "So do I, but we both knew this was temporary. Your dad and I are leaving Friday for Georgia to go check on Mom."

She'd pushed their trip to the back of her mind. "I've forgotten how long you'll be gone."

"Just a few days, but your grandmother has business we need to tend to that can't wait. Too bad you can't come, as well."

"Maybe next summer." With her parents gone, Noah's options slimmed considerably—Matt or the shelter…or another foster family. She hugged her mom. "Enjoy your time with Grams. I better check on Matt and Peter."

Allie returned to the den in time to overhear Peter ask Matt if he planned to take Noah to Memphis if the judge awarded him custody.

Matt stood with his back to her, and she held her breath, waiting for the answer.

"My job is there. I don't have any choice."

Peter caught her eye as if to say, *See, I told you he'd take Noah to Memphis.*

"No." Allie shook her head.

Matt winced. "I assumed you realized..."

She rubbed her forehead. Of course she had known, whether she admitted it or not. She had just hoped—what? That Matt would turn his back on everything he'd worked for? Her insides cringed at her naive assumptions.

Peter squeezed her shoulder. "Do you want me to run you home?"

"No. I'll get Dad to take me."

"I'll see you tomorrow."

"Look," Matt said when the door closed behind Peter. "I'm sorry, but—"

"Don't you see, you're dragging him away from his mom, putting him in a new school. There's no telling how he might react."

"Allie, I don't know what else to do other than take Noah back to Memphis with me."

"But he just had a grand mal seizure today—what if he has another one?"

"He may never have another one—you said so yourself. But if he does, there are excellent neurologists in Memphis."

"That's—"

"Come on, Allie, try to understand. I have contracts waiting on me, a staff meeting first thing Wednesday morning. I can't stay here past Tuesday."

"What are you going to do with him? Take him to work with you?"

"No… I talked with Jessica this afternoon, and she's going to get him enrolled in a very good private school."

He had it all figured out. Except how it would affect Noah. There had to be another answer.

MATT WAVED AT NOAH, who was sitting beside Allie across the aisle in the courtroom. His nephew twisted his hands and barely acknowledged him. Peter stood on the other side of the railing, conferring with the youth court prosecutor. Matt hadn't expected a prosecutor. Or an actual courtroom. He'd thought it'd be him and Peter, and Noah, maybe Allie, in a judge's chambers, where the judge would simply look at Mariah's letter giving Matt temporary custody and sign the custody papers.

The pitcher of water on the judge's bench only reminded him how dry his mouth was. He should've had his attorney show up, or taken up Jessica on her offer to contact their family lawyer. He rubbed his hands on his thighs, glad they were the first case on the docket.

Peter approached him. "You don't have a lawyer?"

"I didn't realize I needed one. Mariah signed consent for me to take custody of Noah. What else do I have to do?"

"You'll have to have a home study, to start with."

Matt hadn't thought about that, and it irritated him that Peter knew he hadn't. He didn't understand what Allie saw in him. Certainly didn't understand why she'd had him over for dinner last night. Home study. How would that happen with him living in another state? He was certain Peter would tell him.

"It always helps to have someone who knows what he's doing at your side." Peter's mouth twitched.

His words struck their mark, doing little for Matt's confidence. "I'll make it just fine, but thanks for your concern." Then he lowered his voice. "And don't get too comfortable at Allie's place."

"Excuse me?" Peter shot him a sideways glance. "Don't you have a girlfriend in Memphis? I don't think who Allie sees is any of your business."

Matt clamped his molars so tight pain shot through his jaw. He had no idea why he'd said what he did. That Peter was right only made it worse.

The judge entered from a side door and everyone stood until she took her seat. As he'd expected, their case was called first. The prosecutor laid out the state's case for Noah remaining in state custody until his mother could resume her responsibilities. When he mentioned Mariah's drug use, Noah slumped in his chair and looked toward Matt, his eyes pleading for him to do something.

Matt stood. "Excuse me, Your Honor, but I don't see why this has to be drawn out. I have my sister's—"

The judge banged her gavel. "Mr....ah—" she looked over the papers on the bench "—Jefferies. We do things in an orderly way in my courtroom, and you are out of order."

Matt's face burned. He should've gotten a lawyer. "Thought I might save the court some time."

"You'll get your turn. Now, please be seated."

Matt lifted his shoulders in apology at Noah. Noah's returning smile was more of a wince. When the prosecutor finished, the judge turned to Matt. "All right, Mr. Jefferies, tell me why you think you should have custody of your nephew."

Matt took a deep breath and slipped into his salesman mode. "Thank you, Your Honor. I'm sorry for being out of order earlier, and that I don't have an attorney. But it was short notice." He glanced at his notes. "You have my sister's letter granting me temporary custody and quite simply, that should be enough. I'm Noah's uncle, his only blood kin, and kin should be with kin."

The prosecutor stood. "Your Honor, normally I would agree with that, but Mr. Jefferies has not had a home study performed, and we have a more than adequate children's shelter here. Mr. Jefferies also plans to withdraw Noah from school here and enroll him in classes in Memphis. We—"

"Uncle Matt can't do that," Noah cried. "I can't leave Mom."

Matt caught sight of Noah's white face as the boy tugged at Peter's arm. Allie leaned over and wrapped Noah in her arms.

The judge banged her gavel. "Order in this courtroom." She peered at Matt over her half glasses. "Mr. Jefferies. Is this true? Do you plan to move Noah to Memphis?"

"Your Honor, I live and work in Memphis. As much as I'd like to keep Noah here, I have no other choice."

"What is your occupation?"

"I am the food and beverage director for the Winthrop Corporation."

"Does that entail working a lot of hours?"

Matt hesitated. "Yes, ma'am. I oversee catering, staffing, contracts, that sort of thing."

"And what do you propose to do with the boy while you are doing your job?"

"He, ah, there's school, and then my fiancée plans to help watch him...." His voice trailed off as the judge's soured expression went south.

Allie raised her hand. "I may have a solution, Judge Stafford."

The judge raised her eyebrows. "Ms. Carson, would you please identify yourself for the court record?"

She addressed the court reporter. "Allie Carson. I am Noah's school counselor, and I am familiar with his case. Noah is presently staying with my parents, who are approved foster parents, but unfortunately, they're going out of town at the end of the week. I believe except for a few technicalities, I am approved to be a foster parent."

The judge turned to Peter. "How many technicalities are we talking about, Mr. Elliott?"

"None, Your Honor. I looked over Ms. Carson's paperwork first thing this morning and signed it. She is now a certified foster parent."

Matt leaned forward. Excitement danced from Allie's eyes. He was glad she was happy. Evidently being a foster parent was important to her, but where was she going with this?

"Your Honor, Noah has been through enough. He needs to stay in familiar surroundings, whatever it takes. If Mr. Jefferies is agreeable, Noah could continue to stay in Cedar Grove with me during the week, and then on weekends Mr. Jefferies can take charge of him. A home study could be conducted in Memphis during this time."

Judge Stafford studied the papers in front of her. Finally, she directed her attention to Matt. "How do you feel about this?"

"Your Honor, can I take a minute to think about it?"

"Do I need to recess court?"

"No, Your Honor. Just give me a minute." Matt rubbed the bridge of his nose. The enormity of caring for a nine-year-old hit him, and even with Jessica's help, it would be a daunting task. Neither of them knew the first thing about caring for a child full-time.

Allie's solution grew on him. It would solve so many problems, like what he would do with Noah when he had to work until midnight. The one it wouldn't solve was the biggest one—he'd be forced to make regular trips to Cedar Grove.

The judge jotted notes on a pad then pinned her gaze on Noah. "While you're thinking, why don't we ask the young man involved? Noah, would this arrangement be suitable with you?"

Noah sat straighter in his chair and locked his fingers in front of him on the table. "I don't want to leave my mom. And I really like Miss Allie."

Judge Stafford's face softened. "I take that as a yes."

She turned back to Matt. "Do you have any objections?"

Matt stood. "I'm agreeable, Your Honor."

The judge brought her gavel down. "I hereby grant temporary custody of Noah Connors to his uncle, Matthew Jefferies, until Mariah Connors is able to care for her son, with the stipulation that Noah remain in Cedar Grove until Mr. Jefferies's home study is complete. Mr. Elliott, would you please make the necessary arrangements?"

Peter looked none too pleased, but Matt didn't care. He drew a deep breath through his nose. He'd won. Sort of. As the next case came forward, he hurried out of the courtroom behind Allie and Noah. When he caught up with them in the hallway, Allie was trying to smooth Noah's unruly cowlick. "Thank you so much," he said.

"I'm not doing this for you."

How well he knew that. He squeezed his nephew's shoulder. "Well, we appreciate it, don't we, Noah?"

The boy wiggled out of his grip and planted his feet wide. "You didn't tell me I had to go to Memphis. Mom was right, I never should've trusted you."

Matt had been trying to do right by Noah, but still, he felt he'd let the boy down. "I thought you understood. Besides, Memphis is a great place. There's all kinds of things you can do…play ball, go to the movies—"

"I can do all that here."

Matt's head throbbed over his left eyebrow, and he massaged the spot. "Well, you're staying here, thanks to Miss Allie." He shot Allie a help-me-out-here look.

She put a reassuring hand on the boy's shoulder. "Let's focus on that, Noah. Okay?"

Matt mouthed a thank-you, which she ignored. He checked his watch. "It's almost lunchtime. Why don't I treat us to another one of those burgers like we had the other night?"

Noah crossed his arms. "I'm not hungry. I want to go see my mom."

Matt got a call from Jessica. "Excuse me just a sec," he said and walked away as he answered his cell phone. "Hey," he said, his voice husky.

"I've been thinking about you. How did it go?" Jessica said.

At last, a friendly voice. "We just finished."

"So you'll be bringing your nephew with you this afternoon?"

"Ah…not exactly. He'll be staying here for the time being."

"What happened?"

"I should've listened to you and brought in your attorney. It's complicated, but probably for the best. I'll explain when I get home later today."

Her sigh came through the phone. "I can't wait to see you. Have you missed me?"

"Of course I've missed you." He caught a glimpse of Allie and Noah. "I'll call you when I get on the road."

"Be careful on the drive back. Love you, 'bye."

"You, too—'bye."

Matt approached Allie and Noah. "Okay, have you decided where you want to eat? The hamburger place, maybe?"

Refusal flashed in Allie's eyes. "We don't want to hinder your departure to Memphis."

He counted to five. He had more to do than stand around arguing. "I have time to take you two for a burger. Besides, we need to discuss a few things, like Patches and clothes for Noah."

The *no* morphed into a *maybe,* and she knelt beside Noah. "We can't visit your mom until two o'clock, and those are pretty good burgers. How about it?"

Noah shrugged an indifferent okay. "He can't make me leave Mom, can he?"

Oh, great, now it was back to "he" instead of Uncle Matt. He squatted to reach eye level with his nephew. "Noah, I'm doing the best I can here. Until Miss Allie offered for you to stay with her, Memphis was my only option. I promise you from now on, I'll make sure you know my plans, and I'll try to work with what you want, but I'm not going to promise you'll always like my decisions."

Noah stood up straighter. "I'm not leaving my mom."

"I hope you never have to." He stood on creaking knees. "So, are we going to get something to eat or not?"

NOAH BLEW ON the French fry then popped it in his mouth. He'd quit listening to his uncle and Miss Allie after they decided Patches would stay with him in Cedar Grove. He kicked the side of the booth and tried to read Matt's upside-down watch. "What time is it?"

"Five minutes past the last time you asked," Matt said. "And stop kicking the booth."

Noah stilled his foot. His uncle didn't have to be so grouchy.

Miss Allie patted his back. "One o'clock."

He huffed a sigh and sagged into the booth

just as the door to the restaurant opened, and an older black woman and twin boys walked in. He gulped and sank deeper, trying to make himself invisible. He hadn't seen Miss Sarah since he ran away.

"Hey, look! There's Noah!"

The twins might be hard to tell apart sometimes, but he'd recognize Lucas's voice anywhere. And they were coming to the table. Today Lucas was dressed in a plain blue shirt and Logan wore another sweatshirt with stars on it.

Miss Sarah stopped at their table. "Why, hello, Allie. And, Noah, I'm so glad to see you and hear your mom is better."

He ducked his head and mumbled a thank-you. The care in her voice made Noah feel bad that he'd run away from the shelter. He hoped Miss Sarah didn't get in any trouble about it.

"Would you like to join us?" Allie asked. "We can put the boys at the next table. That way you can meet Noah's uncle, Matthew Jefferies."

Since that suited Miss Sarah, Noah reluctantly moved his plate and drink to the table Lucas and Logan had claimed. He tried to listen as the adults talked, but when Lucas swiped one of his French fries, he covered his plate with his hand. "Hey, that's mine. And I don't give anything to rat finks."

"What're you talking about?" Lucas bit the end of the fry and eyed Noah's ketchup.

"You told on me, and they sent Jason to find me."

"No, we didn't," Logan cried. "I told you there was an alarm on the door. Thanks to you, they're watching us like hawks now."

They didn't tell on him? Noah removed his hand from his plate, yet he was still skeptical.

"What'd they do to you?" Lucas grabbed another fry and dragged it through the ketchup.

"Nothing. They're letting me stay with Miss Allie during the week while my uncle is in Memphis."

"Why didn't you go with him to Memphis?"

Leave it to Lucas to want to know something dumb. "'Cause my mom's here. I'm not leaving her."

The waitress set fountain drinks in front of the boys, and Logan eyed his fries. Noah shoved his plate toward him. "You can have one, but I want one of yours when your plate gets here."

Logan drew a circle in the ketchup. "School starts tomorrow."

"But we're only going to be here this week," Lucas added. His brother elbowed him, and Lucas clapped his hand over his mouth.

"What's going on?" Noah asked.

Lucas lowered his voice to a whisper and

glanced toward the table with the adults. "Our dad's coming to get us."

"Then you'll have to go to court, like I did today. There's nothing to it."

"You don't get it. We're running away," Logan said. "We don't want to go with him."

Noah shook his head to clear it. "But…I thought you said he was in jail."

Lucas scowled at him. "I told you before, he's gonna bust out. Our cousins said so."

"You're crazy. Your dad wouldn't tell if he was going do that. Your cousins are just messing with you. Maybe he's getting out on bail."

"I told him that," Logan said.

Lucas shot out his jaw. "It doesn't matter how he gets out. He's coming, and we're not going to be here. You can come with us, if you want."

"Uh-uh. I'm staying where my mom is."

Lucas sent him a warning glance as the waitress approached with their hamburgers and set them on the table. "Here you go, boys," she said. "Eat up."

Noah sipped his drink while the twins dived into their food. Maybe he should tell Miss Allie about Lucas and Logan's dad, just in case it was true. Just as fast as the thought came, he shook it off. That'd be snitching. And he wasn't a snitch.

AFTER MATT CHECKED his watch for the second time, Allie patted Sarah's arm. "As much as I'm enjoying your company, I need to get a couple of things from Matt before he leaves."

Sarah leaned forward. "Didn't mean to hinder you...but could we talk a minute in private before you leave?"

Allie shifted her gaze to Matt, and he nodded. "I'll get Patches and wait for you at your house. Maybe take Noah with me?"

"Good idea."

At first Noah seemed hesitant to go with Matt, and Allie resisted the impulse to intervene. Matt had to learn how to reach his nephew on his own. She hid a smile when he mentioned Patches and Noah immediately jumped up. Matt would do okay. As soon as they were out the door, she turned to Sarah. "What's going on?"

She held up her finger. "Let me take care of the twins first." She fished a couple of dollars from her purse and called them over to the table. "You boys finished?"

"Yes, ma'am." Even though Allie taught the mischievous twins in her reading class, she'd never been able to tell them apart. Sometimes she believed they even switched identities.

Sarah nodded her head toward the arcade in the back of the restaurant. "How would you like to play a couple of video games?"

"Really?"

"Cool."

As the boys raced toward the arcade, she called after them, "Don't run!" They barely slowed to a walk, and she shook her head. "Those two will keep you on your toes."

"How do you tell them apart?"

"Logan always wears a shirt with stars on it. Unless they decide to switch. But they're good boys. Only…"

"Only?"

Sarah glanced back toward the arcade. "They're at the shelter because their dad was arrested for cooking and selling crystal meth and none of the family could take them. I think there are distant cousins here. At any rate, the dad has arranged for bond and will most likely get out this week. Somehow he's found out where they are, and I'm afraid he's going to try to kidnap them."

"He won't regain custody of them automatically?"

"Oh, no. That man is pure evil. Robbery, drugs—he even made the boys deliver packages of crystal meth to his customers. Department of Human Services will never let those boys go back to him."

"What happened to the mother?"

"Died less than a year ago." Sarah glanced back toward the arcade. "I don't know what to do. They won't talk about their dad or their mom."

"Is Peter aware of the situation?"

"We talked this morning. He mentioned moving them to another shelter, but you know how it is when shelter kids start a new school. The other kids can be brutal, and Lucas and Logan seemed to be doing pretty well in Cedar Grove. Besides, none of the other shelters in the state have room for two boys. They'd have to be split up, and I don't want that."

"No, that wouldn't be good. Let me think about it. How long do you think we have?"

"Maybe a couple of weeks," Sarah said. "I put in a call to the sheriff in the county where he's being held, but haven't heard back."

"Maybe it's all talk, from the father, I mean."

Sarah shook her head. "That kind of man doesn't make idle threats."

CHAPTER NINE

MATT GLANCED IN his rearview mirror and caught Noah rubbing the arm of his jacket. "You like it?" He certainly hoped so, since he'd shelled out a hundred bucks for it. When did kids' clothes get so expensive?

Noah nodded. "I never had a coat this nice before."

Matt hadn't intended on shopping for a coat much less buying such an expensive one before he left for Memphis. He had other pressing needs, like two texts, one from his client, J. Phillip Bradford, requesting a meeting for later in the afternoon. The other message was from his boss, William Winthrop. Jessica's dad had given him no idea what he wanted, just said to call him when he could.

He'd intended on calling his boss when he and Noah left the restaurant, but a cold north wind reminded Matt it was January, and that the thin windbreaker Noah wore would do little to keep the boy warm. At the store, the longing in his nephew's eyes when he spied the jacket among the cheaper coats loosened the strings on Matt's billfold. They'd walked out of the department store with Noah wearing the jacket, and his windbreaker in the bag.

Matt glanced in the rearview mirror at Noah. "So, are we good again?"

Noah shrugged. "I guess."

Translation—not yet. "Noah—"

Patches let out a yowl bigger than she was. The boy leaned over and spoke soothing words to the kitten, and then he lifted his head. "Are we almost there? She doesn't like traveling."

"Almost." Matt made the turn onto Allie's street. She stood by her car in the drive, and he parked in front of her ranch-style house. It shouldn't take any longer than an hour to wrap up things, and with any luck at all, he would be at his office by four and in his client's office by five.

As Matt unloaded the kitten and the litter box, Noah scrambled out of the car and raced to Allie's car, showing off his new coat. At the front porch, Matt sent Noah to get Patches's bed. He held up the carrier. "Where do you want her?"

Allie raised her eyebrows. "This will be temporary, right?"

He grinned. "I figure the kitty will be wherever Noah is."

She shook her head. "You're probably right.

Put her down anywhere. We'll put the litter box in the laundry room. Oh, by the way, nice coat you bought him."

At least he pleased someone. "Thanks. I'll give you a check to buy whatever else he needs." He followed her into the house and set the carrier down as Noah clattered in behind him.

"Can she sleep in my room? Please?" Noah begged.

"I suppose," Allie said. "I'll help you get her settled."

After they left, Matt glanced around the open room. While Allie's house was nothing like the farmhouse, it exuded the same warmth, with touches of her personality everywhere. He wandered to the fireplace and examined the painting that hung over it. She had gotten quite good. How many times had he sat on that pier and watched the sun go down?

He drew his gaze to a smaller painting, one of Allie's horse, and then he caught sight of a framed collage of snapshots on the mantel. In the center was Mrs. C, evidently on a recent birthday, her face bathed in the glow of candles. But the other photos were taken years ago, and for a second he was caught in a time warp. Allie on Bridger, one of her on her bicycle, Clint and Allie at the lake when they were young, Allie holding up a string of catfish, Clint on a Jet Ski. Another one—Mr. C with one arm around a teenage Clint, the other around…Matt?

He remembered that day. His gaze shifted to a photo tucked in the corner of the frame. It was the same golden autumn day Allie had taken the picture of him manning Mr. C's small wooden sailboat. He ran his finger over it, marveling at how she'd captured his intense concentration, one hand on the tiller, the other holding the mainsheet.

It was the day he decided he would have a lake one day, and a sailboat and a Jet Ski. He cocked his head, studying the photos, settling on the one of Mr. C and Clint and him, the three of them laughing, carefree. Belonging. Accepted.

Maybe he'd missed the most important thing that day.

"I think we have Patches all in order," Allie said as she returned.

He swung around, shoving his hands in his pockets. "Uh, good."

Conversation deserted him, and an awkward silence settled between them.

"Well, I hope you have a safe journey home," Allie said.

"Thanks. Oh, wait. I want to give you that check in case Noah needs something." He dashed off a check for two hundred dollars and handed it her. "Call me if you need more."

Allie glanced at it and looked up. "This will be more than adequate."

For a moment, their gazes locked, and deep-down yearning stirred in him, not for Allie, but for…something, and then she looked away. "Okay, then… I better hit the road."

"When should I tell Noah you'll be back?"

"This weekend." That stirring again. "I'll call every night, um, to talk to Noah. Maybe I can overcome the Memphis thing."

"You should've told him."

"I know. I'll try to do better in the future." He turned, searching for his nephew.

"Noah!" Allie called. "Your uncle is leaving. Come say goodbye."

The boy appeared in the hall doorway, Patches draped over his shoulder. Impulsively, Matt pulled out his phone and snapped their picture to show Jessica. Then he gently lifted the kitten, unhooking her claws from Noah's shirt. He rubbed under her neck, surprised at how attached he'd become to the animal. "Be good," he said to the kitten, then tousled Noah's hair. "You, too. I'll see you this weekend."

Noah didn't say anything, just nodded and took the kitten that Matt held out. With one lingering glance at Allie, Matt turned and walked out of the house.

A LITTLE AFTER FIVE, Matt suppressed the urge to flex the tightness out of his shoulders. It had been a long day. The hearing, driving in from Cedar Grove—he hadn't even been by his apartment. Instead he'd come straight to the Bradford Foundation and to J. Phillip's office.

Bradford leaned back in his leather chair and tented his fingers, his expression mirroring the somber moose head mounted on the walnut paneling behind him. "I like you, Matt. And I appreciate you coming by and going over the figures one last time. Your family situation—is it settled now?"

"Yes, sir. My sister is improving and my nephew is settled." Until the weekend. But Bradford didn't have to know that information.

The older man fingered the wedding band on his left hand, slipping it back and forth. "Taking care of family matters is admirable, but don't let it slow your career down. Did you find a band to play at the banquet?"

Matt struggled to keep his face impassive. *Play your cards close to your vest.* One of the few things he remembered from his dad. Bradford wasn't getting the name unless Matt won the contract. He refused to be intimidated by the steel-gray eyes sizing him up and leaned forward. "Yes. If I get the contract, I have an excellent ensemble lined up."

"Very good." Bradford's face actually held a hint of amusement as he picked up Matt's proposal. "These are your final figures?"

"Yes, sir. And I don't believe anyone can match them and still give you the level of service we at the Winthrop Corporation can."

Bradford inserted the proposal into a thick file then looked up. "We'll see tomorrow, won't we? If yours is the winning bid, I'll call you at ten."

"Yes, sir." Matt rose and extended his hand. "Thank you for seeing me this late."

Bradford stood as well and firmly grasped Matt's hand. "No problem. Do you have plans for dinner?"

Matt caught the hint of an offer. "Uh, yes, sir. My f-fiancée…Jessica…is making reservations at the hotel restaurant. Um, would you like to join us?"

The barest of hesitation, then Bradford patted him on the back. "I hardly think your young lady would appreciate that. No, I'll have something here at my desk."

Matt didn't push it. His client was correct in his assumption Jessica would not be pleased if he brought a guest with him. After all, they hadn't seen each other in several days. Bradford walked with him to the elevator. "And your sister…you said she was all right?"

Her physical condition had improved. Matt

wasn't so sure about her mental state. He'd stopped by the hospital on his way out of town to discuss getting treatment for her drug problem, but she'd been asleep. Or playing possum. Either way, this coming weekend his sister had a decision to make. Peter had left no doubt that Mariah would have to go through rehab to get custody of Noah. "She'll be fine. Thank you for asking."

"Good." His lips twitched, as if to say more, but the elevator doors opened. "You'll hear from me tomorrow."

"Yes, sir." Matt hesitated. Bradford seemed distracted, once again fingering his wedding band. Matt held the elevator. "Are you certain you can't join us for dinner?"

"No, Matthew. Go meet your girlfriend. I'm fine here with my work."

"Well, have a good evening." Matt punched the lobby button and the doors silently closed. His client seemed a very lonely man, something Matt found hard to understand, given his wealth and success.

He didn't remember any mention of family from his research other than a wife who had died years ago from cancer and that one of the nonprofits was named for her. From all reports, the CEO's whole life revolved around his work. He'd check again tomorrow and see what he could find on the internet.

By the time Matt pulled out of the parking garage, traffic had settled down from the mad five-o'clock rush. While he loved living in Memphis, he could do without the traffic. Fifteen minutes later, Matt unlocked his apartment. He couldn't wait to get back into his surroundings, his routine. The past four days seemed like four weeks. Inside, the living room looked as picture-perfect as always. Jessica must've come by and straightened up. He tried to imagine Noah here, and a sigh came from somewhere deep inside him.

His nephew would hate it.

Maybe Matt could scatter around a few family photos, if he had any. He rolled his suitcase into his bedroom and unpacked it. Maybe chrome-and-glass wasn't warm and cozy like Allie's house or the farmhouse. It would do the boy good to be exposed to the finer things in life. Like going to dinner at a fancy restaurant.

Weariness settled in his bones. Maybe he could talk Jessica into eating in. He dialed her number. "Hey, babe," he said when she answered. "What do you think about ordering in tonight?"

"But I'd planned a celebration dinner at the hotel restaurant. Thought I'd have the chef pan-fry a couple of flat-iron steaks...."

Dinner at the hotel meant a jacket and tie. He used his salesman voice. "Or, you could come here, maybe pick up Chinese on the way over. Nice romantic dinner, just the two of us?"

There was hesitation on Jessica's end, then a soft sigh. "You do sound tired. And I haven't talked with Chef yet. Moo goo gai pan sound good?"

Tension eased from Matt's shoulders. "I knew there was a reason I was crazy about you."

Her chuckle floated through the phone. "I'll see you in thirty minutes."

Matt tossed the phone on the bed and pulled a pair of jeans and a sweater from his closet. As he slipped an alligator belt through his pant loops, he remembered the strand of pearls and retrieved the black velvet bag from his suitcase. While he wasn't an authority on pearls, the lustrous beads appeared to be high-quality. Just like the wedding ring set. He opened the velvet box holding his grandmother's engagement ring. Like snow crystals sparkling under a morning's sun, the diamond glittered under the lamp's glow. Proof that his mother had a different life once.

You think you're so much better than me. Why don't you take these snotty-nosed brats and go back to your father. His own father's drunken words just days before he wrapped his pickup around a light pole.

But the words had lit a fire in Matt's mind. He'd always known his mother was different. That she had a quiet refinement that set her apart. When he asked what his dad meant, she brushed him off. When he persisted, she snapped at him. "Your grandfather is more interested in money than he is family."

"But if he could help us—"

"We are doing fine, Matthew. We don't need him or anyone else."

"Mom, look around. We live in a dump. Why won't you ask him?"

"The price is too high, son." Pain had filled her hazel eyes that were red with unshed tears as her shoulders bowed from whatever secrets she hid from Matt.

He'd never asked again. But that did not keep him from dreaming of grandparents who could change his life if only he could find them.

Matt never found them. And now he didn't need them. He had the life he wanted, and Jessica was part of that life. Matt snapped the velvet box shut and slipped it into his pocket. Before the night was out, he'd find out what she thought of the ring.

In the living room, flames licked the gas logs, reminding him of the Carsons' real fireplace. Gas might not be as romantic, but it was much easier. He scrolled through a list of movies and selected a comedy so he wouldn't have to think. For now, he chose a jazz radio station to play softly in the background. He checked his watch as he put cushions on the floor around the coffee table for them to sit on.

Maybe he could talk with Noah before Jessica arrived. He took out his phone, and a tug at his heart surprised him when the photo of Noah and Patches popped up on his screen. He speed-dialed Allie's cell number and his call went straight to voice mail.

"Hi. This is Allie. Leave your number and I'll get back to you."

He frowned. Where could they be? *Probably having dinner with Peter.* But wouldn't she have her cell phone with her? Maybe she didn't want to talk to him. His jaw tightened. "Allie, this is Matt. Just checking to see how you and Noah are. Give me a call."

He laid the phone on the coffee table. He should be happy that Allie had Peter to turn to. Peter could be quite charming when he wanted to be. He was in Cedar Grove…. Matt caught himself grinding his teeth.

Yeah, Peter was in Cedar Grove and would have daily contact with Noah if he wanted to—Allie, too. What if his nephew started liking Peter better than him? The doorbell chimed and he hurried to open the door.

Jessica threw her arms around him. "I have missed you!"

"Same here." He swung her around and gently set her down, giving her a light kiss.

"You can do better than that."

He pulled her into his arms and pressed his lips against hers, enjoying their softness and the way her lips responded to him.

"Better, but…" Jessica slipped her arms around his neck and pressed her lips against his once again.

"Hold that thought," he said and unwrapped her arms long enough to grab the wire handles of the take-out boxes Jessica had set down outside the door.

"I can't believe you," she said.

"Hey, I've only had a hamburger all day and I'm starved." He set the to-go containers on the coffee table.

Jessica's brows lifted. "You want us to sit on the floor?"

"It's all about ambience." He held his hands up. "Good music, good food, beautiful lady. What more could you want? Unless maybe a movie later."

"I'd rather learn more about Noah."

"That'll work, too." Thirty minutes later, Matt leaned back against the couch, his stomach full.

Over dinner, he'd explained about the custody arrangement and had shown her Noah's picture.

"He's a cute kid. I have so many plans for when you bring him here."

"Like?"

"The Pink Palace, the zoo, the art gallery, the planetarium, the—"

"You're going to wear the boy out." He handed her a fortune cookie.

She broke it open and laughed.

"What does it say?"

"'Remember what happened to the early worm.'"

He laughed with her. "That's something you'll never have to worry about."

"Okay, Mr. Smarty, what does yours say?"

He snapped his open. "'Help, I'm being held prisoner in a fortune cookie factory.'"

"It does not." She grabbed the thin paper. "'Be true to yourself.'"

The words were like an arrow to his heart. How many times had his mother said those very words? He began stacking their dishes. "How about that movie now?"

She half shrugged. "Are you going to bring Noah to Memphis next weekend?"

"I don't think I can get him that far away from Mariah. Maybe later, when my sister is better."

"And he'll be staying with Allie during the week? Your old girlfriend?"

Matt frowned. He didn't recall ever telling Jessica that he and Allie had dated. "That was a long time ago. How—"

"I called Clint. You haven't been very forthcoming about your past, and he grew up with you, so—"

"You should have asked me."

"*Hello?* Has something changed since the last time I asked you about your life before you came to Memphis?"

He picked up their dirty dishes and stood to take them into the kitchen. "It's hard to talk about that time in my life. I didn't like anything about it."

"According to Clint, you were an outstanding guy. Honors society, star quarterback, scholarships."

"What I remember is wearing ragged jeans before they were the 'in' thing. And secondhand clothes and Mom being so tired we often had scrambled eggs and nothing else for supper."

She tilted her head. "Do you like who you are now better?"

"Of course I do," he said and shoved the kitchen door open. After he'd loaded the dishwasher, he returned, hoping Jessica would get on another subject. He sat on the hard sofa and tried to find a comfortable spot. "What do you think about me buying another sofa? One with softer cushions? And not white."

She snuggled beside him. "I think it would ruin the tone of this room. Now tell me about Allie. What qualifies Clint's sister to have Noah and not you?"

Same subject, different verse. "She's a school counselor and is familiar with his case, she's also part of the foster care system…and she's completed a home study—something I have yet to do."

Jessica tucked her feet under her. "So, tell me what happened to you and Allie. Why did she let a great guy like you get away?"

He fixed his gaze on the only color in the room—Jessica's painting that had a splash of blood-red. "In the first place, she broke up with me, not the other way around."

"You're kidding. Why?"

Can't you see, Matt? You're fighting to be someone you're not. Someone I don't even like. So you go on, turn yourself into whoever you think you have to be, but I can't be part of it. He shoved Allie's words from his mind. "We grew apart. I came to Memphis, she stayed in Cedar Grove."

"Do you ever wish you'd stayed?"

"No." But was that true? Once or twice this

weekend he'd found himself almost envious of Allie and the contentment she radiated. His muscles tensed. If he'd stayed, he'd still be the kid from the wrong side of town.

"Are you sure?"

"I didn't leave anything behind in Cedar Grove that I want to go back for now." He turned to Jessica. "Do you know how hard I've worked to forget who I was there?" He swept his arm around the room. "This is the life I want. You're the wife I want."

Jessica's hand flew to her lips.

Matt's stomach knotted as he took the velvet box from his pocket and opened the top. There was no turning back now. The light caught the facets of the diamond in the engagement ring, the lively stone shimmering a rainbow of color. He slipped the ring on her finger. "Jessica Winthrop, will you marry me?"

Jessica's eyes widened. "Oh, Matt, I don't know what to say."

"'Yes' will do."

"Yes! Yes, a thousand times yes." She threw her arms around his neck.

Matt released the breath he'd been holding. His life was coming together, and until this very second, he hadn't realized how important Jessica was to him. Nothing was going to change that.

"Do you like Mr. Elliott better than you do Uncle Matt?" Noah scrunched his eyebrows together. He was lying on his stomach in front of the fireplace, drawing.

Allie paused as she folded the pile of warm clothes beside her on the couch. This was a question she probably should've expected, especially since Peter had taken them to the Emporium for dinner. "I think he's nice, don't you?"

"But do you like him better?"

It didn't matter whether she liked him better or not. Matt was marrying Jessica. Which was fine. She and Matt didn't belong together anyway. "How about you? Do you like Mr. Elliott?"

Noah stared at her with his huge blue eyes. Sometimes Allie believed he knew exactly what she was thinking. "He's okay, I guess."

"How about Matt? You still mad at him?"

Again that shrug. "He *knew* I wanted to stay where my mom is."

"I think he was doing the best he could."

"Whatever."

She frowned. "Noah. We don't use that word in this house."

His eyes grew even bigger. "But…it's not a dirty word or anything like that."

"It is here. We probably need to lay a few ground rules for when you're here."

"Huh?"

"Ground rules. Like, no talking back. No saying 'whatever,' what chores you'll have, bedtime, that sort of thing."

"Oh. Mom always let me stay up as long as I wanted to."

"Well, around here, bedtime is nine o'clock, maybe nine-thirty on Friday and Saturday night if you happen to be here instead of with your uncle."

"Nine o'clock?" His voice rose to a high pitch.

"Yes. Which is in thirty minutes." She tossed him a warm set of pajamas. "So, you better get your teeth brushed and your pajamas on. School starts back in the morning."

"Aw, come on, Miss Allie, I'm not sleepy. And what if Uncle Matt calls?"

"Sorry, bud. Those are the rules around here. Besides, I thought you were mad at him." He ducked his head and she laughed. "I suppose we can call him."

She took out her phone. "Oh, looks like we missed a call from him." She pressed the callback button and waited as it rang. "I'll put it on speaker."

"Hello?"

She didn't expect his voice to send a shiver through her. "Matt, sorry we missed your call. Peter took us out to eat."

A brief silence followed. "How's Noah?" he asked.

"Good. But he can talk for himself. We're on speakerphone." *Say something,* she mouthed.

"'Lo," Noah mumbled.

"Hey, how's my favorite nephew."

"Fine."

"How's your mom? And Patches?"

"They're good."

Allie rolled her eyes. "Say something that's more than one syllable," she whispered.

"I gotta go brush my teeth and go to bed."

"This early?"

"Yeah. 'Bye." He handed the phone back to Allie and hurried out of the room

"I'm sorry." She took it off the speaker. "He hasn't been real talkative tonight." Except when he asked questions she had no answers for.

"That's okay. I miss you guys." Wistfulness crept into his voice. "I hope to arrive by six Friday night."

"Fine. We'll see you then." Her thumb hovered over the end button on her phone.

"Wait a minute. I need to tell you something," Matt said.

Nothing good ever followed those words. "Okay."

"I, ah, asked Jessica to marry me tonight. And she said yes."

Stunned into silence, she could only grip the phone tighter. She'd known it was coming but so had not expected it tonight.

"Are you still there?"

"Uh, yeah." She remembered her manners. "Congratulations."

"Allie, I—"

"I'll see you Friday, then?" No way did she want to hear anything else from Matthew Jefferies tonight.

"Yeah, sure. Goodbye."

Allie sat on the sofa, not moving. Not understanding the emptiness in her heart. Their relationship ended years ago when Matt had been so blinded by the kind of person he wanted to be. He believed they broke up because she didn't want to leave Cedar Grove, but how could she go anywhere with him when he was trying to shed the person she loved for someone she wanted no part of?

Maybe this would be the closure she needed, and from what she'd gathered, Jessica was the perfect wife for Matt.

So why did it hurt so much?

CHAPTER TEN

AT 10:00 A.M. the next morning, Matt's cell phone rang and the Bradford Foundation showed on caller ID. He let it ring twice before answering. "Jefferies."

"The Matthew Jefferies who is the director of food and beverage for the Winthrop Corporation?" Bradford's voice held a touch of humor.

"Yes, sir."

"Then congratulations. The contract is yours."

He'd won. Tension leached from Matt's muscles. Yes! He pumped his fist. "Thank you, sir."

"See if you're still thanking me February fifteenth. Can you drop by the office later today and sign the contract?"

Matt looked over his to-do list for the morning. Nothing that couldn't be put off for an hour. "I can be there in fifteen minutes."

He ended the call, leaned back in his chair and let the warm glow of satisfaction wash over him. Step one accomplished. He dialed his boss. "Mr. Winthrop," he said when Jessica's father answered. "Just wanted to let you know we won the contract for the Valentine's Day banquet with Bradford."

"First time ever to get that scoundrel's business. Good job, Matthew."

"Thank you, sir. I plan on getting the rest of his business, as well." And if he could accomplish that before his May job evaluation, he stood a good chance of moving up in the Winthrop Corporation, maybe even into consideration for a vice-president position.

"Good luck. Bradford is a difficult taskmaster. Let me know if you have any problems with the Valentine's banquet."

Not that Matt thought he'd need help, but he assured Winthrop he would do so, if necessary, before hanging up. After all, he hadn't gotten this far by failing.

"YES?" ALLIE SAID, not looking up from her paperwork. She had eleven new requests from teachers for student literacy evaluations on her desk, and it was only Wednesday.

"I need you to speak with Mr. Nichols."

The trembling in the secretary's voice brought Allie's head up, but it was the panic in Betty Marshall's face that got Allie to her feet. "What's wrong?"

"He wants to take Logan and Lucas out of school. He's quite insistent."

Evidently he made bond for his crystal meth charge. "Where is Mr. Wright?"

"He's not here. There's a principals' meeting at the district office this morning."

Allie had forgotten that. "Call the sheriff." She hurried to the outer office. Better to err on the side of caution.

Lenny Nichols was not at all what she expected. He stood at the counter that divided the room. Neatly dressed in a button-down shirt, corduroy coat and khakis, he easily could have passed for a businessman. Except for the eyes and body movements. Dilated pupils, the shifting from one foot to another, the twitchy hands. She stood taller and nodded. "I'm the school counselor. May I help you?" Her voice sounded much calmer than she felt.

Nichols folded his arms across his chest. "I want to pick up my boys."

"Let me see if you're on the list." Allie pulled open a file cabinet and pretended to search the records. She knew his name wasn't listed, but every minute she stalled gave the sheriff time to get there.

She glanced over her shoulder. Nichols had dropped his arms and now stood with his feet planted apart. "While I'm looking, why don't you go ahead and sign the checkout sheet. It's on the counter there."

"Where?"

She closed the file drawer and slid the clipboard toward him. "I'll need you to sign in, and I'll need to see some identification first."

He glanced at the clipboard then at Allie. "I'm not signing anything. I'm their father, and I have rights. Now get my boys down here."

"I'm sorry, Mr. Nichols. The boys are in class."

The image of a rational, everyday businessman disappeared as he lunged over the counter and grabbed Allie's wrist, jerking her to him. "You can't keep my boys from me."

The secretary screamed just as sirens filled the air.

For what seemed like an eternity Allie stared into the dilated pupils of Nichols's eyes, then he shoved her. She stumbled over a stool, landing on the floor. When she scrambled up, Nichols was gone.

"Hit the button to unlock all the doors so the sheriff can get in," she yelled to the secretary as she ran into the hall. She feared he might try to find the twins. Out of the corner of her eye, she saw him duck out the back entrance.

Deputies poured into the front entrance. She wanted to shout that he'd gone out the back way, but every ounce of energy deserted her.

The sheriff hurried toward her. "Mrs. Russell said you had someone causing trouble."

"He left by the back door. You might catch him near the railroad tracks." Allie wrapped her arms across her stomach and swallowed the bile that rose in her throat.

The sheriff barked instructions in his mic. "Are you sure the guy's gone?"

She nodded. "But he wants his sons. He may circle around and try to get back into the school." She turned to the secretary, who had followed her into the hallway. "Lock the doors down again."

"How did he get in?"

"I don't know. After the eight-thirty tardy bell rings, all entryways are electronically locked from the outside. If anyone wants in, they have to ring the bell at the entrance you came in, and we check the video to see who it is before they are admitted." Allie caught her breath. "The video cameras. They should show everything."

AN HOUR LATER Allie sat on the sofa in her office with her eyes closed. Her wrist throbbed where Nichols had twisted it. Lenny Nichols had disappeared into thin air. Surveillance video had shown a student opening the back entrance for him to get in—the same place he ran out. A camera on the football field had caught a man running toward the wooded area behind the school. Although the man was too far away to be recognized, it was assumed to be Nichols. Neither was there any sign of a vehicle. But at least the video had provided a clear picture of Nichols, and every law enforcement department within a hundred miles was on the lookout for him.

"Allie? How are you holding up?"

She blinked open her eyes. Peter stood in the doorway, his six-one frame filling it, concern etched in his blue eyes. She lifted her shoulder. "Between a headache that the adrenaline triggered and my wrist, I'm not sure. How did you find out about Nichols?"

"The principal called because it concerns DHS children." He sat beside her on the couch. "You look beat. Why don't you go home?"

She'd already turned down the principal's offer. "Too much to do, especially with the reports Mr. Nichols's little visit will require. I took ibuprofen, so it should be easing soon."

"I expected to find the school closed for the rest of the day."

"If we shut down every time parents came in here and lost their temper, school would be closed at least once a week." She rolled her shoulders. "Recess has been moved to the gym, though. And the sheriff has deputies scattered around. I'm sure everything will be fine now."

"How would you like to have lunch with me?"

She shook her head. "I don't want to leave right now."

"Then I'll go get something and bring it to you. How about one of Norma Jean's famous salads? And her apple cinnamon scones."

Peter was persistent if nothing else, and having someone to look after her wasn't bad at all, especially at a time like this

Peter raised his eyebrows. "What do you say?"

"I say thank you, I would love that."

Allie barely had time to clear off a table and make a pot of coffee before Peter returned with their food. "How did you do that?" she asked as she handed him a cup of coffee. "This time of day it takes forever to get waited on at Norma Jean's."

A grin creased his cheeks as he blew on his fingernails then brushed them against his lapel. "It's all about connections."

Yeah, Peter had connections, all right. She sat across from him at the narrow coffee table where he had spread their food. Everything looked delicious and the cinnamon aroma of the scones made her mouth water. She chuckled as he broke off the corner of one and popped it into his mouth. "You're eating your dessert first?"

"Aren't you? It's the best part of the meal. And these are delicious, by the way."

"They always are, but that's like flipping to the last page of a book to see how it ends."

"And you've never done that?"

"Never." Allie poured raspberry vinaigrette over her salad and forked a wedge of lettuce. "You're quite the puzzle, you know."

Peter cocked his head. "Why? Because I eat my dessert first?"

"Not just that. Since New Year's Day, I've been trying to figure you out. With the money your grandfather left you, you don't even have to work. And yet, here you are in this small town, working for peanuts when you could be rubbing elbows with the movers and shakers in this world."

"So you've been thinking about me." His blue eyes twinkled.

"You didn't answer my question."

"I told you at breakfast the other morning, you're the—"

"Don't feed me that line that it's all because of me."

The corner of his mouth twitched as he poured creamer in his coffee and stirred it, sloshing a little over the top. With deliberate movements, he used a napkin to blot the liquid. "Everyone always remembers the money, but no one remembers how my parents expected me and my brothers to work, to volunteer in the community. 'Everyone has a purpose for their lives'—growing up, that was their favorite thing to quote to us."

He looked up at her and grinned. "I guess they did too good of a job. I got bored with jetting around and volunteered at a homeless shelter in New York. The men especially, really got to me, some well-educated, had lost their jobs, their families, and many of them, their hope. I'm afraid I burned out pretty quick. So, see, I'm not perfect."

She laughed. "Never in my wildest dreams did I think that."

He speared a tomato. "You certainly know how to wound a guy."

"You'll probably survive." She'd never seen this side of Peter. "So what did you do next?"

His eyes darkened and he became serious again. "Working with those men, seeing them and their families in such pain made me want to do something to help. That's when I went to work for the Department of Human Services in D.C., which led to me going back for my master's. Last summer, my dad told me the director of social services in Cedar Grove was retiring, and I remembered a blond-haired girl who challenged me in high school to be more than I was. She wouldn't give me the time of day back then, but I had to give it one last try. And here I am."

Her heartbeat quickened as he held her gaze. For once, words escaped her.

Peter leaned toward her. "Have dinner with me tonight. We can get a sitter for Noah and go to the new place in town. I've heard it's quite private, and we could get to know each other a little better. How about it?"

"Dinner? Again tonight?" She almost dropped her fork. He was moving too fast for her. "It's the middle of the first week after holidays. And what happened this morning has put me so far behind, school will be out before I catch up. And I don't really want to leave Noah with a sitter."

"Okay. No harm in trying to squeeze in another dinner with you before Friday night. Matt is picking Noah up Friday afternoon?"

Matt. She'd kept thoughts of him at bay since last night, partly because of the charming man sitting across from her. Maybe it was time to shake things up. She picked up a scone and bit into it, savoring the buttery apple-and-cinnamon taste. Peter was right. It was delicious. She licked her fingers. "Yes, he is. And I'm looking forward to going out with you."

His eyes widened. "You are?"

"Yes." At least she wouldn't be hanging around the house thinking about Matt.

CHAPTER ELEVEN

THURSDAY MORNING, MATT took his coffee into his living room and tried to get comfortable on the damask sofa. An impossible feat. Not to mention, he dropped a piece of buttered toast on the white material, which left a faint stain even though he cleaned it right away. He could imagine what the sofa would look like a month after Noah came to stay. He dialed Jessica's number.

"'Lo."

"I woke you up, didn't I? I'm sorry."

"What time is it?" Sleepiness slurred her words.

"Eight-thirty. I wanted to ask if you'd have lunch with me and help me pick out a new sofa, one that's not white."

"What? There's nothing wrong with the sofa you have."

That had woken her. "Not for me and you, but it's not going to wear well with Noah here. I thought I'd get something a little easier to keep clean. Then after he goes back to his mother, we can bring the damask sofa out again."

"You may have a point. Noonish? At the furniture store downtown?"

"Perfect." That way he wouldn't lose much time.

Or so he thought. Jessica found something wrong with every sofa he picked out. It was either the wrong color or the wrong style.

"You keep choosing the same kind." Jessica waved her hands, the diamond on her left ring finger catching the light. "And it doesn't go with the rest of your furniture."

"But it won't be for that long." He glanced at the last sofa he'd chosen. It was similar to the one in Allie's house, with soft cushions and big arms. "It's leather, so it'll go with the chairs."

"But it's too bulky." She turned and pointed to an alternate. "What's wrong with this one?"

Everything. It was thin and hard and a light fabric. He wanted something he could sink back in, something comfortable, something he didn't have to worry about Noah spilling chocolate milk on. What he thought must have shown on his face.

"You don't like my tastes, do you?" She blinked rapidly. "I bet you hate all of your furniture."

"Nooo." He took her hands. "I love my apartment, but as long as Noah is going to be there, we need to think about something practical. I don't want to be on him every minute about furniture."

She put her hands on her hips. "Well, so far, he isn't even here."

"I'm bringing him back with me next weekend." He turned to the last sofa he'd chosen. "And I'd like to have this at the apartment when he gets there." He ducked down so he could see her eyes. "Okay?"

Jessica shrugged. "It's your apartment. And I suppose you're right that the other one would soon be ruined."

"Good." He motioned to the salesclerk hovering nearby. "I'd like to buy this one."

MATT FLIPPED THE heater up a notch. He didn't care what the salesman said. Convertibles were not made for cold weather, not even a Beemer. Where was that sixty-five the weatherman had predicted?

He checked the time and groaned. After eleven and he was still ten minutes away from Cedar Grove. He'd promised Noah he'd pick him up on Friday, only to have to break his word, and thought he'd have to cancel the whole weekend until his assistant agreed to take care of a dinner for the mayor's birthday tonight. Even so, Saturday was half-gone. And he wanted to stop at the hospital to see Mariah before he drove to Allie's house. His sister had pneumonia now.

The hospital came into view, and Matt pulled into the parking lot. He would bring Noah back later. He arrived at Mariah's room as a respiratory therapist finished up a breathing treatment.

Matt tweaked her foot. "How are you feeling?"

"About like I look."

He could barely hear her wispy voice. "That bad, huh?" He kept his tone light, but her emaciated frame and the dark circles under her eyes pierced Matt's heart.

The therapist held up a small device that Matt recognized from his mother's hospital stays. "How often are you using your incentive spirometer?"

"When I think of it."

"You need to do better than that. Your lungs are still congested, Ms. Connors, and I can't stress how important it is to use this device." He rubbed his jaw. "Do you watch TV?"

Mariah nodded.

"Okay, when a commercial comes on, I want you to grab this and try to get the cylinder a little higher each time. You're only pulling about five hundred milliliters now. By tomorrow I'd like to see that number up to seven-fifty."

Closing her eyes, she nodded again. "I'll try."

The therapist caught Matt's eye and shook his head. "Encourage her to use this." He set the device on the table by the bed.

When they were alone, Matt nudged her foot again. "Hey, kiddo."

Her lips curled into a faint smile, but she didn't open her eyes.

"You have to do what they say."

The smile disappeared, replaced by a coughing fit. She hugged her chest until the spell ended. "That hurts so bad I don't even want to breathe. Do you think the nurse would give me something for pain?"

"Are you sure you need it?"

"What?" She snapped her eyes open. "Are you on the drug squad now, little brother?"

"If I have to be."

Her jaw clamped down as beads of sweat popped out on her face. "Why are you here anyway? Go back to whatever penthouse you crawled out of."

He flinched. "Look, I would have helped you if you'd called. Or if you'd told me about Noah."

Her chin quivered, and he turned away, unable to take seeing her tears. Mariah had never been one to cry, even in the face of their drunken father's rages. No, she'd been the one to stand up to him, protecting Matt.

"I'm sorry."

He wasn't sure he heard her right. He turned to face her. "What?"

Mariah took a shaky breath and winced. "Growing up in Cedar Grove with Luke Jefferies for a father scarred us both. We just dealt with it in different ways. At least you have something to show for it." Did he? Matt wasn't so sure anymore. Was his obsessive search for wealth and recognition any different than Mariah numbing herself with drugs? What if he hadn't been so self-centered about leaving Cedar Grove and all it represented behind, perhaps Mariah wouldn't be lying in a hospital bed, and he wouldn't be trying to figure out why his life seemed so empty.

"Maybe both of us can do better from here on out," he said. "Are you up to seeing your son?"

MATT PULLED IN front of Allie's house. She had not sounded too happy yesterday afternoon when he'd called to say he couldn't make it to Cedar Grove. Noah's attitude had been one of indifference. At least the temperature had warmed up again. Maybe Noah would enjoy riding around with the top down.

When the door opened, Allie's face matched her red plaid shirt. A strand of blond hair curled under her jaw. Behind her, a din of shouting and groans filled the room. "Come on in. The boys are in the middle of a game of Wii boxing."

"Boys?" Matt tried to look around her.

Before Allie could answer, a boy who seemed the same age as Noah bounded to the door. He looked familiar. "Miss Allie, Noah's hitting below the belt."

"Lucas," Allie said, "work it out yourselves."

The boy raced back to the TV and joined Noah and another boy that was his mirror image. Ah, the twins from the hamburger place last week, Lucas and Logan. Matt frowned. "What's going on?"

She shut the door behind him. "Noah was disappointed when you didn't come yesterday, and when you called to say you were going to be late today, I picked up a couple of his friends to keep him company."

So, Noah had been disappointed. Surprise to Matt.

"I admire your courage, but question your sanity," he said as he followed her into the living room.

"You and me both. I'm trying to let them work off a little energy with the Wii." She turned to the boys. "Noah, say hello to your uncle, then get your bag. And Logan and Lucas, I'll drop you off at the shelter on my way to the grocery store."

Noah reluctantly pulled his gaze away from the Wii. "'Lo, Uncle Matt."

Matt would've liked a little more enthusiasm. "You ready to have some fun?"

Noah shrugged. "I'm having fun now."

It was going to be a long weekend. He rubbed the bridge of his nose.

"What're we going to do?"

"Ah…" Matt hadn't thought that far ahead. "I don't know. It's a pretty day. We could go to the park and throw the football around. Later we'll go see your mom."

Noah's eyes widened. "Maybe we could have a picnic and Miss Allie and Logan and Lucas could come! We can even take Patches."

Allie's shoulders stiffened. "I don't know, Noah. Your uncle might want to spend time with just you."

"That won't be any fun. Can they come, Uncle Matt? Please? We could have a real game, me and Miss Allie against you and the twins."

"I don't know. Miss Allie is probably busy." Matt shot a questioning glance at Allie. It was crazy, but he found himself wanting her to say yes. The closed expression on her face, stiff body…*no* would be the next thing out of her mouth. If he let her be the one to say no, at least he wouldn't be the bad guy for once. "Why don't we leave it up to Miss Allie to decide?"

"Please, Miss Allie! Could we?"

As all three boys begged to go on a picnic, Allie shot him a dark look. Finally she sighed. "It *is* a pretty day," she admitted. "And warm enough for the boys to use up some of this energy. But not the park. There's a spot at my dad's farm that would be better. And we'll stop and pick up a bucket of chicken."

He hadn't expected her to agree. As the boys yelled and jumped up and down, he glanced at the painting over her fireplace. Surely not... One glance at her stoic expression told him that was exactly where she meant. Noah brought him back to earth when he tugged on his hand.

"Miss Allie says she doesn't have a football. Can we stop and get yours, Uncle Matt?"

"What?"

"Your football, the one at your house."

"Yeah, sure." He glanced at Allie.

"I'll grab a couple of old quilts and throw a few things in a picnic basket and we'll get going."

The boys set the kitten carrier in the front seat of Allie's car while Matt loaded the things she handed him into the trunk of her sedan. When he'd finished, she tossed him the keys. "You can drive. That way I can ride herd on the boys."

When they reached the house on Beaker Street, Matt hurried to the shed behind the house and retrieved the football. Back in the car, he enjoyed the boys' reaction.

"You mean, this was in a real game?" Awe filled Noah's voice.

"Yep. Last game of the season." Matt backed out of the drive. "Who wants chicken legs, and who wants the breast?"

Except for Allie, chicken legs it was. As Matt navigated traffic through town, he noticed she kept watching her side mirror. "Expecting someone to follow us?"

She startled. "No. I just don't usually sit on the passenger side."

That made sense, but still, something seemed off. He glanced her way, and she gave him an imperceptible shake of her head. What was going on?

ALLIE HOPED GOING with Matt on a picnic didn't prove to be a mistake. For more than one reason. Lenny Nichols had not been arrested, and no one had seen him since Wednesday.

She glanced at Matt. As soon as they were alone, she'd tell him what was going on. Alone. The other reason she shouldn't be here. She needed to keep in mind he was an engaged man. She glanced in the side mirror again. No one *seemed* to be following, but... "Take the back road to Dad's place."

"What?"

"I'd like to show the boys Dad's cutting horses. The back road takes us right past their pasture." She'd know in a minute if anyone was following them. When the road behind them remained empty, tension eased from her shoulders. Now if she could just get through the day with Matt.

By two o'clock, the boys had eaten every piece of chicken, even the crumbs, and finally had tired of football. When they asked to explore the nearby woods, she hesitated. "Just don't climb—"

"Don't waste your breath." Matt turned to the boys. "Try not to break a leg. Okay?"

She laughed as they raced off. "You're right. Besides, we never broke a leg. How did you get so good with kids?"

He stretched out on the quilt, propping his head up with his hand, and finished off the bag of chips. Patches climbed over him and pounced on the empty sack. "Who knows?" he said as he stroked the kitten's head. "I'm as surprised as you are. Now do you want to tell me what's going on, and why your eyes were glued to the side mirror?"

She gathered the utensils, placing them in the picnic basket while matter-of-factly recounting what had happened at school. "When I called the shelter this morning, Sarah had not let Logan and Lucas play outside for fear their dad might drive by and kidnap them. I think all three of them were going crazy. She was as happy as Noah when I called."

"Did you think that guy was following us?"

"No, just making sure he wasn't. Very few people know the location of the shelter, and I doubt Nichols knows where I live. My phone number and address aren't in the book."

"There's always the internet," he said.

"There are precautions you can take, you know. I've done a search of my name before and my address did not come up."

"I've always wanted people to find me." Matt rolled over on his back and laced his fingers behind his head and stared at the sky. "This farm is the only place in Cedar Grove I like to be. Even the sky seems bluer. Do you remember the time we tried to cross the creek on that log, and you fell in?"

It wasn't falling in the creek she remembered. It was the kiss that followed after he fished her out. She grabbed Noah's jacket that he'd left behind and folded it neatly. "At least the weather's good today. We don't usually have such warm temperatures in January."

"Just wait a couple of days, and the cold will be back with a vengeance." Matt rolled over and sat up, his knees dangerously close to hers.

The woodsy scent of his aftershave sent a shiver through her body, and she looked away from his chocolate-brown eyes, aware that he was remembering the kiss, as well. When he leaned toward her, she wanted him to kiss her again. But he was marrying Jessica. She stiffened.

"Allie—"

"Why didn't Jessica come with you?"

A harsh laugh erupted from his lips. "Like I'm going to bring her to the house on Beaker Street."

The pain in his voice raised goose bumps on her arms. "There is nothing wrong with that house. Or the fact that you weren't born with a silver spoon in your mouth."

"Says the lady with impeccable credentials." He stood. "Let's don't argue today. Walk with me, and I will tell you about the really important contract I landed this week."

Walking would be safe enough. At least there would be space between them. She took his hand and let him pull her up, ignoring the tingle that shot up her arm. She scooped up the kitten and put her in the carrier. "Why was this contract so important?"

They strolled toward the woods, where the boys had gone to explore.

"Because the Winthrop Corporation had never before won a contract from J. Phillip Bradford."

"Why is that name familiar?"

"Bradford heads up several nonprofit organizations under the Bradford Foundation. They hold conferences, workshops, banquets, that sort of thing. This one contract will open the door to all the rest."

"I know the Bradford Foundation. The school receives grants from it. Sounds like Bradford has been doing this awhile. Why isn't he using whoever he used last year?"

Matt laughed out loud. "That's the rub. Brad ford is a *little* difficult to work with. Just before Christmas, the people he used last year quit on him. Now that I've gotten the contract, the challenge will be to keep it. He's already changed the menu, the decorations, and last night, he requested a different ballroom."

She stopped and looked up at him. "Why in the world do you want to be in that kind of business?"

He gazed down at her. "At this moment, I don't know."

Her breath hitched. A current she couldn't ignore charged the air between them, pulling her toward Matt. He cupped her face in his hands, and hesitantly kissed her. When they parted, she was about to speak, but he put his finger on her lips. "Shhh."

Matt held her captive with his eyes. As his hands trailed down her neck, she wanted him to kiss her again and allowed him to pull her close. This time there was no hesitation as he claimed her lips. She slipped her arms around his waist and gave in to the moment, losing herself to the passion she'd locked away for so long.

He's going to marry someone else. Allie stopped. She couldn't do this. She couldn't let him break her heart again.

His eyes clouded, and he frowned. "What's wrong?"

She sucked air into her lungs. "*You have to ask?* You're marrying someone else, that's what's wrong."

Matt's face lost its color, and he stepped back. His Adam's apple bobbed as he swallowed. "I, ah…" He glanced toward the woods. "Guess I better go see where the boys are."

Without another word, he turned and walked away from her.

WAS HE CRAZY? Or just a jerk? He had no right to kiss Allie. Even if she did look so beautiful today, just like she had ten years ago when they'd walked that log. And the kiss had been every bit as sweet.

He scrubbed his face. He was engaged. How could he kiss Allie when he loved Jessica? His cell phone rang, and he pulled if from his pocket. What could the chef at the Winthrop want? "Jefferies," he answered.

"Why am I just getting the menu for this party for the mayor tonight? Do you expect me to snap my fingers and come up with steaks for two hundred people?"

"What are you talking about, Drew? I emailed it to you Monday morning and handed your secretary a hard copy on Thursday." Next time he'd put it in the man's hands personally.

"Well, I never received it. I was busy with the details for the Baxter anniversary party when your assistant mentioned the mayor's affair."

A pain started in Matt's jaw and worked its way to his temple. He should've got Noah and returned to Memphis to oversee the dinner. But his assistant was more than capable of overseeing the event. Susie McClain was organized, creative, a go-getter and would probably have his job when he moved up the ladder. "I'll be at the hotel in two hours."

"You might want to locate two hundred flat-iron steaks while you're at it. I'm out." The chef disconnected, leaving Matt holding a dead phone.

He blew a hard breath through his clenched

teeth. The mayor's wife wanted a fiftieth birthday her husband would remember. Matt didn't want it to be because there was no meat for the main course. It was his job to see that mistakes like this didn't happen. Even worse, his boss would be attending.

He checked his watch, calculating how soon he could be in Memphis. It was three now. *If* he could get Allie to take Noah for tonight, and *if* he could get her to take him back to his car right away, he might make it by six. The dinner party was at eight. Matt speed-dialed his assistant. "Susie, I need you to locate two hundred flat-iron steaks."

"I started calling our distributors as soon as I realized Chef knew nothing about the party, but it's Saturday." Her frustration sounded loud and clear over the phone.

"I have our main distributor's home number. If he has what we need, can you take one of the hotel vans and collect them?"

"Yes."

"Good. I'll be there by six. Call me if you need anything before then." He immediately scrolled his contacts and dialed the salesman's number. Luck was with him, and he texted Susie to go after the steaks.

Matt then found the boys and shepherded them

back to where Allie was waiting. When he told her his problem, she seemed almost relieved.

"Don't worry about Noah," she said. "He has an essay he needs to finish, anyway."

"I'll be back to get him first thing in the morning." He took the picnic basket from her hand and carried it toward her car. "In fact, I'll take you all out for breakfast."

"No."

The cold north wind that whipped across the meadow was almost as cold as her voice.

Allie drew her jacket close. "Noah, put your coat on." She turned to the twins. "You guys, too."

Protesting, they shrugged into their jackets and headed for the car. When they reached her house, Matt parked and handed her the keys as the boys climbed out and raced to the backyard. He met her at the trunk to get the picnic basket, but she'd grabbed it already. He wanted to apologize, except he didn't know what to say. Instead, he shoved his hands in his pockets. "Can we talk sometime tomorrow?"

She glanced away and took a deep breath, then turned back to face him. He flinched against the pain in her eyes.

"We don't have anything to talk about, Matt. Let's just leave it at that." Without another word, she sprinted for the house.

"Allie, wait. Please, we need to—"

His chest ached as she unlocked the door and stepped inside.

It was several moments before he trudged to his shiny convertible.

CHAPTER TWELVE

THE MAYOR'S WIFE extended her hand to Matt. "The party couldn't have been better. Those steaks were melt-in-your-mouth good, and I loved the black roses and that cane—it was the perfect touch."

"Thank you, Mrs. Miller." Matt's business grin stretched a little wider. "When you called late this afternoon and told my assistant you wanted to tease your husband a little about turning fifty, Susie came up with the idea."

Annette Miller's gaze slid past Matt to Jessica as she joined them. Winthrop trailed just behind his daughter. "I understand you've snagged this young lady. I want to see the ring."

Jessica slipped her arm through Matt's as she held her hand out for Annette to admire her engagement ring. Since Jessica never mentioned she planned to attend the party, he'd been surprised to see her. But then, he'd barely talked to her all day.

"What a beautiful setting." The older woman patted Jessica's arm. "When is the big day?"

Jessica tilted her head toward him, and his chest tightened at the adoration in her eyes. The memory of Allie's kiss seared his conscience. What had he been thinking this afternoon?

"We haven't gotten that far, have we, Matt?"

He tugged at his collar as the air in the room turned stuffy.

"That's something I'd like to know, as well." William Winthrop slapped him on the back. "The house next door goes on the market next week, and I'd like to put a bid in for you two."

Jessica pecked her father on the cheek. "Oh, Daddy! That's so sweet, but we are not moving next door to you and Mother." She turned to Matt. "Right?"

That was something he could definitely agree on. "Jessica did such a great job decorating the apartment, I hate to leave it."

He tugged Jessica away from the others. "I'm returning to Cedar Grove first thing in the morning, so I need to get home. How about a cup of coffee in the shop downstairs to finish off the evening?"

She beamed at him. "Yes! I can tell you my plans for Noah next weekend."

This probably wasn't a good time to tell Jessica he hadn't mentioned to Noah that they would be coming back to Memphis. Hadn't mentioned it to Allie, either. The memory of her intensely blue eyes filled with hurt haunted him.

They were soon settled at a small table in a quiet corner on the lower floor. Bone-tired weariness set in as he sipped black coffee.

Jessica stirred the white chocolate latte she'd ordered. "Is something wrong?"

"No, I'm just tired."

"Are you sure that's all it is? You seemed reluctant when Annette asked about a wedding date."

"I told you that I'm tired. I didn't mean to return for the party until everything went crazy, and then I was surprised you were there with your father."

"Mother had a headache, and I filled in." She sipped her latte. "Have you thought about a date?"

His mind raced. "Valentine's Day?"

She rolled her eyes. "Silly boy, I can't plan a wedding in four weeks."

"I meant next year."

Jessica plopped the mug down with a thud. "You are kidding, right? Because I'm not waiting over a year to be married."

He rubbed the bridge of his nose.

"You're not kidding." She eyed him. "Or maybe you don't want to get married at all."

"It's not that I don't want to get married…"

Until this afternoon, he'd been so sure of what he wanted out of life. Wealth, success, Jessica. The three were intricately woven. How could one kiss throw everything into such disarray?

"It's just that I want to get Bradford's project and the other dozen parties for February out of the way before we even think about a date. And I'd like to get Noah situated."

"If you're going back tomorrow, why don't I go with you?"

He shook his head. "Tomorrow isn't a good day. We're mostly going to be at the hospital, and you'd get bored. And next week he'll be coming here."

Her eyes lit up. "That's right. Let me tell you what I have set up. We can take him to the zoo on Saturday and maybe even the Brooks Art Gallery. Then on Sunday we'll go to the Pink Palace. It will be such fun."

Yes, fun. And it would be. And maybe by then, he could sort out why he felt so empty when everything he'd ever wanted was within his grasp.

"Scoot over, Lucas." Noah nudged the twin with his hip then flopped over on his back. Somehow Miss Allie had arranged for the twins to spend the night at her house, and her queen-size bed would be plenty big enough for the three of them if Lucas wouldn't try to hog the whole thing. Patches mewed from her carrier. Maybe he'd get up and put the kitten in bed with them. Then he could go to sleep. On the other side of him, Logan sneezed. "You awake?" Noah asked.

"Yeah," Logan whispered back. "I can't sleep."

"Me, neither." Noah stared up at the shadows on the ceiling from the night-light. He wished he could've seen his mom today. "Why can't you sleep?"

"I…I thought I saw my dad today."

"Where?"

"When we were coming home from the picnic."

Unease settled in Noah's stomach. "You need to tell Miss Allie."

Logan was quiet, and then he sighed. "I'm scared my dad's going to try to get us."

"Miss Allie won't let him."

"I don't think she can stop him if that's what he wants to do. I'm scared of him. Lucas is, too."

"Why?"

Logan's silence grew in the dark room. "I can't tell."

"Aw, come on, I won't tell nobody."

"Cross your heart, hope to die you won't tell?"

Noah thought on that for a minute. It was serious stuff when you did that. He swallowed. "Cross my heart, hope to die."

It was minutes before Logan spoke again, and Noah thought maybe he'd gone to sleep. "He beat our mama, and she got sick and died. Then he started hitting me and Lucas."

A shiver ran through Noah. He and his mom had been in some bad places, but nothing like that. "Is that why he went to jail?"

"No. We never told anybody what he did. He got caught selling drugs."

"You have to tell Miss Allie. Or you'll have to go when he comes to get you."

"No. He said if we ever told, he'd kill us."

The door creaked open, and a sliver of light slipped into the room. Maybe it was Logan's dad. Noah pulled the blanket almost to his nose.

"You boys should be asleep. It's after ten."

Miss Allie. She almost scared him to death. "Yes, ma'am," he said. He nudged Logan and whispered, "Tell her."

"You promised," Logan hissed back.

"Tell me what?" Miss Allie crossed the room to their bed.

Logan hesitated. "I…I don't want to go back to the shelter. Miss Sarah is nice, but I like it here." That wasn't what Noah wanted him to tell.

The light shone on Miss Allie's face as soft laughter warmed the whole room. "Why thank you, Logan. I wish you could stay here, too, but right now you have to live at the shelter. Today and tonight are special, but you'll have to go back in the morning."

"What if my dad comes to get us?"

"He can't get you." Miss Allie wasn't laughing anymore.

Noah couldn't stand it. "Miss Allie, Logan thought—"

"I'm sleepy now." Logan turned on his side away from Noah. "G'night, Miss Allie."

"Good night, boys." At the door, she turned. "Noah, did you finish your essay?"

"Yes, ma'am."

"Do you want to share with me what you wrote about?"

"Why you shouldn't use drugs."

"Oh." Miss Allie sounded sad, and then she shut the door, taking the light with her.

Logan rolled onto his back. "You can't tell, you promised."

"I know." Heaviness wrapped Noah's chest. He didn't want to break his promise, but something told him he should.

ALLIE STOOD BY the door after she closed it. What a difference a week made. Her house had gone from empty to overflowing, even if it was for only one night. She padded to the kitchen and made a cup of cocoa. Taking it to the living room, she sank onto the couch and tucked her feet under her. Thoughts of Matt's kisses fluttered her heart, and she shoved them away. Time to put Matt Jefferies where he belonged—in a box in the far recesses of her mind…and labeled "Jessica's."

The memory of his kiss burned the label away, and he wouldn't stay in the box. Instead, he loomed in her mind, tantalizing her with his dark eyes and crooked smile. Her cell phone vibrated on the table beside her with an incoming message from Peter. Are you still up?

Allie hesitated before she answered. Because Matt hadn't shown up Friday night they'd canceled their date to go dancing. Why couldn't she fall in love with Peter? She stared at the phone. There was no reason she couldn't. And he had all the qualities she wanted in a husband. He was kind. Caring. Persistent. Compassionate.

Things Matt had been once.

The message dinged again, and she dialed Peter's number before she could change her mind. "Good evening, Mr. Elliott," she said when he answered.

"Evening, Ms. Carson. I'm surprised you're not in bed. Didn't the boys wear you out?"

His rich baritone sent goose bumps over her skin. She could do this, redirect her feelings. An image of Matt popped in her mind. *No, you can't.* She'd show him. "Definitely. I thought I'd take

Logan and Lucas to church tomorrow. Would you like to go with us? Then perhaps come back to my house for a sandwich?"

"How about Noah?"

"Matt's picking him up at nine." If Matt showed up.

Peter suggested they all go to church, and then eat at Norma Jean's. "After that we'll drop the twins off at the shelter and maybe take in a movie."

Did she want Peter to take her to Norma Jean's? Silly thought. She hadn't avoided the little diner after Matt left, why not go there with Peter? Maybe it was time to create new memories at Norma Jean's with someone other than Matt. "That sounds great. See you in the morning."

THE TWINS WERE on their best behavior at lunch the next day, although every time the diner door opened, Logan checked out who entered. Something was bothering him, but Allie couldn't figure out what. When they finished eating, she practically had to pry him out of his seat to go play the video games in the back of the diner. She looked up and caught Peter watching her. "Do I have barbecue sauce on my face?" Allie rubbed her chin.

"No. Just thinking how good you are with the boys. You really should have some of your own."

"Yeah, well…" She paused as the front door swung open and Noah and Matt walked into the diner. Of all the places in Cedar Grove, why did he have to bring Noah here? Noah spied them and made a straight line to their table. Matt stopped at the counter then walked slowly toward them.

"Hey, Miss Allie. I told Matt you were coming here with Mr. Elliott." Noah glanced at Peter. "'Lo, Mr. Elliott."

"Hey, Noah, how's it going?" Peter tousled Noah's hair, and the boy ducked away from him. "Hello, Matt."

"Peter."

Noah's face wrinkled into a frown. "Where's Lucas and Logan?"

Allie smoothed his hair. "They're in the back, playing games." The relief that flooded his face puzzled her. What was going on with these boys?

He looked up at his uncle. "Can I go play the games?"

"Sure. I'll come get you when our sandwiches are ready. I ordered you a plain hamburger, no pickles. Is that good?"

Noah nodded and hurried to the game room.

"You want to join us?" Allie asked.

Matt looked from Allie to Peter. "We're getting our burgers to-go and taking them to the house to eat. Noah hasn't seen his mom yet so we're going back to the hospital afterward. She was getting some sort of test earlier."

"You can wait here," Allie said. Peter helped her shift her chair over, then he left his arm draped across the back, touching her shoulder.

Matt sat stiffly in the chair, his face flushed. "Noah did say I could find you here. Do you know when you'll be home?"

Allie glanced at Peter. "Couple of hours. Why?"

"Just wondering. Thought maybe we could discuss what's going to happen when Mariah is discharged."

"Sure." Silence filled the dead air. "How did your dinner party go last night?" she said.

"Fine. The mayor's wife said it was a success."

Peter leaned back in his chair. "What is it you do again, Matt?"

"Director of food and beverage for the Winthrop Corporation. I handle everything from sales to developing the operating budget to overseeing events."

"Sounds like an important job. Congratulations." Peter offered his hand.

Matt hesitated briefly before he took the offered hand. "Thanks."

The waitress behind the counter called out a

number, and Matt glanced at his ticket. "That's us." He stood. "I'll bring Noah home around four. Do you think you'll be there by then?"

"I'll make it a point to. Tell Mariah I'll see her tomorrow."

Heaviness settled in Allie's heart as he walked away.

Peter shoved his chair back. "So, do you think Logan or Lucas would be interested in a game of Scrabble?"

She stared at him. Surely he wasn't serious. He was. She did not look around as the door to the diner closed. "No, but they might join us in a game of Wii football."

MATT PULLED OUT of the restaurant parking lot and glanced in the rearview mirror at Noah's solemn face. Talking to the IRS was easier than connecting with his nephew. "I didn't get a chance to ask yesterday, but have you had a good last few days at Miss Allie's?"

Noah nodded his head, but no verbal answer. So far today he'd been quieter than usual, like something bothered him. Or he just didn't like Matt. Wouldn't Peter love to know that. Then he could take away his nephew. Matt winced. If he admitted the truth, Peter was a decent man. Just not the man for Allie.

Noah kicked the back of his seat. "Are we almost there yet?"

"Two minutes. How's school?"

Again, only a shrug. Matt almost asked if the cat had his tongue, but memories of adults saying that to him when he was a kid dried up the words. "How about Patches? Does she like it at Allie's?"

Finally. A smile.

"She sleeps with me." Noah unbuckled his seat belt as Matt parked beside the house. "After we eat, can we throw the football around some?"

Matt's heart warmed that he actually suggested doing something. "You bet. Then we'll go see your mom."

In the house, Matt put their sandwiches on the red Formica table. This was the one place in the world he missed his mom the most.

"What's this?" Noah traced his finger over initials Matt had carved into the table.

"Uh, something that got me into a lot of trouble."

"You mean you get into trouble with people besides Miss Allie?"

"Sometimes. This particular time I got a Case knife for my birthday." He couldn't remember who gave it to him, only that his mother was not pleased. "It made perfect sense to me to carve my initials in our table. Unfortunately, it didn't make sense to my mom."

Noah leaned toward him. "Did you get punished?"

"Oh, yeah, but you know what the worst part was? My mom crying because I'd ruined her new table."

"I know. I hate it when I make my mom cry. What'd you do after that?"

"There was nothing I could do except to buy her a new table, and you can see I didn't do that. But she forgave me. And took my knife away. And grounded me. I hated being grounded."

Noah's eyes softened and he patted Matt's arm. "I get it. Being grounded is tough."

If Matt could, he'd freeze this moment, but it was gone too quickly.

"Can we go throw the football?"

"Eat your sandwich first."

Noah rolled his eyes, but picked up a packet of ketchup and squirted the red sauce on his plate. He dipped a French fry in the ketchup, and then tackled his burger.

After he drained the last of his drink, Noah swiped his mouth on his shirt and folded his arms, waiting.

Matt stuffed the napkins and to-go box in the trash. "You ready to throw the football around?"

Noah grabbed the ball and tossed it up. Matt

snagged it in midair. "Wait until you get outside," he said, tousling Noah's hair.

The unusually warm weather of a week ago had deserted them, but it wasn't uncomfortably cold as the January sun filtered through the bare trees. In the spring, he'd need to get someone to clean up the yard since the last tenants hadn't raked the leaves. Maybe one of the neighbors would know who to hire.

He told Noah to run deep then spiraled the ball through the air. Noah caught it and came closer to lob it back. "Show me how you do that."

Matt bent down and showed Noah how to grip the ball with his thumb and index finger. "Then you place these fingers over the laces." He positioned Noah's fingers where he wanted them, then showed him how to stand. "It's not about how hard you throw. The power comes from your legs. Now you throw and I'll catch."

Noah practiced the steps. "Dig your back foot in the ground," Matt called out. "That'll give you more leverage when you rotate your hip." He clapped when Noah made a decent throw. "That's great. Next time hold the ball closer to your head."

Soon, Noah's passes lengthened, sending Matt all the way to the shed. The boy had a natural arm. After a few passes, Matt held on to the ball. "That's enough for today. Don't want to make your arm sore. And it's time to go see your mom."

"Do you have any more stuff in the shed like this football?"

Matt scratched his chin. "I don't know. I think I saw some boxes with your mom's name on them."

"Could we take them today and show them to her?"

"Maybe one box." Matt unlocked the shed and scanned the boxes, spying one marked report cards and dolls. Evidently his mother indexed by the last word so everything in the box should begin with the *c* or *d*.

Noah traced his fingers over the boxes at the other end of the shed. "Can we see what's in some of these?"

"Sure." Matt scooted him out of the shed. "Maybe next week."

They loaded the boxes in the front seat of his car, then Noah climbed into the back and fastened his seat belt. "Can we put the top down?"

"It's a little too chilly today. Maybe some other time." They drove the short distance to the hospital and found a parking spot near the door.

When they entered Mariah's room, she sat in a chair by the window, reading a newspaper.

"Mom! You're out of bed!" Noah ran to his mom and hugged her.

Mariah looked much better than yesterday. Someone had shampooed her hair and fluffed it up a bit. "Are you using the breathing thing?"

"Yes, little brother." She gazed at Noah. "You look so handsome."

"Aw, Mom. Guess what Uncle Matt's been doing? Teaching me to throw a football."

Mariah smiled at him, her eyes bright. "Thanks."

"No problem. We brought you a surprise."

"Yeah!" Noah grabbed the box and put it in his mom's lap. "It's stuff from when you were a littlc girl."

When Mariah read the end of the box, her fingers flew to her lips. "Oh, my word," she whispered. "My dolls." She glanced up at Matt. "Where—"

"In the shed behind the house. Our childhood. It's all there, neatly boxed up."

She blinked back tears. "I didn't know. I haven't been back in years, not since mom—"

"I know. But that's going to change."

"Yeah, Matt put all our stuff in his house."

"And you're welcome to move in after you're released from—"

She shook her head. "Not now."

"Mom, open it. I want to see what's inside."

She stroked Noah's back. "Okay. But I'm tired. Help me in bed first."

Matt and Noah helped Mariah to the bed then Matt took the chair she vacated. When she asked for the box, he took a small penknife from his pocket and sliced through the tape.

Noah stared at the knife. "Is that—"

"No, I never saw that knife again." He closed the blade and started to slip the knife in his pocket when he noticed the longing in his nephew's eyes. "Would you like to have this?"

"Matt—"

"Every boy should have a pocketknife, sis. I'm sure he'll be careful with it." He turned to Noah. "Won't you?"

"You bet. I won't take it to school or anything." Noah took the knife and ran his fingers over the grooved bone handle. "Thanks, Uncle Matt. You're the greatest!"

All it took was a knife to win his nephew over? "Don't cut yourself with it, because if you do, your mom will kill me. And don't carve your initials in Miss Allie's table."

Noah rolled his eyes. "I'm not crazy. And I'll be careful."

Mariah reached for the box. "Well, I want to see what's in here." She removed the lid and a gasp slid from her lips. "I can't believe Mom kept these dolls all these years."

Matt and Noah exchanged a boy-to-man look. "Mom, what's in there besides dolls?"

Mariah laid the dolls on the bed and peered inside the box. "Here's a deck of cards. Matt, remember how we used to play Crazy Eights?"

Noah opened the deck. "I know how to play that."

As Noah dealt the cards and Mariah sorted through the box, Matt settled back in the chair, observing the two. "Look here." She held up envelopes. "My report cards."

"I want to see." Noah looked over her shoulder. "Wow, Mom, you really did make A's and B's."

"I told you. Oh, look, here's a can of pick-up sticks."

Noah shook the box. "What's that?"

"I'll show you." Matt took the box to the shelf under the window. "You hold the sticks in one hand and let them fall and then you see how many you can pick up without disturbing the others."

Mariah picked up another envelope. "My birth certificate. I've been trying to find this for ages." She frowned and looked up. "This doesn't make sense. Mom listed her married name instead of her maiden name."

"What?" Matt left Noah and crossed to the bed.

"Here, see for yourself." She handed him the certificate.

Matt scanned the document. Their mother's married name was on the line for her maiden name. "Maybe that's what you're supposed to do."

"My maiden name is on Noah's. Not my married name."

Matt rubbed his neck. "Why would she do that?"

"Maybe for the same reason she wouldn't discuss her family, except for Grandmother Rae."

"Did you ever know our grandmother?"

Mariah twisted a strand of hair around her index finger. "I think so...sometimes I remember this older woman holding me. Don't remember what she looked like, just a fuzzy impression."

"I don't remember her at all. I used to ask Mom why we didn't have grandparents like all the other kids, and she'd cry and then I felt bad about asking."

"Yeah, I know. Mom was really secretive. When I was a kid, I thought she was some sort of princess who ran away from the castle."

He grinned. "I thought she was a spy."

They both laughed.

"She was so different from Dad," Matt said. "I've often wondered why she married him."

"He wasn't always mean. That happened after he lost his job and started drinking. You were too young to remember when he would get down on the floor and wrestle with us." Mariah folded the birth certificate and slipped it back into the envelope. "I remember something that happened one Christmas. She and Dad thought we were asleep, and you were. But I wanted to see Santa. I'd crept into the hall, and I heard Dad ask Mom if she wanted to call her father. She started yelling at him, saying, 'I'll never call that man ever. And don't mention his name again.' That's why I hadn't asked anything about our grandparents."

Matt slipped his hand in his pocket and jingled the change. "You know, we could probably fill in all of these gaps."

"What do you mean?"

"If we had her social security number, we could run a background check."

"Do you have it?"

If he did, it was probably buried in one of those boxes in the shed. "Do you know where they were married?"

"Memphis, I think. Why?"

"We could at least find out what her maiden name was. And who knows what else we might discover."

CHAPTER THIRTEEN

MATT GLANCED UP at the address over the double doors. One Bradford Plaza. Some day he would walk into an office building that carried his name on it. As he crossed the slate floor, he couldn't help but notice the panorama of the Mississippi River and the two bridges across it. He punched the penthouse button. The first step began with climbing to the top at the Winthrop Corporation. To do that, Matt had to convince J. Phillip Bradford to let him handle the conference needs of the CEO's other charitable organizations. Matt intended to accomplish that today. The elevator door slid open, and he stepped inside.

"Hold the elevator, please!"

Matt jabbed the open button as Bradford's secretary hurried toward him with a Starbucks cup in her hand. "Thank you, Matt." She leaned against the rail and caught her breath. "FYI, Mr. Bradford is in a mood today—which is unusual for a Wednesday. He usually doesn't get this bad until much later in the week."

"Good to know." Matt had heard that Elizabeth Jones had been with Bradford since he started his first business and was certain she was past retirement age. Not that he would ask. While Ms. Jones seemed to like him, everything about her advertised top-notch executive secretary, from her wedge-cut silver hair to the black business suit and smart heels she wore. She would not find age-related questions entertaining or appropriate. "Is that a peace offering?"

"No, this is for me. J. Phillip can get his own coffee." She brushed a speck of lint from her suit. "I noticed you have a nine o'clock appointment. Good idea to get here early."

Matt checked his watch. Twenty minutes early might be overkill. The doors opened, and he waited for Ms. Jones to exit then followed her into the reception area, which was already full of people waiting to see Bradford. Definitely not overkill.

The secretary turned back to him. "Why don't you wait in my office? I'll let him know you're here."

He trailed her inside the spacious office, grateful for the favor. The room's simple elegance continued the theme he'd seen everywhere else at the Bradford Foundation. He nodded his head toward the waiting room. "What do they all want?"

"Donations. On the second Wednesday of

each month Mr. Bradford sits down with repre-
sentatives of the nonprofits that provide services
to the Memphis needy. With the economy the
way it is, I'm sure they're here to ask for bigger
allocations."

She paused and pressed her lips together, almost like she wanted to say more. Her phone
buzzed and she picked up the receiver. "Yes,
Mr. Bradford. Matt's in my office. I'll send him
right in."

Matt started toward the door, but she held her
hand up. "Yes, sir, I'll have someone get it for
you." She paused and two red splotches appeared
on her cheeks. "Yes, sir."

Ms. Jones's hand rested on the receiver, and
she muttered something under her breath Matt
didn't catch. Then she straightened, and her de-
meanor changed from obvious irritation to san-
guine as she pressed a button on her desk. A soft
buzzer sounded, and the door unlocked. "You
may go in, but I'd be pleased if you'd stop by
here before you leave."

"Yes, ma'am." Matt straightened his tie and
stepped through the door that fed directly into
Bradford's corner office. Floor-to-ceiling windows comprised the two outside walls, and the
CEO stood with his back to him as he gazed out
the window that faced west.

"Good morning, Matthew." The older man

turned and motioned for Matt to join him. "Last night's rain washed away the smog…come get a great view of the Mississippi."

Bradford was a study in contradictions. Where his employees wore strict business attire, the CEO dressed expensively casual in a Robert Graham cotton shirt—Matt recognized the brand because Jessica had wanted him to buy a similar shirt before Christmas. He'd said no because of the cost. Bradford also wore khakis. Matt had never seen him in a power suit and wondered if the old man would wear khakis to the banquet. He joined Bradford at the window. A barge rippled the water as it drifted south toward the I-55 bridge. It occurred to Matt that the scene reflected the same panorama that hung in the entrance foyer.

"From here, I've seen the Mississippi at flood stage, and I've seen it low enough to ground barges, but even at its lowest, it's a powerful, beautiful river. Ten dams can't contain it when it's at flood stage." Bradford smiled at him. "But you're not here to talk about the river. Have a seat."

Matt chose a straight-back chair he wouldn't sink into and waited while Bradford sat behind his desk. Matt couldn't help calculating the cost of the weathered cherry desk. At least three grand, maybe four. The side door opened, startling him, and Ms. Jones entered with a Starbucks cup.

"Your coffee, *sir*."

Bradford took it with a slight twinkle in his eyes. "Thank you, Ms. Jones."

She turned and crossed her eyes as she passed Matt. He gulped down the laughter that threatened to escape his mouth.

As the door closed, Bradford took the lid off the cup. "Impossible woman. Thinks she runs this place. Sometimes, I have to remind her otherwise. Now for you." He fixed his gaze on Matt. "Let's cut to the chase. You're here to snag the conference business for all three nonprofits, but I have another offer for you."

Matt leaned forward, not quite sure what to expect.

"Your talent is being wasted as director of food and beverage at the Winthrop Corporation." Bradford sat back in his chair and sipped his coffee. "You are nothing more than a glorified event planner."

"Excuse me, sir? There's a little more to my job than that."

Bradford waved him off. "You will admit Winthrop is not utilizing you effectively?"

Matt shifted in his chair. He couldn't argue that point, but he remained quiet.

The older man set his coffee on the desk. "It's

time for me to slow down a little, to turn loose a few things, so I'm creating a new position here at the Bradford Foundation. I'll come up with a fancy title later, but for now, let's just say I want someone to come under my wing, learn every aspect of this foundation. Eventually this person will become CEO in my place. Are you interested?"

Did Matt just hear him right? "Why…why me?"

"You've finessed everything I've thrown at you, and you keep smiling. Don't you think you can handle the job?"

Matt sat straighter. "Oh, I can handle it. I just figured you'd want to give it to a vice president or someone who's come up through the ranks."

"I thought about that, but I want someone more like me in the job. Someone who's willing to put in the hours that will be needed. I think you fit the bill. So, can you give me an answer now, or do you need to think about it?"

Matt raised an eyebrow. "You didn't mention the salary."

A glint of admiration flashed in Bradford's eyes just before he cracked a wry grin. "I didn't, did I?"

He named a figure, and Matt struggled to keep from blinking. Twice his salary at Winthrop. For once he was speechless, but not for long. "When do you want me to start?"

"How soon can you?"

Matt thought a minute. "After Valentine's Day."

"That's a little over four weeks. Why so long?"

"I can pass most of my contracts over to my associate, but there are a few that will wrap up Valentine's Day that I personally want to take care of."

Bradford's gray eyes darkened as he rocked back in his chair and stroked his jaw. Maybe Matt had blown it. He held his breath as the CEO cleared his throat.

"I would expect nothing less of you." Bradford stood. "We'll make your effective date of employment February fifteenth."

Matt scrambled to his feet and shook the hand his new boss extended. "Yes, sir."

"And in the meantime, we have a banquet to put together." Bradford picked up a yellow envelope and handed it to him. "Suggestions for a few changes. And on your way out, stop and see Ms. Jones. She has another packet for you. A portfolio on the Bradford Foundation for you to study. I want you to know this company inside out."

So, Bradford had been certain of Matt's answer before he ever arrived. "Yes, sir!" He stepped back and strode toward the door.

"Oh… Matt, how's your sister?"

He paused with his hand on the doorknob and turned to address Bradford. "She's better and hopefully will be released from the hospital this weekend."

"Good. I'm assuming you'll be able to get her sorted out before you start work here."

A twinge of unease settled on Matt. How much did Bradford know about Mariah? "Yes, sir, this weekend."

"You may want to move her and your nephew to Memphis. That way you won't have to run back and forth to…what was the name of that little town?"

"Cedar Grove." With the resources at his fingertips, Bradford knew exactly where Mariah and Noah were, so why this game? "Yes, sir, that's a thought."

"I make it a point to get to know my employees and their families. I'd like to meet them sometime."

"I'm sure that can be arranged."

"Good."

Employee. Excitement surged through Matt's veins, but he contained himself until he was on the other side of the door and inside Ms. Jones's office. Evidently the secretary had stepped out, and he allowed the reality of what had just happened to wash over him. His fingers curled into fists, and he pumped the air. *Yes!* Home run, touchdown, slam dunk. All rolled into one. At this second, he could drop a basketball through the hoop and not even have to jump.

"Be careful you don't bump the ceiling." Ms. Jones's calm voice penetrated his haze. She'd slipped in the other door and now walked to her desk.

"You knew," he said, turning to her.

She gave a slight nod and handed him a white packet.

"Then why did you tell me to be sure and stop by your desk when I left?"

She took her seat and indicated a chair for him. "I wasn't completely sure you would answer in the affirmative."

He was too jumpy to sit and elected to pace. "If I'd said no, were you going to try to change my mind?"

"Oh, no," she replied with a somber smile.

A little of the excitement dimmed, and he paused to stare at her. "You were going to congratulate me for turning his offer down?"

"No."

"Then, what?" The words came out edgier than he'd meant.

"I had thought you might ask for time to consider the offer."

Matt detected…not disappointment in her voice, but something else. Something he couldn't quite put his finger on. "If I had done that, ask for time, what would your advice have been?"

"But you said yes, so it's of no consequence."

Ms. Jones reminded him of his mother when she wanted him to figure out something for himself. He was curious to know what advice she would have given him. "Please?"

Tapping her lips, she seemed to consider his question. "All right, but you have too many stars in your eyes, so you probably won't agree with what I have to say.

"First I want you to know I've been J. Phillip Bradford's secretary since he went into business. We're friends, and I was friends with his wife. While I haven't always agreed with his decisions, I admire and respect him. However, I saw what happened to him and his family when work became the most important thing to him. And you will have that same choice—at some point, you will have to choose between your job and your family."

"I know I'll be working a lot of hours," Matt said. "I think I know what I'm getting into."

"Are you sure? J. Phillip Bradford is a generous, compassionate person. His standards are higher than most, but he expects no more than he gives." She smiled. "The problem is he gives two hundred percent. He's married to his job and will expect the same from you. Make sure that's what you want, Matthew. He will accept no excuses, especially since he's taken you under his wing."

"But, why me?"

"Obviously, you have impressed him. If you think there are other reasons, my dear Matthew, you will have to ask him." She slapped her palms on the desk and stood. "I have to get back to work."

Matt all but bounced on his feet as he waited at the elevator, the portfolio tucked securely in his briefcase. In less than an hour, his life had changed. The downside was telling his current boss he was quitting. And Jessica. His excitement dampened slightly. She might not be happy he was leaving her father's corporation.

He willed the elevator to hurry. Next on his agenda was a drive out east to the register of deeds archive office to apply for a copy of his parents' marriage license. Maybe he should let it go for today. No, he'd penciled the time in, and if he didn't go ahead and do it, he wouldn't have time later.

Matt shifted his briefcase to his right hand. Lots of puzzles today...like Ms. Jones's tone when she found out he'd accepted Bradford's offer. The door to the elevator slid silently open, and as he stepped into the glass cage, it came to him.

Sadness.

That was the tone he hadn't been able to identify.

ALLIE HESITATED OUTSIDE the hospital door. Matt should be the one talking to his sister about entering rehab. But Mariah had called Allie. Now if she could find the right words. She pushed open the door and halted inside the room, her pulse racing at the sight of the empty bed. Mariah had resisted any talk of getting help. What if she had run away? "Mariah?"

"In here." She emerged from the bathroom wearing the clothes Allie had bought the day before. Mariah's long black hair was pulled into a ponytail. She straightened the new shirt. "Thanks for getting these. I'll pay you as soon as I get back to work."

The breathy words matched Mariah's pale face. Allie winced at the size-two jeans that hung loosely on her thin frame. "Don't worry about it."

Mariah's lips formed a thin line. "I don't accept charity."

Allie had seen that same streak of independence in Noah. "Matt gave me money to buy anything you or Noah needed."

The tight lines eased. Evidently help from Matt didn't constitute charity.

"Well, thanks for taking the time to buy them."

"You look nice." For an instant, Mariah reminded Allie of the girl she'd known in high school—before drugs and alcohol took their toll. "How do you feel?"

Mariah collapsed in a chair by the window and stared out. Beads of sweat dotted her forehead. A strand of hair had escaped the ponytail, and her right hand shook as she tucked it behind her ear. She turned from the window and leveled her gaze at Allie. "I don't have enough energy to swat a fly, I hurt all over and I could use something for pain."

Allie frowned.

"Don't worry, I'm not taking anything stronger than aspirin." She closed her eyes and took a deep breath. "I'm scared. If I go to rehab, I'll be locked away from Noah for no telling how long."

"Rehab isn't jail, Mariah."

"It'll seem like it. That's…what I wanted to talk to you about." She wiped her forehead then rolled her lips in, pressing them together as she looked upward. "You're a psychologist, can't you help me?"

"Mariah, I'm only an elementary school counselor, and I'm not trained in drug rehab."

Her thin shoulders sagged. "I just don't want to be locked away where I can't see Noah."

Allie knelt beside her and took her hands. Mariah's body shook. "If you don't go into rehab, I have it on good authority that the state will not release Noah to your care."

Mariah's eyes widened. "Would they do that?"

"I'm afraid so. You need to get help, Mariah. For your sake and for Noah's." Allie moved from her kneeling position to the chair beside Mariah. "I talked with the administrator of the program here at the hospital. It has one of the lowest rates of recidivism in the state, and you'd be able to stay in the building behind the hospital for the ninety-day program."

"Ninety days?" Her face became even paler than before. "I can't afford to stay here that long."

"You can't afford not to. And Matt's paying for it."

Again, Mariah stared out the window. A minute passed. "Can Noah come see me?"

"After two weeks."

Mariah closed her eyes and shuddered as she took another deep breath and let it out. "I can't go on like I am now, but I know I can't do it by myself...I've tried before."

Abruptly, she squared her shoulders. "Okay.

The doc said he'd release me today if I had somewhere to live. I might as well go straight to the facility…would you set it up?"

Allie reached for her hand again and squeezed it. "You're doing the right thing. I'll call the administrator on my way back to school. She's already said if you agreed, she'd take care of the paperwork."

"Thanks." Mariah's voice cracked as she whispered the word and her chin quivered as she blinked back tears. "Would you…" She took another shaky breath. "I'd like to tell Noah myself. Is there any chance you can bring him to the hospital before I leave?"

Tears stung Allie's own eyes as she nodded. "It's almost his lunchtime, and then I think he has recess. We'll see you within the hour."

"Allie?" Mariah gave her a tremulous smile. "Thanks for everything you've done."

Allie grinned. "I haven't done anything."

"Oh, but you have. You took Noah in and now you're helping me get clean. And you put up with my brother. There for a while, I thought maybe the two of you…" Mariah leaned back in the chair. "What happened to you and Matt?"

Allie had asked herself that same question a dozen times lately and always came up with the same answer. "He wanted a different kind of life than I do. Still does. He wanted me to leave Cedar Grove, and I couldn't, not—"

"But if you loved him, you would have gone with him," Mariah said.

"Mariah, think back. Matt was so driven to change, to become this…this other person that he believed he had to be."

"He has changed—look how he's helped me and Noah."

"I'll give him that, but he's marrying someone else."

"No, Matt still loves you. I can see it in his eyes when he's around you."

Allie shook her head. "It's too late for us. Matt's all set to marry Jessica Winthrop. It's a done deal."

"I don't know who this Jessica is, but I know she can't hold a candle to you."

"You're sweet, Mariah." She opened the door. "And now I have to go pick up your son."

ALLIE CONTACTED THE rehab administrator as soon as she was in her car and set up Mariah's transfer. When Allie reached her office she dialed Matt's number. She hadn't talked to him since he'd dropped off Noah on Sunday, and they hadn't really talked then. She pressed his number before she could change her mind.

"This is Matthew Jefferies. Sorry I missed your—"

She ended the call. At least she tried. She noticed a memo from the school secretary. Noah's essay on drugs was one of three that had been selected to be read at the end of assembly on Friday. He would be so excited. His English teacher had shown it to Allie and she'd been surprised at how good it was. But it was a subject he knew well. She wished Mariah could be there—then again, maybe not. Maybe she could record it and let her watch it in private.

Her cell rang, and she answered, expecting it to be Matt. "Thanks for getting back to me."

"What?"

Allie held her phone out. Peter. "Oh, sorry, thought you were someone else. What's going on?"

"Lunch, maybe? Me and you?"

"Afraid not. I'm taking Noah to see his mom during lunch. How about lunch tomorrow?"

"I have appointments. How about dinner tonight?"

"Fine, if you're up for mac and cheese and hot dogs. It's Noah's favorites."

"Why don't I bring barbecue for the two of us?"

Sunday with Peter had been fun. After they left Norma Jean's, they'd brought Logan and

Lucas back to her house to get their things and Peter had actually gotten the boys to play Scrabble, after a game of Wii football. Later she and Peter had walked in the park. Another call beeped in, and she checked the phone. Matt. He'd have to wait. "Barbecue sounds wonderful. See you at six?"

"Absolutely."

She ended the call and switched to Matt. "Hello."

"Sorry I missed your call, but I was tied up with a clerk at the register's office."

Why did his voice have to send shivers down her spine? "What in the world were you doing there?"

"Trying to get a copy of my parents' marriage license."

"Whatever for?"

"It's too long a story to get into now. Has something happened? Is that why you called?"

"I talked to Mariah today, and she's agreed to enter the rehab program at the hospital. They're accepting her today."

"Allie, that's great. Does Noah know?"

It surprised her that he'd thought of Noah. "Not yet. I'm taking him to see her as soon as this next class period ends. She wants to tell him herself."

"I wish I could be there."

"So do I. Are you coming Friday?"

"Planning on it. Why?"

She picked up the memo. "Noah's essay was picked to be read at the school assembly Friday afternoon, and since his mom can't be here…"

"What time?"

She could almost hear his brain working on the excuse he'd have to not be there. "Two-fifteen, last period of the day."

"I think I can make that."

There shouldn't be any thinking to it. "It'll be important to Noah."

"I'll be there. And, thanks for everything you're doing. I doubt I could've talked Mariah into rehab. I'll give her a call in a minute."

Matt sounded different today, upbeat and energetic. "Mariah probably would have listened to you. She wants to get custody of Noah again, and she knows this is the only way."

"Well, thanks, anyway." He hesitated. "Look, I've got to tell someone—Bradford offered me a job with the foundation, at twice my current salary. He said my talent and abilities were being wasted."

So that was it. Maybe Matt would be satisfied now. A job with the world-renowned Bradford Foundation leapfrogged him from somewhere near the middle of the corporate ladder to practically the top rung.

"Well? Don't you have anything to say?"

An arrow loaded with guilt pierced her conscience. She should be happy for him—his dreams were coming true. So they weren't her dreams, but if making more money was what made him happy, so be it. She just hoped one day he would realize that life wasn't about the salary a person made. "Congratulations. I'm excited for you, Matt. Have you told Jessica?"

"Not yet. But I think she'll understand, although her dad might not be as understanding."

The door to her office opened, and Noah lingered in the entryway. She waved him in. "Look, I have an appointment. I'll see you Friday." She ended the call and smiled at the boy. "How would you like to go see your mom?"

His eyes grew round. "Is she sick again?"

"No, she wants to see you." She herded him out the door, stopping long enough to sign him out. In the car, Noah seemed quieter than usual. "Everything okay?" she asked.

He shrugged. "I guess."

Must be her day to pick up on undertones. Unlike Matt's, Noah's voice clearly expressed a problem. "So, everything okay with you and the twins?"

Instead of answering, Noah kept silent for two blocks. "Miss Allie, if somebody tells you something and you cross-your-heart-and-hope-to-die promise you won't tell, will you die if you do?"

Allie pressed her lips together to keep from smiling. Children were so literal. "No, you won't die. Did the twins tell you something that you promised not to tell?"

He nodded.

Oh, boy. There were so many directions she could go here. They approached the hospital, and she bought time as she scanned the area and found a parking spot. Once she switched off the ignition, she turned to him. "Promises are important, but sometimes you have to break them."

His face pinched in a frown. "But if I tell, Logan will be really angry."

There had to be a way to help him understand. "Let me ask you a question. Let's say it was really cold, and you and Logan found a pond that was frozen over, and you played on it. And let's say you both promised you wouldn't tell anyone because you knew adults wouldn't want you to do that. You go back the next day and while you're skating on the ice, it cracks and Logan falls into the water. Should you keep your promise not to tell anybody?"

"No! He might die." Then his worry lines smoothed, and his eyes lightened. "Oh, yeah, I get it. If somebody might get hurt bad, you don't have to keep your promise."

"Something like that." She smiled at him. "You want to share what Logan told you?"

He narrowed his eyes. "I want to think about it a little longer."

"Okay." She patted his arm. "Let's go see your mom."

Just outside Mariah's door, Allie gestured to Noah. "Why don't you go in? I need to, uh, make a call to the school."

He gave her a curious glance.

Allie took her cell phone from her purse as she waved him in with her hand. "Go ahead. I'll be in shortly."

Noah shrugged and pushed open the door. She slipped the phone back in her purse and walked up to the waiting area near the nurses' station. Mother and son needed time to themselves

CHAPTER FOURTEEN

NOAH STILL FELT CONFUSED. Was Miss Allie right? He didn't really think he'd die if he told Logan's secret, but it didn't seem right. He'd promised, and his mom always said you kept your promises. But what if the twins' dad took them and something terrible happened? Maybe his mom would know what to do. If she told him the same thing that Miss Allie did, then he'd tell. With a lighter heart, he pushed open the door. His mom sat in a chair by the window. "Mom! You're better! You're dressed."

A smile stretched across her face. "I'm going to be okay, Noah. Better than okay. Come give me a hug."

He ran to her outstretched arm, not caring at the moment that she'd said that before. He buried his head in her shoulder. "I was so worried about you."

She held him at arm's length and stroked his cheek. "I know."

Her eyes were shiny, and for a minute, he thought she was going to cry as she bit her bottom lip. "Everything is going to be okay, Mom. You're going to come home, and I'll take care of you." Tears rolled down her cheeks. "Mom, don't cry."

"I'm not crying." She wiped her nose with the back of her hand. "My eyes are just leaking."

"Mom, eyes don't leak."

She laughed. "Noah, you're so funny." She dabbed her eyes with a tissue. "I'm so sorry for what I put you through, and I promise you it won't happen again."

His shoulders drooped. She always said that after she got sick, and she meant to keep her promise, but she never did. Maybe that was why it was so important that he keep his promise to Logan.

"Honey, this time it's for real. That's why I asked Miss Allie to bring you here. This afternoon I'm going somewhere to get help."

"You're going away? No! You can't do that. I'll take care of you."

"*I'm* supposed to take care of you, not the other way around. I'll still be here in Cedar Grove, and it'll only be for three months. You can stay with Miss Allie during the week and your Uncle Matt on weekends, like now."

Noah stared at his mom. What if she never came back? What if she was like his dad and decided she didn't want him anymore? He folded his arms across his chest.

"Noah, I need to do this. It's the only way I can stop using the drugs."

He trembled. She'd never, ever admitted she was using drugs before. "You promise you'll come back and get me?"

"Oh, Noah, you're the main reason I'm doing this, and I'm not going anywhere. The state won't let me have you back unless I get help. And I don't want to live like this anymore."

"Can I come see you?"

"After two weeks. And stop frowning. It's their rules, and it's only fourteen days, and today counts…so technically it'll only be thirteen days."

He tried not to grin, but he couldn't help it. Only his mom could turn fourteen into thirteen. "You promise?"

"I promise."

Noah glanced down at the floor. His promise to Logan weighed on his mind. "Is it ever okay to break a promise?"

She heaved a sigh. "No, it's never okay to break a promise. That's why I want to get help— so I'll never do that again. Always remember—"

The door swung open. "Okay to come in?" Miss Allie asked.

"We're good," Mariah answered. "Thanks for giving us some time."

"No problem," Miss Allie said as she came into the room. She turned to Noah. "I think rehab is a good thing, don't you?"

"It's a long time."

"Not as long as Christmas or even summer break."

He hadn't thought of it like that. "So Mom will be home before school is out?"

Miss Allie smiled. "Way before. Speaking of school, you have to get to class, but first I have an announcement." She pointed toward Noah. "Drum roll, maestro."

Puzzled, Noah imitated a drum roll.

"I am proud to announce that Mr. Noah Connors has been chosen to read his winning essay this Friday afternoon in the school assembly."

"What?" His essay won?

"Oh, son, that's awesome. I wish I could be there to hear you read it."

Read it? In front of everyone? Noah's happiness disappeared.

"I'll record it with my phone," Miss Allie said. "And your Uncle Matt is coming."

He shook his head. "Do I have to read it? Can't someone else do that?"

His mom put her arm around him. "You'll

do great. Just pretend everyone's in their underwear."

"Mom!" Sheesh.

"You'll do great, and you won't be the only one. Two other students are reading essays." Miss Allie nodded as she smiled. "We'll practice at night."

He couldn't get up in front of the whole school. He just couldn't.

MATT DRUMMED HIS fingers on the leather steering wheel. Allie was right. He needed to tell Jessica he'd accepted a job with Bradford. And then tell her father, his boss, that his last day would be February fourteenth. Or maybe not. He had more than four weeks. Why not wait until the end of January? Two weeks was the customary notice.

No. That wasn't the right way to handle this. He had a sales meeting at four that Winthrop was sitting in on. He'd tell him after that. Yes, that's what he'd do. And he couldn't tell Jessica until he was ready to tell her dad. Maybe he should give her a call, though, and check on plans for this evening.

She answered on the third ring. "Good afternoon, Mr. Jefferies. How did your meeting with J. Phillip Bradford go?"

"Better than I expected. I'll tell you about it over dinner."

"That will be perfect since I'm making duck l'orange for you tonight."

"Wow."

"I take it you're pleased?"

"I feel special."

"I assumed we'd be celebrating your success, landing those other accounts with Mr. Bradford, and I wanted to do it at home."

"What time? Your dad has scheduled a sales meeting at four, and you know how long that can go."

"It will be coming out of the oven at six o'clock sharp. I've invited him and mother to dinner as well, and he knows better than to be late for me."

"You've already invited them?" Matt swallowed. Maybe he'd wait and break the news to both of them at the same time—after dinner.

AS THE CLOCK inched toward five-thirty, Matt tried to focus on the sales project a junior member of the team described, but his mind kept wandering to his job offer from Bradford. The sheer size of the foundation staggered him. Rachel's Hope alone distributed millions of dollars to various breast cancer research projects. Named after Bradford's wife, who had died from breast cancer, it was the largest of the three charities. Charities that were largely funded by an investment Bradford made in the sixties.

With a start, he realized Winthrop had asked him a question. "Yes, sir?"

A ripple of laughter went around the room. Wrong answer. Heat rising in his face, Matt palmed his hand up. "Sorry, I guess I was thinking of that duck Jessica is cooking."

Winthrop's eyes widened, and he checked his watch. "Time to adjourn this meeting." He glanced at Matt. "Do you mind if I ride with you? Evelyn is meeting me at Jessica's."

"Not at all." Like he could say anything else. "I'm parked on the second level, so give me a minute to pull my car out front."

Traffic was light as Matt drove the short distance to Jessica's apartment on the river bluff.

"Nice car," Winthrop commented.

"Thank you, sir. Too bad it's so chilly or we could have the top down."

"Hmm. How did the meeting with Bradford go today? Did you lock in the rest of the foundation's banquet business for us?"

Matt pulled up in front of Jessica's apartment building. Winthrop had always been more than fair with him. It wasn't right for him to be less than honest now. "Actually, sir—" he swallowed "—Bradford offered me a job...at twice my current salary."

"I see."

Silence filled the small car. Maybe he should have waited.

Winthrop cleared his throat. "I'll match the salary and make you a junior vice president of the company."

For once in his life, Matt was speechless. His mouth worked, but no words formed.

Winthrop grinned like a Cheshire cat. "It's okay, son, you don't have to decide this minute. But remember, you are marrying into the Winthrop family—and there's no limit to how high you can go in the corporation."

"I have to say I never expected this. Thank you for your confidence, sir." Matt's mind whirled as Winthrop opened the door and climbed out of the car. A job offer that he'd accepted and now a counteroffer. All in one day. Robotlike, he put the car in Drive and pulled away from the curb to find a parking space. He had some serious thinking to do.

THE EVENING PASSED in a blur. He kept quiet as Jessica raved about a porcelain doll she'd bought for her collection. He admired the dainty doll when she brought it out, and gathered from her mother that this something-or-other Bebe was a good find. He didn't see that it was much different from all the other dolls in the collection.

Dolls Jessica had had since she was a little girl, her mother had once told him.

He'd always liked Evelyn Winthrop. Poised and gracious—nothing ruffled her, not even her husband. She was the perfect corporate wife and her daughter was almost a carbon copy. Matt played around with the food, even managing to eat a small amount.

"Crème brûlée?" When he nodded, Jessica whisked his plate away and set a small dessert bowl in front of him.

She was very beautiful tonight, dressed in a black sheath, her coppery hair pulled up in a French twist. And even though dinner was simple, she'd created an atmosphere of elegance, with the meal moving gracefully from one course to the next. Matt traced his finger along the stem of the Waterford goblet. It was easy to imagine Jessica throwing a dinner party for a hundred guests and it going off without a hitch. He'd been right six months ago when he first decided that she would be the perfect wife for him.

He should be on top of the world. A beautiful fiancée, job offer, counteroffer, his salary doubled. So why did emptiness fill him?

A beep came from the kitchen. "That's our coffee," Jessica said. "I'll be right back."

For a nanosecond, it was Allie, not Jessica, smiling at him. He rubbed his hand across his eyes. Too much had happened today. He wasn't himself.

Jessica returned with a silver carafe, and after she'd filled the cups, she leaned in close to him. "Would you like to share your good news about getting Bradford's business?"

Matt glanced toward William Winthrop and the older man gave him a go-ahead nod.

"Well, the meeting didn't turn out quite like I envisioned. J. Phillip Bradford offered me a job."

Jessica gaped at him. "You told him no, of course."

"Actually, I didn't. It was an amazing offer."

"Matt, you can't!" She turned to her father. "Daddy, do something!"

"Let him finish, Jessica."

"When I told your dad, he made a counteroffer. Same salary. Junior vice-president position."

Jessica squealed. "Oh, Daddy!" She kissed her father repeatedly on the cheek, and then pounced on Matt. "You shouldn't have scared me like that." She leaned closer and whispered in his ear. "He's grooming you to take his place, you know."

Matt swallowed hard. Could that be true? Although Winthrop had hinted at it, Matt's mind couldn't process the possibility. But it made his decision so much more difficult.

Winthrop's chair scraped back on the hardwood floor. "Evelyn," the older man said, "I think it's time to take our leave. These young people need time to themselves."

On her way out the door, Evelyn hugged Matt. "I'm so proud of you. And I can't wait to have you for a son-in-law."

"Thank you, Mrs. Winthrop."

"Let's not have any more of this Mrs. Winthrop nonsense. Call me Evelyn."

Matt didn't know if he could do that. "Yes, ma'am."

As soon as the door was closed behind her parents, Jessica wrapped her arms around him. "I'm so proud of you, too."

"I haven't decided if I'll take your dad's offer." There. The words were out.

She stepped back. "Not take his offer? I don't understand."

"I have to think about it."

"What's to think about? We're going to be married. You'll be part of the Winthrop family. Why would you want to work for someone like Bradford, anyway? He's done nothing but give you grief ever since you went after the Valentine's Day contract."

He held up his hand. "My head is going around and around. I don't want to talk about this anymore tonight."

"Fine." Jessica began clearing the table.

He knew that tone, and everything was not fine. "I'll help." He gathered the linen napkins.

"I'd rather do it by myself. Why don't you go home and get your head cleared."

"Come on, Jessica. Just because—"

"Please. Go home."

He stiffened at her sharp tone. "Why are you angry?"

"I'm not angry, but if we can't discuss something as important as your career, what does it say about our relationship?"

"The conversation seems a little one-sided."

"Well, I'm sorry if I want you to do what's best for your career."

He tossed the napkins on the table. "You know, I think you're right. I probably do need to go home."

He shrugged into his overcoat. When he bent to kiss her good-night, she offered her cheek. He turned her to face him. "I'm sorry. I didn't mean to upset you."

She lifted her gaze and tears wet her lashes. "I just want to be part of your life. Sometimes I feel like one of those dolls I collect—something to be admired and taken out of the case only to be shown off."

He brushed a tear from her cheek. "Could you give me a little while to process today?"

She nodded. "Of course. Just don't shut me out."

"I won't." The last thing he wanted to do was hurt Jessica.

"NOAH'S SPEECH...DID you help him with it?" Peter handed Allie the last plate to dry. After they had ended up sharing the take-out sweet-and-sour chicken with Noah, Peter had rolled up his dress-shirt sleeves and commandeered her sink.

"No, he wouldn't let me." She'd finally convinced the boy to read his essay as they sat around the kitchen table, telling him the more he read it to others, the easier it'd be on Friday. It was short, probably shorter than the other two that would be read by fourth- and fifth-graders.

Allie eased to the wall that separated the living room from the kitchen. Noah was engrossed in a television program and not paying any attention to them. When she turned around, Peter had picked up Noah's essay and was rereading it at the table.

She'd been amazed at how well he and Noah were connecting. Even Logan and Lucas enjoyed being around him. After they beat him at Wii football Sunday afternoon, he'd challenged them to learn how to play Scrabble, and the boys loved it. She didn't know why she'd ever thought Peter was a stuffed shirt. "Would you like a cup of coffee? I have almond-toffee creamer."

He looked up. "Eww. Black, please." Then, he tapped the papers. "Noah has quite a way with words for a third-grader. We need to get him into the accelerated writing program."

"His teacher suggested the same thing, and we're working on it." She set a mug of steaming coffee in front of Peter and sat opposite him at the table. "Tonight's been fun."

"I'm glad. You looked pretty stressed when I got here. Anything I should know about?"

Allie cupped her hands around the mug, letting the heat radiate through her fingers. "I'm worried about something Noah said earlier. He's keeping something from me, something to do with Logan and Lucas."

"Has the father been heard from again?"

"No." Allie sipped her coffee. "I did talk to the sheriff this afternoon, and that didn't make me feel any better. He's been in contact with law enforcement officials in the county where the boys lived. The sheriff there suspects Nichols may have killed the boys' mother."

"What?" Peter leaned toward her. "How?"

"They think he beat her. But no one saw it happen, and when she was taken to the hospital, she swore she fell down their basement steps.

She never changed her story and died two days later from a blood clot."

"Do you think the boys saw what happened?"

"The police report indicates they were asleep, but I suspect they weren't. I discovered this afternoon Logan has confided a secret to Noah, but it's one of those cross-your-heart-hope-to-die-you-won't-tell kinds of things. I'm going to talk to them separately at school tomorrow."

"I may need to move the boys to another shelter."

"I hope not. I don't want Logan and Lucas to be put in danger, but it's so hard for shelter kids to go into a new school in the middle of the year. When will you make that decision?"

"I'll have to check and see if one of the other shelters in the state can take them. When I last checked, there wasn't room for both of them at the same facility, and I do want to keep them together. I'll call tomorrow and let you know." Peter held up his hand. "And, if you see anything unusual at school, call the sheriff, and then call me. I've told Sarah at the shelter the same thing."

She shivered. "It's terrible when boys have to fear their fathers, isn't it?"

"Unfortunately, yes." Peter captured her hand, and his blue eyes darkened as he laced his fingers in hers. "I want you to be careful. Nichols may blame you for what happened the other day, and I don't want anything to happen to you."

"Peter…"

"Don't say anything. I know you think you're in love with Matt, but he's all wrong for you, Allie. You need someone who will cherish you. All Matt cherishes his money and his career. He'll never return to Cedar Grove. I'm here, and I love you, Allie."

Peter loved her? Or was she just the prize in Matt and Peter's ongoing competition? "Peter—"

"Don't say anything now. Just give me a chance. Go out with me on the date we've never actually had. Friday night when Noah will be with Matt."

She pulled her hand from Peter's and took her coffee to the microwave and reheated it. He was right about Matt, and she needed to get him out of her system. But she'd loved him since junior high school. How did you just stop loving someone? Maybe by recognizing it was a dead end. The microwave dinged, and she took her cup out and turned to Peter. "Would Friday night include dancing?"

A smile stretched across his face. "Definitely."

He stood and took the cup from her hand before twirling her around the kitchen. When they stopped to catch their breath, he tilted her face up. "I know you don't have the same feelings I do, but I'm a patient man, and I'm willing to wait."

CHAPTER FIFTEEN

WHEN HE REACHED his car, Matt shrugged out of his overcoat and threw it in the backseat. He needed to talk to someone, but who? Allie? No, she hadn't been that enthused about the job with Bradford in the first place. Going back and discussing it with Jessica would only start another argument.

Clint. Allie's brother was the closest thing he had to a friend in Memphis. He slid behind the wheel. It was a sad commentary that he didn't have anyone close to him he could talk to, but he'd been so busy with his career, making close friends hadn't seemed that important.

He should have thought of Clint right away. At least he would be unbiased. Matt scrolled through his contacts and dialed Allie's brother.

Clint answered on the second ring. "Forget your tux again?"

"Something like that. Are you in the middle of anything? I need your opinion on something." Matt really should have touched base with Clint sooner.

"I'm just leaving the Boys and Girls Club. There's a coffee shop on Poplar. Do you want to meet me there?"

"Yeah. Give me the address." Ten minutes later Matt pulled into the parking lot and spied Clint's red Crown Victoria. Inside the café, Matt ordered a black coffee and took it to the booth where his friend waited.

"I like your wheels," Clint said. "Allie keeps bugging me about getting a new car."

"Listen to your sister. That's what, a '97? It's bound to be on its last set of tires."

"Something like that," he said with a laugh. "How's Jessica? I hear you finally popped the question."

"Yeah. But she's much too good for me."

"You can say that again." Alarm crossed Clint's eyes. "That's not why you wanted to talk, is it?"

"No." Matt sipped on his coffee. Strong, exactly the way he liked it. "I need an objective opinion."

He filled in Clint on Bradford's job offer, then Winthrop's counteroffer. "I don't know which one to take."

Clint saluted him. "Man, as the kids would say, that's an awesome problem to have."

Satisfaction flushed through Matt. "It's not

bad, is it? I mean, for someone from the wrong side of town."

A frown creased Clint's brow. "You're not still carrying that baggage around, are you?"

The words stung. Matt jutted his jaw. "You don't have any idea what it was like growing up on Beaker Street."

"You're right, I don't. But can't you see how that gave you the drive to succeed? I don't think either man cares where you grew up, only that you can do the job."

"I didn't come here for a lecture. That I can get from Allic. I want advice on which job to take."

Clint leaned back and folded his arms across his chest. "Give me the pros and cons of each job."

"I would enjoy either job, and both come with long hours and headaches, but Bradford may be the biggest headache. Mr. Winthrop is more than fair. Jessica will be unhappy if I don't take her dad's offer. There will be more prestige and power with Bradford at the foundation— it's a worldwide organization. The money will be about the same…although Bradford offered me more first."

Clint relaxed and bent forward. "Which is more important? The work you'll be doing or the prestige and money?"

Matt frowned. Was that a trick question?

"While you're thinking about that, let me give you a piece of advice. Prestige and money are nice, but if that's all you focus on, it'll leave you empty and wanting more. Along with high blood pressure and heart disease. I know. When I first got out of college, I took the job that paid me the most. It was with a Wall Street brokerage firm. Long hours, lots of pressure, on the phone all day. Great money, though. And I hated the job. Eventually I realized I was only in it for the dough."

"How about the job you have now?" Matt checked his watch. "It's nine o'clock and when I called you earlier, you were just leaving it."

Clint nodded. "I still have long hours at half the pay, but don't you see, I'm giving something back, making a difference in the lives of these high-risk kids. And I don't feel like a hollow shell any longer."

Hollow. Perfect word for the way he felt.

"When do you have to give your answer?"

Matt gave a short laugh. "I've already accepted Bradford's offer. But that was before Winthrop countered." He sighed. "I don't want to burn any bridges with Bradford before I make a decision."

"So you're not going to tell him about Winthrop's counteroffer?"

"I don't know what I'm going to do. Go home

and sleep on it, I guess. Besides, it's getting late. I'm sure you have a busy day tomorrow."

"I'm taking tomorrow off. Going to help dad get caught up with the horses."

"They're back?"

"As of yesterday. How are things going with Noah?"

"Better. On Friday I'm bringing him here to meet Jessica." Matt stared down at the almost empty cup.

"Sounds good."

He felt Clint's gaze and looked up. His friend's eyes held a question. "What?"

"You've been spending a lot of time with my sister. How's that working for you, you know, with your history and everything?"

Matt traced his finger on the cup. If he told Clint that he'd kissed Allie, his friend would probably deck him. "Sometimes when I look back, I think breaking up with Allie is the biggest mistake I ever made. How did I get it so wrong?"

Clint shrugged. "You were young and couldn't see anything but getting ahead. How about now? You do love Jessica, don't you?"

"I wouldn't have asked her to marry me if I didn't."

"But do you love Jessica enough to take what

she wants into consideration as you decide your next career move?"

If he decided he wanted to take Bradford's offer, could he give it up because Jessica didn't agree? "That goes two ways," Matt said. "She should want what will make me the happiest."

"It doesn't work like that, bro. If mama ain't happy…" Clint stood and picked up his cup, carrying it to the trash.

Matt followed him and tossed his, as well. Maybe he wasn't ready to get married. He was at the same place he'd been with Allie seven years ago. He dismissed the thought. Outside, he pressed his key fob and started his car.

"Show-off." Clint unlocked his Crown Vic. "Just remember, money isn't everything."

CHAPTER SIXTEEN

ALLIE PROPPED HER arms on the fence rail as the three boys trotted by, their legs hugging Bridger's sides. Clint stood beside her. "Thanks for saddling him up. How's Kelsey?" She thought that was his girlfriend's name.

"I'm not seeing her anymore."

"What happened?"

Clint gave her a half shrug. "Absence does not make the heart grow fonder. My hours got in the way. Well, not just mine, but hers, too."

"I'm sorry." The north wind picked up, and she pulled her down-filled jacket closer as their dad joined them at the fence. She cocked her head, studying the two men. They were a lot alike, not only in looks but also in the size of their hearts. And while Clint's hands weren't as calloused as their dad's, he'd earned a few blisters mucking out stalls and chopping wood.

The boys passed by once more, their cheeks rosy from the cold and laughter lighting their eyes. Noah rode in the front with the reins, and he handled the horse like he'd been riding since birth. Dad nudged her.

"Makes me think of the old days when you and your friends rode him. Once he finished tossing his head and snorting, he always settled down and let you kids have fun."

"Yeah." Fun wasn't the only reason she'd brought the boys. She hoped the relaxed atmosphere would help her ferret out whatever secret they were keeping from her. She rubbed her arms against the cold.

"You ought to do this more often," Dad said, pulling a tin of butterscotch candies from his Carhartt coat. He'd taken up candy when he quit smoking a few years ago. He offered the tin and she took one. "I figured by now, one of you would have a few little ones of your own out here riding."

She unwrapped the candy. "I figured you'd want us married first."

All three laughed, and then Clint said, "I talked to Matt last night."

The mention of his name stilled her. "Oh? Did he tell you about his new job?"

"Yep, as well as the counteroffer Mr. Winthrop made."

"That doesn't surprise me." She waved at the boys. "It's getting colder. Let's rub Bridger down and then see if we can find some hot cocoa."

She and her dad followed the boys to the barn while Clint deserted them for the warmth of the house. "Get the cocoa started," she called after him.

At the barn, she helped the boys untack the horse and put him in his stall. "I'll feed him," she said. "You three go on to the house and get warm."

While she measured out Bridger's sweet feed, her dad grabbed a flake of hay and tossed it into the stall. "Ran into Peter Elliott in town today."

"Oh?"

"You could do worse."

"Dad!"

"Got to admire a man who'll stop me on the street and tell me his intentions toward my daughter."

Heat crept up her neck. She leaned against the barn door and stared at the ground, feeling his gaze. "He's nice."

"I'd say he was a great deal more than nice. Is Matt Jefferies the problem? Are you still carrying a torch for him?"

"No." Maybe. "I don't have a future with Matt. He's getting married."

"I saw how he looked at you the day we moved Mariah's things." He settled on a bale of hay. "Do you two have unfinished business?"

She jolted as the memory of his kiss gave

her goose bumps. She shook her head. "I don't think Matt even knows why we broke up. He still thinks it's because I didn't want to move to Memphis."

"That's what you told everyone."

"Come on, Dad. You know me better than that."

"You wouldn't talk about it."

"I couldn't back then." She sat beside her father on the hay. "I would have gone anywhere with him. Or at least with the Matt I fell in love with. But he changed that last year in college. Started hanging out with the rich people, trying to act like them. Didn't want to have anything to do with his old way of life, including Mariah. He became so obsessed with making money…. I didn't know him anymore. He lost who he was."

"You've been seeing a lot of him lately. Has that stirred up old feelings?"

"Yeah. I'm afraid it has." She glanced up at him. "But the past few weeks he's seemed like the old Matt. Taking care of Noah, trying to help Mariah."

Kissing her.

Dad wrapped his arm around her shoulder. "Could it be possible he's finding his way back?"

AFTER DINNER, ALLIE checked her watch. Almost six. She needed to get the twins back to the shelter and Noah home in time for them to do their homework. "Have you seen the boys?" she asked her mom.

"Noah and Lucas are in the den with Clint. I think Logan is with your dad in the office. The boy is quite taken with those trophies your dad has."

Allie knew which trophies. In his younger days, Dad had competed with the cutting horses he now raised and had the trophies to show for it. She peeked inside the office, and sure enough, Logan sat on the couch, captivated as her dad talked.

"Hey, you two," she said, entering the room. "Dad bending your ear?"

Logan felt his ear. "No."

She covered her mouth to keep from laughing, and then turned to her dad. "Could you go tell Noah and Lucas to find their coats?"

He looked from her to Logan. "Sure. Want me to keep them entertained a minute."

She beamed at him. "Good idea." She sat on the couch beside the boy and rubbed his shoulders. "Have fun today?"

He nodded. "I wish we could live here."

Maybe her parents... She dismissed the thought. The children they fostered were short-term, like Noah. With no family who could take them, it was likely the twins would enter the long-term foster care system. "Maybe Mr. El-liott will find you an even better place."

"What if my dad finds us?"

"Is that what's been bothering you?"

He hunched his shoulders in a shrug.

"You want to talk about it? Sometimes that helps."

No answer. With a sigh, she patted his back. "You better find your coat so we can leave."

When they reached the door, he stopped. "Miss Allie, sometimes nobody can stop bad things from happening."

The resignation in his voice nearly undid her. She bent over until she was at eye level with him. "But you need to let people try."

He stared at her for a moment, and then ducked his head.

Allie straightened as he scooted past her. Lenny Nichols had to be at the bottom of what-ever was going on with Logan. Maybe tomorrow she could convince Noah to share what he knew.

MATT STEPPED OUT of the elevator on the top floor of the Bradford Building and walked to the re-ceptionist's desk. For once, the waiting area was empty. The clock on the wall said it was five-thirty. No wonder. Where had the day gone?

"Good afternoon, Mr. Jefferies. Mr. Bradford is expecting you."

"You're working late." He searched his memory for the receptionist's name. Carrie? No... something that started with a C, though. Callie...Connie...*Casey*.

The petite redhead laughed. "Around here, late is nine o'clock, except for Ms. Jones. She leaves every day at five sharp. And, now that you've arrived, I am free to leave, too."

So executives weren't the only ones who put in long hours at the foundation. He was curious "Do you like working here, Casey?"

Her face lit up. "Oh, yes, sir. Mr. Bradford is wonderful to work for."

"I've heard around here, it's his way or the highway. You don't mind that?"

Frown lines formed between her eyes. "Well, he *is* the boss. But, his bark is much louder than his bite. Underneath all that gruffness, he has a big heart. When my mom was sick, I had to take off a month, and he paid me as if I were here. And not just me. Other employees who've had to be absent because of illness or family emergencies have never had their pay docked, either."

So Bradford's concern about Mariah was not unusual. "Thanks."

"Always glad to be helpful. Anytime you have a question, just ask."

"I will," Matt said. He walked toward Bradford's door and pushed it open. "The reception-ist said to come on in."

Bradford stood at the window as always. Matt joined him and understood why Bradford liked the view. Sunset faded into night, lending an ethereal glow to the riverfront.

"My father used to call this time of day the gloaming," Bradford said. "Did you finish study-ing the portfolio?"

Matt's mind raced to keep up with his boss. "I think I have one more folder. It's a lot to absorb."

"I understand Winthrop offered you a vice president position."

For a second, Matt didn't breathe.

"Don't look so shocked." The older man went to his desk and sat down. "And don't ever let anyone talk you into playing poker."

In a daze, Matt followed and took his usual chair. "How—"

Bradford chuckled. "I'm surprised you don't know that Winthrop and I meet for lunch. Once a week at Rigatoni's."

Matt gripped the arms of the chair. Nothing made sense…or maybe everything did. Was he some sort of stringed puppet in a game between the two CEOs? "Did Mr. Winthrop know you were going to offer me a job?"

"No." Bradford eased back in his leather chair. "Are you reconsidering my offer?"

Matt rubbed his jaw, the stubby bristles of his five-o'clock shadow prickling his fingers. "May I ask you something?"

"Shoot."

"If you and Winthrop are such good friends, why has the Winthrop Corporation never hosted your galas?"

Bradford reached for a bottle of antacids on the corner of his desk. "This ulcer is killing me." He shook out two blue tablets and popped them into his mouth, chewing with the gusto of a child taking vile-tasting medicine. He wiped his lips with a tissue. "Friendship has nothing to do with business. Winthrop never gave me what I wanted at the price I wanted. You did." He flexed his fingers. "I understand you're marrying Winthrop's daughter."

Evidently, he was a common conversation topic.

The older man chuckled. "Yes, we talk about you often. As for Jessica, if she's anything like her mother, she'll be an advantage to your career."

"Thank you, sir."

"Matthew, you have what it takes to make it in the business world. You're smart, articulate, willing to work to get what you want. Your only weakness is in thinking you can juggle a family life and your career. Both will suffer. You're going to have to decide which you want, but I'll tell you now, if you choose to put your family over your career, you won't make it. Not here." Bradford leveled his gaze at Matt.

Until recently, he'd chosen his career over everything, but since Noah and Mariah had come back into his life, nothing about his life was cut and dried. "Other men juggle family and career. Why can't I? I'm already working a sixty-hour week."

Bradford frowned. "But you're not married yet. And in the beginning you'll be working seventy, eighty hours a week here. Matthew, I have big plans for you, and this position I've offered is only the beginning."

"How did you do it, sir? Build your company and have a family. Didn't they suffer because you're a workaholic?"

"It wasn't a choice for me in the beginning. To put food on the table, I had to work. Do you know how many construction companies vied for business in this area in the sixties? I had to give customers something different. Perfection. My undivided attention and my time. That's how I became successful. And why I had the money to develop the concept that made me wealthy."

"Rental storage units," Matt said.

Bradford nodded. "In the mid-seventies there were very few public storage units in the South, or anywhere else for that matter. I happened to see one in Texas and stopped to inquire what it was. The man I spoke with thought I was asking to rent one of the spaces, and he told me I've have to be put on a waiting list. I came back to Memphis with an idea. Took five years and my own money, because not one banker would give me a loan for the project. But I believed in my idea enough to back myself. Now I'm able to give away millions and still live how I want to.

"But you asked if my family suffered because of my focus on business? Not financially, but emotionally? Probably. I did put work first, them second."

He leveled his gaze at Matt. "My suggestion is to go ahead and marry Jessica—like I said, she'll be a great asset, and she understands the business world. But wait a few years to start your family. Get established here at the foundation. Make your mark in the world. Then, in ten years or so, you'll still have plenty of time to have those children."

Matt's blood thrummed through his body. In ten years, Bradford would be in his eighties, probably looking to step down as CEO....

Bradford looked him in the eye. "So, I'll ask you again. Are you accepting my offer or Winthrop's?"

This was it. He had to choose. The job he

knew or this unknown territory where he would be challenged at every turn. The challenges scared him and at the same time sent excitement coursing through his blood. "I accepted your offer yesterday. Nothing has changed."

"No going back on your choice, even if Winthrop ups the stakes?"

"No, sir."

Bradford extended his hand. "I'll hold you to your word."

IN HIS CAR, he dialed Jessica's dad. "Mr. Winthrop," Matt said when he answered. "I wanted to let you know I've made the decision to go with the Bradford Foundation."

"I see." Winthrop cleared his throat. "Is that set in stone?"

"I'm afraid so, sir. I gave him my word."

"My loss. But there's some consolation since I'll be gaining you as a son-in-law."

Tension eased from Matt's shoulders. "Thank you, sir. I really appreciate everything you've done for me, and my assistant is more than capable of taking over for me, although I plan to stay through the Valentine party rush."

"Good. Have you told Jessica?"

"I'm on my way there now."

"Good luck with that."

Matt thanked him again and hung up. Surely Jessica would understand it was his career.

"YOU WHAT?" JESSICA stared at him. "You don't want to be a part of my family's business? The business my father built from the ground up. You could have taken over when he retired."

"You don't know that."

"I'm his only child. Trust me, you would have taken over."

"That doesn't even make sense, Jessica. And I would not want a job I didn't earn."

Two bright red spots dotted her cheeks. "And what happened to 'we'll discuss this tomorrow'? You didn't even call me. I thought our marriage was going to be a partnership."

He searched for the right words. "I'm sorry about that, but I was in Bradford's office and one thing led to another. He wanted an answer."

"You couldn't tell him you needed to discuss something as important as this with your fiancée before you made a commitment? This doesn't just affect you, Matthew." Tears formed in her eyes and she bit her lip. "I can't believe you did this to us."

He couldn't believe she was so upset about his decision. "I thought you would want me to be where I could thrive." He tried to catch the words. "I didn't mean that the way it sounded, but can't you see the opportunity at the Brad-ford Foundation will challenge me. I'll make a difference there." The hole kept getting deeper. "Let's sleep on this and talk about it tomorrow."

"That's what you told me last night."

"I don't know what to say, other than to repeat that I'm sorry. I…guess I better go."

At the door, he glanced over his shoulder. "I'll call you tomorrow."

She didn't answer.

At his apartment Matt shrugged out of his coat. Even though his stomach rebelled, he needed to eat something. In the kitchen, he read the note he'd left on his refrigerator door this morning. *Call Noah*. He checked his watch. Eight o'clock. The boy should still be up.

Allie answered on the second ring. "Hello, Matt."

There seemed to be a slight warming in her voice. "Hello, Allie. Everything okay?"

"Everything's great. I took the boys out to Dad's and let them ride Bridger. Thought if you wanted to, we'd do it again Saturday."

"I'm planning on bringing Noah back to Mem-phis."

"Oh…okay." The temperature in her voice dropped a few degrees. "Well, we'll do it some other time. Do you want to speak to Noah?"

"Sure."

He heard the phone being passed, and then Allie saying, "It's your uncle."

"'Lo," Noah mumbled.

"Hey. Are you practicing your throw?"

"Miss Allie doesn't know how to make it spin. Can we do it this weekend?"

"You bet. Are you ready for your big day?"

Noah lowered his voice. "Could you talk to Miss Allie? Get her to read my essay?"

"I'm not exactly Miss Allie's favorite person right now."

"Yeah, I know. Maybe I can get Mr. Elliott to talk to her."

Matt's chest tightened. "How's everything else going?"

"Okay. Are you coming tomorrow?"

"It's your big day—wild horses couldn't keep me away." He walked back into the living room. "Uh, how would you feel about coming here to see where I live this weekend?"

"You mean Memphis?"

"That's right, I have someone I want you to meet. We'll probably go to the zoo. How does that sound?"

"You'll bring me back to Miss Allie's?"

"Sunday afternoon."

"Can Logan come?"

If Logan came, Lucas would be there as well, and he didn't know if he could handle three boys. "I don't think I can get permission to bring them."

"Would you ask Miss Allie? Here she is."

Suddenly Matt was on the line with Allie. "What's going on, Matt?"

"Jessica has a big weekend planned for Noah— the zoo, Pink Palace, dinner. He wants Logan to come with him, but I told him it wouldn't work."

"You're right, it won't."

"So is the dad still on the loose?"

"Yep. If there's not anything else, I have work to finish."

"Yeah, sure." Matt gripped his phone long after she'd disconnected. Had it been just a week ago that they'd shared laughter and fun…and a kiss.

He pushed the thought away. Maybe some fresh air would clear his head. He stepped out onto the balcony, ignoring the cold. Overhead the sliver of a new moon hung low in the night sky. Glancing down, street lights illuminated the busy intersection in front of his building.

It was plain how Allie felt about him. That didn't stop him from remembering how blue her eyes were when he cupped her face in his hands and that she responded to his kiss. He raked his hand through his hair. Instead of thinking about Allie, he should be trying to figure out how to

make things right with Jessica. But tonight, past
and present seemed bent on confronting him.

What if he could go back seven years...would
he be so quick to let Allie walk away? He hadn't
even fought for her...instead, he ran in the opposite direction. And what about Jessica? Was
he even being fair to her with these unresolved
feelings for Allie?

Was he marrying Jessica because she fit so
well with the lifestyle he wanted? Hosting dinner parties and chairing fund-raisers and sitting
on various boards. No, he loved Jessica. He truly
did.

Enough to spend the rest of his life with her?

Matt rested against the balcony rail. He should
have talked the job over with her. He even saw
her side. But in his heart, he knew the outcome
would not have changed. Working with J. Phillip
Bradford excited him like nothing ever before.
They were kindred spirits. Driven to succeed.
But it was even more than that.

I'll make a difference there. When he spoke
those words to Jessica, he hadn't known where
they'd come from. But driving home, he figured
it out. The focus of the Bradford Foundation was
to give away money, not take it in.

Maybe he could make Jessica understand that
tomorrow. But did he want to? He was back to

the question of what he should do. He shivered
and realized the temperature had dropped.

Back inside, Matt picked up the last envelope
on the Bradford Foundation. He sat on the white
couch and made a mental note to let the apartment manager know his sofa would be delivered
tomorrow.

He slid the envelope's contents onto the coffee
table. A small packet with a note tumbled out,
and he picked it up.

Matt, J. Phillip asked me to put together
a photo biography of his early days to go
along with the report. Be sure to return
these to me. E. Jones

Matt read the report on the other holdings of
the foundation. On the second page was a black-
and-white photo of Bradford's first rental unit
with him cutting the ribbon and a dark-haired
woman by his side. It had to be Rachel, but the
caption beneath it named her only as Mrs. Phillip Bradford. Matt scanned the rest of the document, searching for any mention of other family
members. He thought somewhere he'd seen the
mention of a child, but he found nothing in the
report. Maybe he'd ask Ms. Jones tomorrow.

Inside the packet, Matt discovered an assort-
ment of old photos, mostly grainy black-and-

whites. He sorted through them, putting those of Bradford in one pile and any of him with other people in another. He paused to examine a faded snapshot of Bradford standing beside the dark-haired woman holding a baby. Nineteen-sixty was stamped at the bottom of the photo. He turned it over. *Our little family* was penned in feminine handwriting. He flipped it over again. It was hard to distinguish whether the child was a boy or girl. Surely this wasn't the only family photo of them.

Matt could tell most of the other photos were from the late seventies and early eighties. They showed Bradford at different construction sites or cutting a ribbon at the opening of one of his storage buildings. Sometimes Rachel was there, but more often than not he was alone. He reexamined the photo of her holding the baby. The photographer had stood too far away to capture her features, but her posture suggested confidence. Matt had read her biography in the folder on Rachel's Hope and the details of her battle with breast cancer during a time when such things weren't talked about, but there'd been no personal information on her. What had become of the child, who would be in his or her fifties by now? Again he would have to rely on information from Ms. Jones…if she was inclined to share it.

He stood and paced the length of the room several times.

He'd read through the entire portfolio, gleaning insights into the man who ran the Bradford Foundation. His wife's bout with cancer and her eventual death sparked the beginning of Rachel's Hope, which in turn spawned the other two charities. Going to work at the foundation was more than his dream job. He would be helping to fund the researchers who might find the cure for the cancer that had killed not only Rachel Bradford, but also his mother and millions of other women.

That was worth a little sacrifice on his part.

BLUE FLAMES LICKED the gas logs in the fireplace, warming the room as Allie tucked her legs under her on the leather couch. She wished she'd been nicer when Matt called, but after he mentioned what Jessica had planned for the weekend, niceness went out the window. Still… *Would've, could've, should've.* The story of her relationship with Matt. She looked up as footsteps padded down the hallway and Noah came into view.

"What are you doing up?" she asked.

"I wanted to know if you had another picture of Bridger. One I could keep." A hopeful smile curled his lips.

"I think I can find you one." She patted the sofa beside her. "Come sit with me a minute."

After he was settled, she wrapped an afghan over his legs. "Have fun today?"

"Yes, ma'am. Can we go back soon?"

"Maybe next week."

Noah looked up at her. "Are you going to marry Mr. Peter?"

Allie laughed. "Where in the world did you get that idea?"

"Well, he comes over a lot, and he looks at you with goo-goo eyes, so I thought…"

Goo-goo eyes? She put her hand over her mouth to keep from laughing again. "No, I doubt Mr. Peter and I will marry."

He heaved a sigh. "Good. Maybe Uncle Matt will quit messing up, and you'll like him. He looks at you with goo-goo eyes, too."

"He does?"

Noah nodded. "When he thinks you're not looking, but we saw him. Me and the twins. We think you should marry him."

Allie rubbed her forehead with her fingertips. The boys had surely misinterpreted what they saw.

"He doesn't like it when Mr. Peter is here, either," Noah added.

"For your information, your uncle already has a fiancée. You'll meet her this weekend."

"I won't like her."

"I've met her, and she's nice. I'm sure you'll

like her." She squeezed the boy's shoulder. Since Noah was in a confiding mood, maybe he'd tell her what was bothering the twins. "Have you, um, thought about sharing your secret with me?"

His body stiffened. "What secret?"

"About what's bugging Logan."

He picked at a thread in the afghan. "I've thought about it."

"And?"

Noah remained silent. Finally, he stretched and yawned. "I'm sleepy now. I think I'll go back to bed."

He threw the afghan aside and climbed off the couch. "G'night," he said when he reached the hall.

"Good night, Noah. And if you change your mind, I won't mind if you wake me up."

He stared at her with his huge blue eyes. "I wish..." He shook his head. "I'm sorry, Miss Allie, but I just can't."

After the bedroom door closed, Allie folded the afghan before she turned off the gas logs. There had to be a way to discover whatever the boys were hiding, but so far she hadn't found it.

A few minutes later as she crawled into bed, she smiled. So, both Peter and Matt had been making goo-goo eyes at her.

CHAPTER SEVENTEEN

"LOOK, BOYS, I know something is wrong, but I can't help you if you won't tell me what it is." Allie tapped her pen on the desk. The three boys squirmed in the chairs across from her. Her gaze traveled from one boy to the next, settling on Logan. "Miss Sarah tells me you're not sleeping. Do you want to tell me why? Is it about your dad?"

Logan caught his breath. "How—"

A sharp look from Lucas stopped him, and then Logan said, "No, ma'am. I mean, I'm sleeping good."

This code of silence had to end. "Boys, your dad is not going to get you."

Logan's spoke up. "Miss Allie, our dad will do whatever he wants to do, and you can't stop him."

"I can if I know what's going on. Have you seen him?"

Logan cut his eyes at his brother. She turned her attention to Lucas. "When did you see him?"

"Didn't say we did, but he's everywhere," Lucas mumbled.

"But have you specifically seen him?"

Lucas barely shrugged his shoulder. "I haven't."

Allie turned to Noah. His eyes widened, and he shook his head. "I haven't."

Her gaze rested on Logan, who fidgeted in his seat. Finally, she sighed. "Okay, go to lunch. But please, think about telling me what's going on."

The boys scrambled from their seats and raced toward the door. Allie cleared her throat. "Noah, would you remain behind just a second?"

Noah looked at Logan before he turned around. "I don't—"

"I want to talk to you about your speech."

"Oh." Noah inched toward her, rubbing his arm where Logan had elbowed him.

When the door closed behind the twins, she folded her hands on the desk. "Are you okay about reading your essay?"

"I guess. Do you think Uncle Matt will be here?"

"I haven't talked to him today, but he said he would. I believe he will be if he can." Noah was clearly nervous. Desperate to reassure the boy, she said, "You'll do fine, Noah. Just be sure to read slowly and speak in your outside voice."

"Yes, ma'am. Can I go to lunch now?"

Her head said to ask him again about what was upsetting the twins, but her gut said to let it go. "Okay…but this afternoon, think about telling me what's going on. I know you promised to keep a secret, but some things are too big to be handled alone. If the twins have seen their dad, I need to know."

His eyes darkened, but he remained silent. She stood. "Go eat your lunch. I'll see you in the gym."

MATT HAD TOSSED and turned all night, finally rising at six. It was all downhill from there. He arrived at the hotel to find the main refrigerator had blown its compressor, and an hour later, the sprinkler system in the Savannah Ballroom activated, soaking the carpet, and he'd just hung up from his sixth call from Bradford or his secretary, Ms. Jones. He massaged the knotted muscles in his neck. He had forty-five minutes to clear his desk and be out of Memphis to make it to Noah's assembly. He set the timer on his phone to beep ten minutes before he needed to leave.

His door opened, and his assistant stuck her head in. "Got time to deal with one more problem?"

A pain shot through his stomach, and he grabbed the bottle of antacids he'd bought earlier in the day. "Don't tell me something else has gone wrong."

She grimaced and started to back out of the room.

He hadn't meant to sound so sharp. "Sorry, what is it?"

"Cara Carpenter's mother called and canceled the wedding."

"What?"

Susie took another deep breath. "The Carpenters' Valentine's Day wedding has been canceled—seems the bride ran off with one of the groomsmen."

Matt groaned as he dropped his head in his hand. The Carpenter wedding and reception had budgeted out at seventy-five thousand dollars. Pain shot just above his left eye, and he pressed his middle finger against it. "Check the reserve list, and see if there's anything big enough to fill that slot."

"I have. The Russell wedding and reception is the only thing that comes close, and I think our quote to them was fifty thousand."

"See if they are still interested." This close to Valentine's Day? He doubted it.

"I will. If they're not interested, do you want me to go down the list?"

"Yes." A text beeped in on his phone. Bradford. Another summons to the tower. He sent a text, agreeing to be there within ten minutes. His desk would have to wait. Maybe he could grab a sandwich somewhere and eat it on the way. He shook two more antacids into his hand.

"More trouble?" his assistant asked.

"Not really." He stood, offering a weak smile. "Let me know what the Russells decide."

"I will," she said and closed the door behind her.

Matt stretched, rolling his neck from side to side. He glanced at his desk and caught sight of yesterday's forgotten mail. As he put on his suit jacket, he flipped through the envelopes, spying one from the Shelby County register's office. The copy of his parents' marriage license. He ripped it open.

His mother's last name was Bradford? Was it possible? No. It had to be a coincidence. Bradford was a common name in Memphis. Although his mother's age was about right. But wouldn't J. Phillip Bradford tell him if he were his grandfather? Maybe they were cousins. His mind reeled with questions. Questions only Bradford could answer. He hurried out the door.

Matt missed his overcoat the instant the icy wind off the river hit his face. He kept walking. If J. Phillip and his mother were connected in any way... He flared his nostrils. The old man's money could've saved his mother's life. That thought kept time with the soles of his shoes as they slapped the pavement. When he exited the elevator on the top floor of Bradford's building, he didn't bother to knock at Ms. Jones's door. "I'm going in to see Bradford."

She stood. "Wait, Matthew."

"No." He reached for the doorknob, then turned around. "Did you know Bradford was my grandfather?" She paled instantly.

"You could have told me."

Ms. Jones sat down. "I wanted to, but it wasn't my place."

Matt shoved the door open. Bradford was at his computer. "I want to hear you say my mother was your daughter."

Bradford turned and frowned. "What?"

Matt threw the copy of the marriage license on the desk. Bradford walked slowly to the desk and picked it up. His lips twitched as he stared at the paper. Finally he looked up, his face devoid of emotion. "Yes. She was my daughter."

Matt's gut wrenched. "And you didn't help her?"

"She refused my help. Her principles were at stake, she said. Told me what I could do with my money."

Matt was stunned. "Why? What did you do to her?"

"I didn't *do* anything."

"I don't believe you."

Bradford returned his gaze, never blinking. "It was about your father. He was a lazy no-good leech with zero ambition." He sat taller in his chair, his eyes challenging Matt. "Would you agree or disagree?"

It was an accurate assessment of the father Matt remembered. But Mariah had said he wasn't always like that. "He must have had some redeeming qualities or my mother wouldn't have married him."

Bradford's gaze slid somewhere past Matt, then he refocused. "He told her what she wanted to hear. Words I never had time to say. Why do you think I suggested you delay starting a family? I didn't want history to repeat itself."

Bradford motioned toward a chair. "Sit down, and I'll try to explain."

"I think I'll stand."

"Suit yourself." Bradford's voice shrank to a whisper. "I tried to dissuade your mother from seeing your father, which was a mistake. Made her all the more determined. Then she got pregnant with your sister. I offered to raise the child for her, and she laughed in my face. Said I hadn't had time for her, and why would she subject her own child to that kind of life.

"I threatened to cut off the purse strings, and she told me to go right ahead. Money made things easier, she said, but not necessarily right. And that your father would take care of her." Bradford snorted. "He couldn't take care of himself, much less her and a child. Susan had some idealistic dream about marriage. I suspect when it didn't turn out the way she thought it would, she was too embarrassed to come to me."

Matt's face burned. His dad may have been everything Bradford said, but that didn't excuse him from not helping his daughter. "You could have gone to her when you knew she was in trouble, but you chose to turn your back, not just on your daughter, but on my sister and me. To think, I wanted to be like you."

"You already are."

"Never."

Victory glittered in Bradford's eyes. "Why haven't you been helping your sister?"

Matt's mind protested. The situation with Mariah was different. *Was it?*

"And how about this girl you're engaged to. Jessica. Do you love her? Is she your soul mate? Or does she just fit into your plans?"

The truth hurt when it was delivered so bluntly. If he truly loved Jessica, he never would have kissed Allie. Matt sank into the chair he'd refused earlier. His hands were as dirty as his grandfather's.

"I wanted to help you and your sister, but

Susan refused. Said she didn't want my money tainting her children. She didn't want anything just handed to you."

Matt's watch beeped the alarm he'd set earlier. *Noah.* He stood. "I have to leave."

"But I need you to—"

"Find someone else. I quit."

"Don't let this little bump deter you from what's rightfully yours."

"Why would I want anything you have? You let my mother die. Your money and the right treatment could have saved her life."

For the first time the granite cracked. "When I found out she had cancer, it was too late. I offered to fly her to M.D. Anderson, but she refused. Said the cancer had spread to her bones and she didn't want to go through more chemo. By then it probably wouldn't have done any good, anyway."

His phone buzzed again. He strode to the door. There was a nine-year-old boy expecting him to show up at his school, and he wasn't going to disappoint him. Before he walked out, he turned around. "How hard did you try?"

MATT DASHED BACK to work to pick up his overcoat. His cell phone beeped as he stepped off the elevator. Elizabeth Jones. Matt shoved it back in the pocket. He wasn't ready to talk to Bradford's secretary. In his office he found his assistant sitting at his desk. "Susie?"

She looked up. "Oh, good, you're back. I was just writing you a note." She laid the pen down. "The Russells had booked a local church, but are very much interested in using the Savannah Room. Mrs. Russell wants to meet with you tomorrow morning to discuss details."

"You take care of it."

"Me? I don't have the authority—"

"I'm giving you the authority to cut a deal with them." He stuffed the marriage license in the breast pocket of his coat. "Just don't give away the hotel."

She saluted him. "Yes, sir. Any suggestions on how much I can shave off?"

He shrugged. "Five percent. Ten, if it's absolutely necessary."

Susie had barely closed his door when it opened again. His heart sank. Jessica. They had to talk, but not today. "I'm just leaving for Cedar Grove."

"This won't take long." She pulled the engagement ring from her left hand and handed it to him.

"What? You're breaking the engagement?"

"No. You'll have to do that…if that's what you want."

"I don't understand."

"Take this weekend and decide if you really want to marry me. If you do, be prepared to tell me why when you give the ring back. And if you don't…" She smiled but it didn't reach her eyes. "Then you won't have to ask for the ring."

"Wait." Matt took the ring and the velvet box she handed him. An ache spread through his chest as tears wet Jessica's eyes. Would it make any difference if he told her he'd quit the job with Bradford? Did he want it to make a difference? If only he knew the answer. "Once the weekend's over. Can we talk then?"

"You just gave me your answer, Matt. If you weren't questioning your love for me, you would have put the ring back on my finger."

"Jessica…I…I don't know what to say."

"I do." She kissed him on the cheek. "Good-bye, Matthew Jefferies."

When Noah stepped out into the hallway, Lucas grabbed his arm. "You didn't tell her anything, did you?"

"No." Noah turned to Logan. "Maybe you ought to tell Miss Allie you saw him following us."

Logan shook his head. "If I did and he found out, he'd beat me for sure."

"How could he find out?"

"I don't know, but he would. He knows ev-crything."

Lucas nodded. "He knows where the shelter is—I saw his pickup go by."

"You lied to Miss Allie!"

"No, I didn't. I didn't see *him*."

"How do you know it was your dad?"

Lucas snorted. "You think I don't know my own daddy's truck?

"We need to tell Miss Allie," said Noah.

"She can't stop him. When the assembly starts, we're going to run away."

Noah swallowed the sick feeling that almost choked him. "You can't do that. Where would you go?"

Logan stuffed his hands in his jacket pockets. "We've been watching the trains that go by the school. There's a train that stops and waits until another train passes. There's always a door open and—"

"Shut up, Logan." Lucas shoved his brother.

Noah had seen the train Logan was talking about from his seventh period window. "You don't know where it's going."

"And neither will he." Lucas folded his arms across his chest.

Noah's heart pounded. This wasn't right. "We have to tell Miss Allie."

Logan grabbed his arm. "No. You promised

you wouldn't tell anything about our dad, and this is part of it. You don't break cross-your-heart-and-hope-to-die promises."

The door to Miss Allie's office opened, and Noah jumped. "What's going on, boys? I thought you were hungry."

Noah gulped. The voice in his head yelled at him. *Tell her.* "Miss—

"We're going, Miss Allie." Logan grabbed Noah's arm and pulled him down the hall, muttering, "You promised."

Noah looked over his shoulder. Miss Allie waved. "See you boys after the assembly. We'll have a little party in my office to celebrate Noah winning the essay contest."

Lucas turned back to answer her. "Yes, ma'am!"

In the cafeteria, Noah's sandwich stuck in his throat, and he sipped milk through a straw to get it down. The voice in his head kept insisting that he tell someone what the twins were going to do. "You can't just run away. Miss Allie will be worried. You gotta tell her."

"No," Logan said through gritted teeth. "Last time we told, something bad happened."

"Yeah." Lucas got in his face. "We told Mom that he was making us take the drugs to people, and she tried to stop him. He beat her up, and she died. Besides, he's gonna come get us today."

Noah stared at the twins. "How do you know?"

Logan pulled a folded piece of paper from his pocket and handed it to Noah. "A kid gave this to me outside."

Noah read the note. Three words in bold letters. *Be ready today.* A shiver ran down his back. "We need to give this to Miss Allie."

Logan snatched it back. "No, and you can't tell her. Don't you understand, she can't stop our dad."

Noah wadded the rest of his sandwich in the paper and put it on the tray. "What about my Uncle Matt? He's a guy. He could help us."

"But he's not here," Lucas said.

"He'll be here for the assembly."

Logan and Lucas exchanged glances. "Not even your uncle," Logan said as the bell rang, ending their lunch period. "You promised."

CHAPTER EIGHTEEN

EVEN WITH HIS foot floorboarding the gas pedal, Matt couldn't outrun his thoughts. He never meant to hurt Jessica. Just like he never meant to hurt Allie seven years ago. What kind of man was he? Selfish. Self-centered. The truth stung. He didn't deserve either woman.

And he did love Jessica. Just not the way a man should love his wife. If he had, he would have taken her feelings into consideration before he took the job with Bradford, and there would have been no kiss with Allie.

Allie. She'd made it plain how she felt about him. Matt blew out a deep breath. He'd certainly made a mess of everything. Yeah, he'd attained success. Success that left him hollow and empty. It had taken him seven years to realize everything he ever wanted was right in Cedar Grove, not in some job or fancy apartment. The thought looped through his mind as he rolled toward Cedar Grove.

He pulled into the school parking lot at two-thirty. Allie had stressed the assembly started at two-fifteen. He hoped he had not missed Noah's speech. Inside the office, he signed the school visitor sheet. "You said the assembly is in the gym?"

"Yes, sir." The student tilted her head. "You've missed half the pep rally. Would you like me to show you the way?"

"I know where it is."

Matt raced down the hallways that had not changed since he was a student here. He arrived just as the cheerleaders walked to the sidelines, and Noah stepped up to the microphone. The boy scanned the bleachers expectantly then his shoulders drooped. He hadn't seen him. Matt stepped to the outer edge of the gym.

"Way to go, Noah!" Matt's shout carried over the noise of the students, and Noah's head jerked up. When he saw Matt, his face broke into a grin, and he stood a little straighter as he spoke into the microphone.

"Hi, I'm N-Noah Connors." His nervousness blared from the speakers. "I want to r-read you my essay."

A twitter of laughter rippled across the gym.

"You can do it, Noah," Matt whispered.

"I knew someone who wanted to be a singer. She was really good, good enough to get a meeting with a record producer in Nashville." His voice grew stronger. "But she was scared, and a friend gave her a pill so she wouldn't be nervous. She sang for the producer, and he wanted her to come back and audition again for some more people. After a while he wanted to sign her to a contract, but she had started taking more pills and doing other drugs, and she didn't show up on time.

"She never did get a contract, and this year she almost died." Noah stopped and took a deep breath. "The singer is my mom and I knew she was doing drugs." Matt closed his eyes. He'd never even known Mariah wanted to be a singer. He'd been a lousy brother.

"Drug a-abuse hurts everyone."

Noah took a deep breath and continued. "It hurts parents when their kids do drugs, and when it's the parents, it hurts the kids." Noah's voice gained strength. "I know because my mom almost died from drugs. If that had happened earlier this year, part of it would have been my fault because I didn't tell anyone. If you know anybody who takes drugs, even if it's an adult, don't keep their secret. Tell a teacher you trust or our counselor, Miss Allie. And if you ever think about taking one of your parents' pain pills or any other drug, don't do it. Othewise it may be the biggest mistake you ever make in your life. Remember, drug abuse hurts everyone. Thank you."

Matt blinked back tears as applause swept across the gym. He was proud of Noah, and maybe if Mariah heard his speech, it would give her even more reason to stay clean. Noah bowed slightly and carefully folded his notes as he stepped aside for the next student.

After two more speeches, the principal spoke a few words and dismissed the students to their homerooms. Matt scanned the crowd for Allie. His stomach soured when he found her exiting the gym with Peter, his hand resting on the small of her back.

Jealousy struck with the power of a bolt of lightning. His heart belonged to Allie, always had, always would. Why hadn't he been able to see that earlier, before Peter staked his claim? What if it was too late? He had to tell Allie how he felt. Not that he'd blame her if she turned him down and chose Peter. She'd be crazy not to.

He'd noticed her office next to where he signed in. Maybe that's where they were going. He turned and hurried back the way he came.

"NOAH DID A great job. I'm glad Matt made it in time to hear him." Allie ushered Peter into her office. When she'd heard Matt's voice encouraging his nephew, she swung the video camera around just in time to catch him clapping.

"Me, too. Even though he almost missed it."

Peter caught her by the hand. "Noah's pretty special, isn't he?"

"He sure is." She walked to the small refrigerator in the corner of her office and took out a box of ice cream sandwiches. "Want to stay for his party? He and the twins are coming when the bell rings."

"Sounds like fun." He cocked his head. "Are we still on for tonight?" he asked. "Dining and dancing?"

A knock at her door prevented her from answering. "It must be the kids. Come in."

The door opened and Matt stepped in. He looked from her to Peter. "Can I speak—"

Noah pushed past him and grabbed her hand. "Miss Allie, you gotta stop Logan and Lucas. I didn't think they'd do it, but I can't find them."

She knelt in front of Noah. "Stop them from what?"

"They're running away on the train. I told them not to, but I know they did." He stopped to get his breath.

"Slow down," Matt said. "What train?"

Noah's bottom lip trembled. "I'm sorry. I should've told you, Miss Allie. But I didn't believe they'd do it. And they made me promise."

Allie covered her mouth with her hand. "Was this their secret?"

He shook his head. "No. They saw their dad

hit their mom and then she died. They're running away on the train so he won't find them."

Peter stepped forward. "Is it the train that stops behind the school?"

Noah nodded.

"Do you know which boxcar they got on?"

"No, sir. They just said there was always one open."

Matt stood. "I'm going to see if I can find them."

"I'll come with you." Peter turned to Allie. "Call the sheriff's department and tell them to make sure that train doesn't move."

Allie punched in 911 as the two men bolted from the office. When the dispatcher answered, she identified herself and explained the problem. Then, pocketing her cell phone, she caught Noah as he edged toward the door. "Hold on, young man. You're staying right here until we get back with the twins."

"But I want to help."

"You've already helped by telling."

"Do you think they'll be mad?"

She smiled at him. "We'll worry about that later. Now sit on the couch until I get back."

He cut his eyes toward the door.

"Noah, promise me you'll stay here."

"Yes, ma'am."

With a glance back, Allie closed the door behind her, thankful he'd finally come forward with the truth.

FOR THE FIRST five minutes after Miss Allie left, Noah sat on the couch, his feet dangling above the floor. What if the twins' dad showed up? He caught his breath. He forgot to tell Miss Allie that he was coming to get them today. What if their dad saw them go to the train? And he was there…and Miss Allie was there.

Noah had to tell her. But he'd promised to stay in the office. He didn't care. Miss Allie said that sometimes, if somebody might get hurt, you had to break your promise. He hopped off the couch. He knew a shortcut through the woods to the train.

The cold air hurt Noah's throat as he ran across the deserted schoolyard and slipped under the hole in the fence. He tucked his head against the wind and sprinted to the trees. Once he made it past the woods, he'd be at the tracks. The strong smell of pine trees met him at the edge of the woods, and he paused, panting for his next breath. He couldn't see the tracks and didn't remember the woods being so big. Noah bit his lip. He had to find Miss Allie. He edged past the first line of trees.

A hand wrapped around his neck and jerked Noah in a choke hold.

"Just keep your mouth shut, and you won't get hurt. Where are my boys?" the gravelly voice breathed against his cheek.

The twins' dad? Chills shivered down Noah's back. He wrinkled his nose against the sour odor of alcohol. "What boys?"

The choke hold tightened. "Logan and Lucas. I've seen you with them. You know where they are."

Noah couldn't breathe. Black dots filled his eyes. He thought he heard Miss Allie calling the twins' names. The man loosened his hold on Noah's neck. "The train? Is that where they are?"

More voices yelled for Logan and Lucas.

Logan's dad grabbed Noah by the back of his neck, squeezing hard. "You got a choice. Walk or be carried. It's up to you. And you better keep your mouth shut."

"I…I'll w-walk."

The hold loosened, then he grabbed Noah's collar, pulling his coat tight until the zipper cut into his throat. Noah tried not to stumble on the thick floor of pine straw as the twins' dad pushed him through the trees. They stopped at the tree line right next to the train.

"Don't move. You hear me, boy?"

"Y-yes, sir." Noah risked a peek. He wore a

dirty cap, and he needed to shave, but he looked strong. No wonder the boys were scared of him. Then Nichols pulled a bag from his coat with white stuff in it. Noah's chest got tight as the man took a straw from his pocket and used it to breathe in the bag. *No!* He'd seen his mom do that and then act really crazy. He bunched his muscles…maybe if he ran.

"Don't even think it, kid." Nichols leaned against a tree. "Why are they looking for my boys on the train?"

Noah didn't answer and the man shook him. "I asked you a question."

"Th-they were running a-away."

"From that shelter?"

Noah shook his head. "From you."

"Did they tell you why?" When Noah didn't answer, he shook him again. "They told you, didn't they? I've got to get them before they tell someone else. Let's go." The man pushed Noah out of the woods onto the bare rocks near the train.

Farther along the track, Uncle Matt hopped up into a boxcar, then turned and helped a man with a blue uniform on. Noah squinted. *Jason, the deputy sheriff.* He had a gun, and he could save them.

"They're checking the boxcars one by one,"

Nichols muttered. "I'll let them do the work of finding them."

Miss Allie stepped from the other side of the train. She was so close, only five boxcars away, and Jason was way down the track. Noah wanted to yell for her to run, but she disappeared into the open boxcar. In an instant she was back at the door. "I found them! They're okay." Then she disappeared again.

"Come on." The man jerked Noah up. In his hand was the biggest gun Noah had ever seen. Bigger than Jason's. What if he hurt Miss Allie with it? Maybe Noah shouldn't have told her where the twins were. He cringed as Uncle Matt and Mr. Peter ran to the boxcar. What if everybody got killed?

"WHAT WERE YOU THINKING? You scared us half to death," Matt said as he handed one of the twins down from the boxcar to Peter.

"Not now, Matt. First, let's get them warm." Allie hopped off the car and knelt, hugging both of the boys. "It's okay. We'll sort this out back at the…"

Her eyes widened, and she stood, shoving the boys behind her.

Frowning, Matt turned to see what had frightened her. His heart dropped to his knees. A man holding a gun had Noah positioned in front him as a shield. Matt stepped in front of Allie. "I don't know what you want, but how about letting my nephew go."

"As soon as I have my boys. Now just step away from them."

"You're not getting them." Allie moved beside Matt.

"Get behind me." The words rasped from his mouth. From the corner of his eye, a flash of blue appeared in the boxcar the boys had hidden in, and then disappeared. *Jason.*

Peter pulled Allie back and stood beside Matt. "Mr. Nichols, you can't escape with the boys... they'll slow you down. Why don't you put your gun away and just leave?"

Nichols cackled. "That's where you're wrong. When I get my boys, I'll fly out of here like an eagle. Now give them to me...." He eyed Matt. "Or I'll start shooting, and your nephew will be the first casualty, and then the little lady will be next."

The man was crazy...or high. Where was Jason?

"I wanna talk to the little lady."

"No." Matt didn't give Allie a chance to speak.

"You can't tell me no. I got the gun. What do you say I shoot *you* first?" He raised the pistol.

"No, wait!" Allie squeezed between Matt and Peter.

"Don't shoot her!" Noah leaped, shoving Nich ols's arm as the gun fired.

Matt threw himself across Allie, knocking her to the ground. Another gun fired, but pinpointing who fired it eluded him. Jason, maybe? He couldn't think, couldn't breathe. When did it get so dark?

"Matt! Talk to me, Matt!"

Allie? He tried to answer, but his mouth wouldn't work. If he could just close his eyes a minute…

"MATT! STAY AWAKE." Allie wanted to shake him, do anything that would make him open his eyes again. Instead she continued to press against the wound in his chest, shaking Peter off when he tried to relieve her. Why didn't the bleeding stop? Blood soaked the coat that she'd shed and stuffed against the bullet hole. The muscles in her arms screamed for relief. She'd heard an ambulance. Where was it?

"Let me take over."

Allie looked up as an EMT slid his latex-gloved hands under hers and continued pressing against the flow of blood.

Peter gently pried her away from Matt's side. "Let them do their job."

The paramedics worked quickly, hooking up an IV, taking Matt's blood pressure. Allie took Matt's coat that Peter handed her. He had stripped it off Matt earlier so they could make sure there was only the one injury. Blood ringed the spot where the bullet went in, but she didn't care—the coat still held Matt's woodsy cologne, and she breathed in, filling her nostrils with his scent. He had to make it. He just had to.

Allie caught phrases like *clipped a major vein* and *loss of blood* and *shocky*. She stepped aside as a medic rolled a gurney to where Matt lay. While other EMTs loaded him, the lead paramedic turned to her. "Is he on any medication? Allergic to anything?"

She hugged the coat closer. "I don't know. I've never seen him take anything."

"Is there anyone who would know?"

"His fiancée, maybe, but I don't have her phone number." Maybe his cell phone was in his coat pocket. She patted the front two pockets. Empty. Her fingers fumbled inside the breast pocket, relief surging through her when she touched the hard case. "Give me a second."

She scrolled through his favorites. Jessica's name was first, then hers. She touched the number, and it immediately dialed. Jessica answered on the first ring.

"I don't believe we have anything more to talk about, Matthew."

Allie put the phone on speaker. "This isn't

Matt. He's been hurt. Do you know if he is allergic to anything?"

"What? Who is this?"

"It's Allie. Is he allergic to—"

"No, not that I know of. What happened?"

Allie turned to the medic. "Did you get that?"

The EMT nodded. "How about meds?"

Allie spoke into the phone again. "Is he on any kind of medication?"

"No. Tell me what this is about!"

The EMT gave her a thumbs-up. "We're transporting to Cedar Grove General."

"What's going on?" Panic edged her voice.

Allie punched it off speaker. "Matt's been shot. He's being transported to the hospital here in Cedar Grove now."

"Shot? How?"

"It's a long story. I'll tell you when you get here."

Silence answered her, and Allie glanced to see if the call had been dropped. No, they were still connected. "Jessica?"

"I'm here. Where's the hospital?"

Allie gave her directions then disconnected the call as the EMTs picked up the gurney and carried Matt toward the waiting ambulance.

"Miss Allie?" Noah pulled at her arm. "Is Uncle Matt going to be okay?"

She'd almost forgotten the boys were here. "I hope so, Noah. I hope so."

The boy sounded on the verge of tears, and she put her arms around him. The twins stood with Peter, their eyes glued to where another team of EMTs worked on their father only a few yards away. "Peter, would you ask if we can leave?"

He went and returned shortly. "We can go. The sheriff said he'd get your statement later. I'll take you home."

She shook her head. "I can drive. Would you take the boys to Miss Sarah? I'll call my parents to come get Noah."

"I want to go with you." Noah's eyes pleaded with her.

Unable to say no, she nodded then hugged each of the twins.

Logan glanced toward his father. "Miss Allie, is my daddy going to live?"

Lucas crowded next to her. "Yeah, Miss Allie."

"I don't know. I hope so." Her answer was so inadequate, but Allie didn't know what else to say. No matter how bad a person Lenny Nichols was, he was still their father. The boys had enough to deal with seeing him shot in front of their eyes. They didn't need to deal with his death right now.

CHAPTER NINTEEN

In ICU, Allie stood at the foot of Matt's bed with Mariah at her side. Two hours of surgery, an hour in recovery. The minutes had ticked by like days. Afterward, a surgeon had talked with them and explained how the bullet had punctured Matt's left lung and nicked a major vein. It'd been the pressure Allie had kept on the wound, along with the quick arrival of the EMTs, that had saved his life.

Although they were given five minutes with him, his nurse hovered nearby. She'd already told them they would have to leave if the monitors registered any negatives. From the way Matt looked, that could be any second. She tried to count the tubes running from his body and stopped at four. Thank goodness they hadn't allowed Noah to come in with them.

Mariah stepped closer to the bed. "Why is he on a ventilator?"

"It's only temporary," the nurse replied. "It's to rest his heart."

Mariah dried her eyes and then backed toward the door. "I...I better check on Noah."

Allie didn't remember the doctor saying anything about his heart. "May I stay a little longer?"

The nurse nodded, and Allie dragged the one chair in the room to Matt's bedside as the nurse stepped out of the cubicle. Allie stroked his hand, barely touching his skin. He'd saved her life, and now he might lose his own. "Matt, you have to get better," she whispered. "Noah and Mariah need you. I need you."

She glanced up at the monitor as his heartbeat jumped to ninety-five and held her breath until it settled back to a steady eight-six beats. Content to just hold his hand, she sat quietly as his chest rose and fell with the ventilator. When the nurse tapped her on the shoulder, she stood and brushed her lips against his cheek. "I love you," she whispered in his ear. One last time, she squeezed his hand.

Back in the waiting area, Allie tucked her feet under her and picked up Matt's jacket, laying it across her lap. She really should ask for a bag to put it in, but she couldn't bear the thought of giving the coat up. Her finger touched the hole just above the breast pocket, and the skin on the back of her neck prickled. If Noah hadn't shoved

Lenny Nichols's arm, the hole would've been dead center of Matt's chest.

Pushing the thought away, she checked her watch. Where was Jessica? She should've made it to Cedar Grove by now. Across from her, Noah slept, curled up on the other half of the couch beside his mother. Mariah gave her a tired smile.

"Are you okay?"

"Nothing I can't deal with. Can I borrow your cell phone and call the rehab? I'm not returning until Matt is out of the woods."

A phone rang, and she exchanged glances with Mariah.

"I think it's coming from your purse," Mariah said.

Allie opened her bag. It was Matt's phone. Jessica's name showed on the ID. She grabbed it. "Hello?"

"Allie? How is Matt?"

"Critical, but he made it through the surgery. Are you almost to the hospital?"

After a brief pause, Jessica said, "I decided not to come."

"I don't understand."

"Matt will. Could you please keep me updated on his recovery?"

"Of course. What do you want me to tell him?"

"Tell him I called to check on him."

The line went dead. "That was strange."

"What do you mean?"

"The caller was Matt's fiancée, and she's not coming, said he would understand."

"That is strange."

Allie tapped the phone. There were probably other people she needed to notify. Like his new boss, J. Phillip Bradford. She found Bradford's number and dialed. The call went to voice mail. "Mr. Bradford, this is Allie Carson, a friend of Matthew Jefferies. Matt's been injured. Could you please call me back?"

Allie laid the phone on the seat beside her. She nudged Mariah's foot. "Would you like a cup of coffee?"

"Desperately."

"Me, too. I'll get it." Allie walked to the small canteen in the waiting area and poured two cups. She hadn't asked Mariah about sugar and cream, so she grabbed two packets of each. When she returned to the small area they'd carved out, Peter sat talking with Mariah. He rose. "Mariah was telling me he's still critical."

"He's on a ventilator." She handed Mariah one of the cups. She held out the sugar and creamer, and Mariah shook her head. Allie took a sip from her cup and turned back to Peter. "Did you get the twins to the shelter?"

"Yes. I explained what happened to Sarah."

"She's good with them. Any word on their dad?"

"He didn't make it. I've told Logan and Lucas, and they didn't say much."

She stared at her coffee, the bitter aroma turning her stomach. The twins had been through a lot and they would need help dealing with it. Her gaze went to the couch. As would Noah. That he could sleep was a good sign, though. Her hand shook as fatigue swept through her body.

Peter took the cup. "It's not too cold out, and you look like you could use some fresh air. How about taking a walk with me?"

A walk sounded wonderful. Allie glanced at Mariah.

"Go. I'll find you if you're needed. But leave me your phone so I can call you if there's any change."

Outside, Allie breathed in a cleansing breath of cold air and exhaled a cloud of vapor from her lips. She glanced toward the heavens. The parking lights kept her from seeing any stars, but a new moon was visible. In another couple of months it would still be daylight at six-thirty. If she were at the farm, she'd be able to see the Milky Way. Would she and Matt ever again lie on a blanket by the lake and stare at the stars? She pulled her coat close as a shiver slid down her back.

Neither she nor Peter spoke as they strolled toward a small park beside the hospital. He broke the silence first. "Matt's going to be all right. He's too stubborn to die."

"He saved my life." Dead leaves crunched beneath her feet as they walked the path lit by overhead security lamps.

"What he did was very brave." Admiration laced Peter's words.

"I never believed Lenny Nichols would pull the trigger."

Peter guided her around a mud hole. "It was the drugs. The sheriff told me they found a bag of cocaine and a straw in his pocket. I'm certain blood tests will reveal a high level of the drug... and no telling what else."

That explained why he thought he could fly.

Peter halted on the path and turned Allie to face him. "Don't let your past beat you up, and don't let it keep you from your future."

She tilted her head. "My future? What are you talking about?"

Peter brushed a strand of hair from her cheek. "Matt risked his life for you. He loves you."

She wasn't sure Matt saving her life meant he loved her.

"The question is, do you love him?"

Love shone from Peter's eyes, and conflicting thoughts battled in her mind. Peter was safe, predictable. But she would never love him the way she loved Matt. He deserved to know that. Tears stung her eyes. She nodded, not trusting her voice.

His shoulders drooped, and he looked away. She leaned toward him and kissed his cheek. "I'm sorry, Peter."

He wrapped Allie in a hug. "I am, too."

The husky words pierced her heart. She stepped back, hating goodbyes. "I better get back."

"I think I'll stay here awhile."

MATT DRIFTED TOWARD the light. He'd been dreaming about Allie, and didn't want to leave the dream. *I love you.* She'd whispered the words in his ear. Trying to recapture that world, he ignored the voices murmuring in the background of a soft whooshing sound. His nose tickled. Needed to scratch it, but something caught his hand. Matt cringed against the shriek above his head and blinked his eyes open.

"He's waking up."

A glaring light flooded the room, and he squeezed his eyes shut again. If only he could shut his ears to the cacophony of bells and buzzers assaulting them.

He sensed someone hovering over him and cracked his eyelids again. "Mr. Jefferies, try not to move. Wiggle your fingers if you can hear me."

"Yes." The word garbled in his throat.

"Don't try to talk. You're in the hospital in Cedar Grove, and you're on a ventilator."

Hospital? Matt strained to sit up.

"Lie still, Mr. Jefferies. I'm going to give you something to help you relax."

A warm sensation spread through Matt's body, and the light faded into blackness.

"Excuse me. Are either of you with Matthew Jefferies's family?"

Allie opened her eyes, and the ICU waiting room swam into focus. She must've dozed off. A woman in her early twenties held a clipboard and a plastic bag in her hands. Rubbing the sleep from her eyes, Allie nodded. "I'm a friend and this is his sister." She pointed at Mariah.

"I'm Tina Darby with Admitting, and I need insurance information. Actually, I need everything. Would've been here sooner, but it's been a crazy night."

Mariah raised her eyebrows. "Would you mind?"

"Sure." Allie turned to Tina. "I don't have any of his personal information, but I'll do what I can."

"I'm sure all the information I need is in the

bag. It contains Mr. Jefferies's pants and his wallet, but I can't go through them. Hospital rules." Tina handed Allie the bag.

Allie took a leather wallet from the bag and opened it. Matt's driver's license and insurance cards were inside, and she was able to provide the information Tina needed.

After she'd received the answer to her last question, Tina stood. "Thank you so much. I'm sure if I need any additional information Mr. Jefferies can provide it in a couple of days."

After Tina left, Mariah glanced toward the ICU doors. "When do you think we can see him again?"

"Soon, I hope. I'm sure he's still asleep from the anesthetic." Allie shifted the wallet from one hand to the other, looking for somewhere safe to put it other than her small purse.

"Why don't you put it inside his coat?" Mariah asked.

"Good idea." Paper rustled when Allie slid the wallet in the pocket. Curious, she extracted the paper. A marriage license? A memory nagged. Matt had said something about getting his parents' marriage certificate. She handed the papers to Mariah. "I think this is yours."

Mariah's brow creased in a frown. She took the paper and the frown eased. "Matt said he was going to get this. So my mom's maiden name was Bradford."

As in J. Phillip Bradford? Allie's mouth dropped. Was it possible he was their grandfather? "May I see that?"

She took the paper Mariah handed her. Susan R. Bradford. It would be too much of a coincidence for them to have the same last name and not be related. Was that why he hired Matt? If that was the case, why hadn't Bradford returned her phone call? Surely, he would want to know about Matt's condition.

"Who is this man?" Mariah asked.

"J. Phillip Bradford heads a huge foundation. Matt just agreed to go to work for him." Maybe she should give him another call. She redialed Bradford's number. Once again it went to voice mail. And once again she left a message.

Mariah rubbed her injured arm. "I can't believe we might have a living, breathing grandfather. Why do you suppose he never contacted us?"

Allie had no idea. Her cell phone rang and she glanced at her ID. Mom. She answered and told her there'd been little change in Matt's condition.

"I'm sorry, honey. How are you and Noah holding up?"

"Noah's been asleep, but I think he's waking up. Mariah's here, too."

"The hospital is no place for a boy. Your dad and I are coming to get him and let him stay here awhile."

"Oh, Mom, that'd be great. Let me check with Mariah first." She put her hand over the phone. "My folks want Noah to come out to the farm. Is that okay with you?"

"Be great," Mariah replied.

Allie relayed the message.

"Your dad wants to talk to you."

"How about Matt's car?" Dad asked. "Someone mentioned it was at the school. Does it need to be moved?"

She hadn't given the car a thought. "That's a good idea. I have his clothes, and his keys are probably in his pocket."

"Your mom and I will be there in fifteen minutes."

She disconnected and reached for the bag with Matt's clothes as Mariah gently shook Noah awake. Allie patted the slacks and found the keys in the left pocket, along with a small velvet box.

Mariah gasped when Allie pulled out the box. "Grandmother Rae's ring box! Check and see if the rings are in it."

Allie flipped the lid up and almost dropped the box. A stunning antique engagement ring sparkled against the white satin. She thought he had given the ring to Jessica.

So why was it in his pocket?

CHAPTER TWENTY

SUNDAY MORNING, ALLIE rode the elevator up to ICU. About midnight last night, her mom had finally talked her into going home to sleep. As usual, Mom was right. Sleeping in her own bed made a world of difference. Now if only Matt would wake up. But at least he was stable. Mariah sat in their usual corner, and she waved. Mariah had returned to rehab on the condition that she would be allowed to visit Matt.

Her face lit up as Allie approached. "I talked to Noah. He's having a ball at the farm."

"Mom and Dad love having him." She sat in the chair opposite Mariah. Other families drifted in as visiting time neared. She'd connected with several of them and now asked if there'd been any improvement in their loved ones. One was being moved out on the floor, but the others were unchanged. How well she knew their feelings. To go in time after time yesterday and see Matt so still and pale broke her heart. Maybe today...

The doors to the unit opened. "Why don't you go back first? Then I'll go," she suggested.

She wanted to give Mariah time alone with her brother.

"Thanks." She started to say more, but instead rose and hurried toward the doors.

While Allie waited, she checked Matt's cell phone to see if somehow Jessica had returned her call and she'd missed it. No, and neither had J. Phillip Bradford. In less than ten minutes Mariah returned, her eyes wet.

Allie's heart leaped into her throat. "Is he all right?"

Mariah lifted her shoulders in a defeated shrug. "Just like yesterday. Is he ever going to wake up?"

"Did you ask his nurse?"

She shook her head.

"When I go back, I'll ask and let you know. Okay?" Allie worried Mariah might lose what progress she'd made toward recovery.

She stopped at the nurses' station just outside Matt's door. "Any change, Traci?" She knew the nurses on each shift by name.

Traci's smile was encouraging. "We're weaning him off the ventilator, and his vitals are holding good. The doctor said something about waking him up."

Best news she'd heard all weekend. She thanked Traci and stepped inside the cubicle. Her excitement faded at the sight of Matt's still form. No wonder Mariah seemed depressed. Even though Allie knew the doctors had induced a coma to let his body rest, would he ever come out of it?

Allie slid a hand in her pocket where she carried his grandmother's ring. For some reason, touching the velvet box calmed her, gave her encouragement. She sat in the chair beside the bed and took his hand. Traci had said to talk to him, that perhaps he could hear her. "Good morning, Matt. It's a beautiful day outside."

No response other than the occasional whoosh of the ventilator.

"They said you might wake up today." Her voice broke, and she rubbed her throat, trying to relax the tight muscles. When she thought her voice wouldn't betray her, she began again. "Noah said to tell you hi. And that he's riding Bridger every day.

"Matt, if you'll just get better, I'll leave Cedar Grove with you. If you still want me to." The words slipped past her lips. She hadn't meant to say them, but now that she had, a weight lifted from her heart. "I was wrong to let you go without a fight. I'm sorry."

Was that a flicker of his eyelid? Allie moved closer, but the only thing that moved was his chest as he breathed in and out. Three soft chimes sounded throughout the unit, signaling an end to visiting time. She stood and stroked his cheek. He needed a shave. She leaned over and whispered in his ear the same thing she said each time. "I love you, Matthew Jefferies. Please come back to me and give us a second chance."

EXCRUCIATING PAIN WOKE MATT. Pain in his chest. Pain in his head. Pain just to breathe. He moaned, and a nurse moved instantly to his side. He gripped her wrist. "Hurting. I need…" Her image blurred.

"Mr. Jefferies, my name is Traci, and I'm your nurse. Do you know where you are?"

He blinked, and Traci's features sharpened. Intense blue eyes behind black-rimmed glasses appraised him. He focused on the stethoscope hanging around her neck. "Hospital." But why was he in the hospital? And why did he hurt so much?

"Good. Can you tell me your name?"

Was she crazy? She'd just called him by his name. Burning pain shot through his chest again. "Please. I'm hurting."

Her brows almost touched in a frown. "Your name."

He licked his dry lips. "Matthew Jefferies."

The frown disappeared, and she inserted a needle into his IV. "I'm sorry, but I have protocols I have to follow. This will help." She patted his arm as she slipped the stethoscope from around her neck and put the buds in her ears. "At least you're off the ventilator and breathing on your own."

Ventilator? Explained why his throat hurt so bad. As the burning eased to a dull throbbing, more questions crowded his mind. "How long have I been here?" Was that him? "And why do I sound like a frog?"

Traci pulled the buds away from her ears. "The ventilator. And you've been here almost two days. Do you remember anything that happened?"

He shook his head, and pain rocked it. He wouldn't do that again. "What day is it?"

"Sunday. And it's afternoon. Now, let me listen to your chest, and then we'll talk."

Matt lay still while Traci moved the chestpiece over his body, breathing when she instructed. "Why does it hurt when I breathe?" he croaked when she finished.

She folded the stethoscope and slipped it in her pocket. "You had a collapsed lung, among other things, but that's improving."

He lifted his right hand to touch his chest.

"I wouldn't do that. You have a tube in your left side—just above where you were shot."

Shot? A fuzzy image surfaced in his memory.

A man. A gun. Matt gripped the nurse's wrist again. "Allie. Is she…"

"Your friend?" Traci smiled. "She's fine. Would you like to see her?"

ALLIE HURRIED THROUGH the ICU corridor. The receptionist hadn't said why Matt's nurse wanted her, and her mind created a thousand things that could be wrong. She hesitated outside Matt's cubicle. What if… She rubbed the velvet box in her pocket for reassurance as Traci walked past with an IV bag in her hand. "You can go in." Allie must have given her a look of panic because the nurse smiled. "I promise, he looks much better."

Gathering her courage, Allie stepped around the opening. Matt lay with his eyes closed, his lashes dark against his pale skin. A gown covered his chest, hiding the bandage. The ventilator was gone, replaced by a nasal cannula. She released the breath she'd been holding. The nurse was right—he looked better. He wasn't going to die.

His eyes opened, and for a minute, he stared at her. "You're beautiful."

The raspy words spoken barely above a whisper sent her heart into orbit. She took a shuddering breath. "Oh, Matt…"

She flew to the bedside and leaned over,

brushing his lips with her own. Alarms buzzed over his head, and she jerked back.

Traci chuckled and pressed a button. "Nothing to worry about unless his heart rate keeps climbing. Then I'll have to ask you to leave." The nurse peered over her glasses at them. "I'll be outside the room if you need me."

"Slow your heart rate down," Allie ordered as she sat in the chair. "I want to stay."

"Yes, ma'am." Matt gave her a lazy smile and took her hand again. "What happened? I'm not too clear on how I got here."

She rubbed her thumb over his knuckles. "You saved my life when Nichols fired that gun." She closed her eyes, trying to keep the tears at bay. When she blinked them open, Matt had slipped into a deep sleep. She'd worn him out. Slowly she rose and walked out of the room. "He's asleep again," she said to Traci.

"It'll probably be like that off and on all day. I think he's being moved out on the floor tomorrow."

"You think he's well enough for that?"

"Oh, yeah. He's strong, his lung has re-inflated, and it may not look like it now, but he's on the mend."

Her heart lifted at Traci's words.

CHAPTER TWENTY-ONE

EARLY MONDAY MORNING after Allie called the school and arranged to take a personal day, she hopped into the shower. Just as Traci had predicted, Matt was being moved out on the floor. No more short visits. Each time she had seen him Sunday after he'd woken she'd found Matt a little stronger, a little more alert. But the visits had been shared with either Traci or Mariah. She wanted a little private time with him.

As she dressed, an alert sounded on Matt's cell phone. She hadn't heard the phone ring, but it showed he had a missed call and a voice mail from J. Phillip Bradford requesting that Matt or someone call him back. About time. She hit the call-back button, and he answered on the first ring.

"Bradford. Is this Matt?"

"No, this is Allie Carson. Matt's in ICU."

A full five seconds passed in silence. "Why? What's wrong with him?"

"He was shot Friday afternoon."

"Sh-shot? Why?"

"It's a long story better told in person. Why didn't you call back Friday after I left you the message that he'd been injured?" Bradford wasn't the only one who got to ask questions. "Or yesterday," she added.

"I didn't listen to your messages until today." An exasperated sigh sounded over the phone. "Confound it, girl, what happened and what's his prognosis?"

"There was a shooting here in Cedar Grove. Matt was one of the victims. He's recovering from a gunshot wound and a collapsed lung. It was on the news."

"Not in Memphis."

Allie didn't try to fill the silence between them.

He drew in a breath and released it. "Is he… how is he?"

"His condition has been upgraded to good, and he's being moved to a room."

"Thank you, Miss Carson."

The dismissal in his voice angered her. "Wait! Aren't you coming to see him?"

When he didn't answer she held the cell phone out to see if he was still there. He'd disconnected.

At eleven o'clock, Allie stepped off the elevator onto the fourth floor of the hospital. Traci had called and let her know Matt was in his room, and doing well. She touched the ring box in her pocket. The velvet box had become her security blanket, giving comfort when she touched it. It would be hard to give it up, but it belonged to Matt, not her.

She hesitated outside room 435, then swallowed the anxiety that crawled into her throat and pushed the door open.

Matt sat propped up in bed. "I wondered where you were. Mariah's already been here and gone back to rehab."

"You must be better. You're grouchy."

"And you're beautiful."

Tears sprang to her eyes, and she blinked them back. She managed a smile for him. "How do you feel?"

"Like I could run a race if it was a half inch long."

It was good to hear his voice almost back to normal. She leaned over the bed to kiss his forehead, and he shook his head.

"Before I woke up, I had dreams that you were kissing me…and not on my head." His hands framed her face. "You were kissing me like this."

His lips captured hers, and she lost herself in the kiss.

"I love you." He murmured the words against her lips.

She pulled away from him. "I love you, too, and I'm sorry…."

Alarm flashed in his eyes. "Sorry? About what?"

"That I didn't go with you all those years ago when you asked me, but I was so angry with you."

"No, you were right. I thought I had to be someone different if I wanted to succeed. I turned my back on you, Mariah, my friends. I forgot about loyalty and kindness, all for greed." His voice cracked.

She waited, wanting to make it easier. Anything to ease the anguish in his eyes.

He took a breath. "I couldn't see you standing in front of me, loving me the way I was. If you had gone with me, I would have destroyed your love. Like I destroyed Jessica's."

She held the jewelry box out to him. "Is that why this was in your pocket?"

He took the box. "I loved her, but not the way she deserved to be loved. I couldn't. Not when I've always loved you. And she saw that and gave the ring back to me." He lifted his gaze, his blue eyes holding hers. "I grew up on Beaker Street, and I've learned it's nothing to be ashamed of. I want to ask you to marry me, but…"

Her heart almost stopped. Marry him? "But?"

"I don't have a job."

She gaped at him. "I don't understand."

"I don't expect Winthrop will hire me again given everything that's happened, and I quit the Bradford Foundation. By the way, he's my grandfather."

She nodded. "The marriage certificate. Your mom's name was Bradford."

"I won't work for a man like him...." Matt's gaze slid past her.

She turned. J. Phillip Bradford, dressed in a black overcoat and as tall as Matt, stood just inside the room.

"I hope I can change your mind about that, Matthew." He came forward and faced her. "You must be Miss Carson."

Ms., she wanted to say. Instead she accepted the offered hand. "And you must be Matt's grandfather."

His gray eyes studied her. "Yes." He stepped closer to the bed and shifted his gaze to Matt. "Can we talk? Privately?"

"Anything you want to say, you can say in front of Allie. We're going to be married, if she will have me." He opened the velvet box.

"Rachel's rings?" Bradford crossed the room and took the box from Matt's hands. Reverently, he stared at the ring inside. Then he looked first at her then at Matt. "Where did you get these? Where's the wedding band?"

"It's in my safe. And the rings came from my mother, actually my Grandmother Rae." Understanding crossed Matt's face. "Rachel."

Bradford pressed his lips together, but not before Allie noticed them tremble. He turned to her. "Please. Could we have a few minutes in private?"

THE DOOR CLOSED behind Allie, and Matt wanted to call her back.

Bradford shut the box and cupped it in his hand. "May I sit down?"

Matt nodded. His grandfather took off his coat and sat in the chair nearest the bed. "I'm sorry I didn't come earlier, but I didn't know about the shooting. After you left Friday…" He folded his arms across his chest. "Anyway, when I saw you had called, I was too angry to talk. I didn't listen to the messages until this morning."

Bradford stood and walked to the window that overlooked the parking lot. "Matt, I've made so many mistakes. First with Susan, and now with you and Mariah. I asked for your mother's forgiveness years ago, and she gave it." He licked his lips. "Now I'd like to ask for yours…and Mariah's."

Matt wanted to block out his grandfather's voice. He didn't want to forgive him. "My mom might be alive—"

His grandfather walked back to the foot of the bed. "I can't change the past, Matthew. But I want to repeat what I said Friday. I offered to get her help. She said it was too late, that the cancer had spread. I'll live the rest of my life knowing I possibly could've made a difference with her cancer if I'd tried just a little harder. But at least we made our peace—albeit at a price. I had to promise not to intrude in your life or Mariah's. I kept my promise until you came to me, wanting the contract for the Winthrop Corporation. If you didn't realize I was your grandfather, I didn't see it as breaking my promise."

Matt's throat tightened, and he tried to swallow the lump choking him. Forgiveness was a choice. He could be like his mom had been for so long and hold on to his anger. Refusing to forgive him would hurt his grandfather, maybe even destroy him. But Bradford wouldn't be the only one destroyed. It would eat at Matt just like it had his mother. "What if we start out by getting to know each other first?"

His grandfather drew in a deep breath and released it. "I can handle that." He wrapped his hand around Matt's. "Now I have to go find your sister."

Matt wiped his eyes with the sleeve of his free hand. "She's in the rehab building behind the hospital. I'm sure you'll know how to get past the rules and regulations about visitors."

The older man smiled at him. "Probably so." He grabbed his coat. "I hope you'll reconsider the job at the foundation. You're perfect for it, and you can make a difference in the war against cancer."

"I'll talk with Allie about it."

His grandfather looked down at the box he still held. "I believe this belongs to you…or maybe Miss Carson?"

"Hopefully, the future Mrs. Jefferies." Matt clasped the box to his chest. "Would you tell her we're finished talking…for now?"

"I will."

The door closed and Matt sank into the bed. His shoulder burned, and his body ached, and he probably needed sleep. But he wasn't about to give in to it. Not until Allie said yes, and he placed the ring on her finger. He smiled as she slipped into the room. "He asked me to forgive him."

She returned his smile. "Did you?"

"We'll see. He wants me to come back to work

for him at the foundation. If I do, would you consider moving to Memphis? Not in the city, but maybe out in the country?"

"I'll move wherever you are."

"Help me up," he said.

"Should you get out of bed? You've had a tiring morning."

"Yes. But a man can't propose flat on his back."

He made it as far as the side of the bed. "This'll have to do. Sit here, beside me."

She eased onto the bed, and he took her hand and slipped the engagement ring on her finger. He looked into her eyes and saw his past, his present and his future. "Allie Carson, will you marry me?"

She pressed her lips together as tears spilled onto her cheeks. "Yes, Matthew Jefferies, I will."

Six months later...

MATT STARED IN the mirror at his crooked bow tie. Where was Allie when he needed her?

In the bride's room getting dressed, of course. He yanked the end of the tie, then turned when someone knocked at his door. "Come in."

Clint entered and grinned. "Allie sent me to help you with that." He pointed to the tie dangling in Matt's hands.

"Thanks." He handed Clint the tie, then stood still while his friend expertly knotted it. "I don't know why I can't learn how to tie those confounded things."

Clint laughed. "Not nervous, are you?"

Matt wiped his damp hands on his pants leg. "Probably no more than any other groom on his wedding day. Is Noah dressed?"

"The ring bearer is dressed and waiting at the back of the church with your granddad."

Granddad. Over the past six months, their relationship had grown into more than Matt had ever expected. Partly because J. Phillip Bradford had changed, mellowed even, and was not so work-driven. Everyone said it was because of Matt, but personally Matt believed it was Noah. The kid had a way of getting next to a person.

The first chord of the processional began.

"I think that's our cue," Clint said.

Matt nodded and followed his best man through the doorway and joined the pastor at the front of the church. Finally. The day he'd waited for since asking Allie to marry him. The nervousness he'd felt earlier faded as Allie's mom was escorted down the aisle. How he wished his own mother were here.

Soon the music flowed into a light minuet, and Noah walked toward him, carefully carrying the white pillow. Mariah was next as matron of honor, and Matt's chest swelled. He was so proud of his sister. Clean and sober since January, taking college courses, but most of all, being the mother Noah needed. Their grandfather had offered Mariah a part-time job, and they were thinking about moving to Memphis, close to where Matt and Allie had bought a house.

Then the unmistakable start of the bridal chorus began. Matt's heart thumped against his chest as Allie appeared in the doorway on the arm of her father, beautiful in her white A-line dress.

Men weren't supposed to cry, but tears stung his eyes as Allie's gaze sought his. He stood a little straighter as she walked toward him and took her hand from her father.

He couldn't stop beaming at Allie. Her eyes glistened as the pastor began.

"Dearly beloved, we are gathered here…"

As he talked, Matt rehearsed the words he'd written for their ceremony…then he began. "Allie, you are the most generous, loving and unselfish person I know. I don't deserve you, but I'm so thankful you've chosen to spend your life with me, and that we will grow old together. I, Matthew Jefferies, do take you, Allie Carson, to be my lawful wedded wife. I promise to love and honor you, to care for you, to be faithful to you from this day forward for the rest of our lives."

Tears rimmed Allie's eyes. She blinked them back and smiled. "Matthew, you are my heart, my one true love. I vow to love you in sickness and in health, in good times and bad times, to respect your successes and your failures. I will cherish our marriage, and I want to grow old with you. I give you my hand, my heart and my love from this day forward as long as we both shall live."

The minister smiled his approval, and then asked, "What token of love do you offer?"

Noah stepped forward and the rings were handed to him. "The wedding ring symbolizes the unending love you vow." He handed Matt the wedding ring that had belonged to his grandmother. With a steady hand, Matt slid the ring on Allie's finger.

"With this ring, I pledge my love for now and all eternity."

Allie took the ring for him and slid it on his finger. "I give you this ring as a token of my love now and always."

The pastor looked up. "May you always keep the vows you have made today. Treat one another with love and honor and faithfulness.

"And so, by the power vested in me by the

State of Mississippi, I now pronounce you husband and wife. You may kiss your bride."

Matt leaned over. "I love you," he said and gently pressed his lips against Allie's.

He hooked his arm in hers, and they walked up the aisle, stopping to hug her mom, and nodding to others.

The doors to the church opened, and together they ran down the steps amid the ringing of bells.

* * * * *

LARGER-PRINT BOOKS!

GET 2 FREE LARGER-PRINT NOVELS PLUS 2 FREE MYSTERY GIFTS

Love Inspired®

Larger-print novels are now available...